TAXI

(a Take It Off novel)

The meter is running…

One night as Rose Crawford steps out of a bar, she gives no second thought to lifting her hand to signal a cab. After all, it's the responsible thing to do.

A common occurrence.

Far safer than walking several blocks, alone, in the dark.

A familiar-looking yellow taxi with black, faux-leather seats, running meter on the dash, and a smiling driver pulls up to the curb.

Rose slides in. Gives the driver her address…

But she never reaches her destination.

Instead, she finds herself captive, at the will of a man who isn't a driver, but a bona fide psychopath.

Trapped in a taxi she can't escape, Rose begins to panic. As the miles between her and safety grow, hope dwindles. It isn't until someone else joins her in captivity that her spark of hope is rekindled.

Derek is strong, capable, and surely together they can fight their way to freedom.

Then Rose finds out exactly why she's been driven into hell. Derek may be an unwilling captive, but he isn't going to help her.

In fact, he's there to do the exact opposite.

TAXI

Take It Off Series

CAMBRIA HEBERT

DEDICATION

For anyone who has an irrational fear.
This book probably won't help with that.
My bad.

TAXI

1

Rose

I was going to regret this.

It was hard enough to drag my butt out of bed at the ungodly hour of four a.m., but add the heavy weight of regret, and yeah, I was pretty much guaranteed a hellacious morning of kicking my own ass as well as nursing a hangover.

Well, at least I'd have good coffee.

Good coffee always made any situation just a little more tolerable.

People that didn't drink coffee? I didn't understand them.

How could you not enjoy the aromatic, rich scent of freshly ground roasted beans as it wafted up to tickle the underside of your nose in the form of curling steam? The mug would permeate your palms and fingers with warmth, soothing any kind of frazzled nerves or just plain offering comfort in a world that moved so fast it was almost impossible to keep up.

Coffee wasn't just a drink.

It was an opportunity.

A chance to not only refuel low energy stores, but to rejuvenate the mind. It was a brief reprieve in a cup, a chance to have something exactly the way you wanted it. Made just for you. It was basically a selfish desire, and no one ever criticized you for it because everyone could be selfish when it came to coffee. There was enough for everyone to have some exactly as they wanted it.

And if they wanted it black?

Well, who was I to judge?

I'd pour it. I'd serve it with a smile.

In the back of my head, I might recall the article I read stating those who drank black coffee were likely psycho… but I wouldn't say it out loud.

A girl could learn a lot about a person from the way they took their coffee.

My mind was wandering. Blabbering on and on about my passion. At least I wasn't saying all this out loud. Good grief, I'd never get a cab standing here on the sidewalk visibly talking to myself.

I was drunk. Maybe not full-on drunk… just tipsy.

Slightly smashed.

I giggled.

I liked that. I needed to create a drink to go with it for my menu.

I stepped out of the slightly covered doorway of the pub and farther onto the sidewalk. The familiar sight of a yellow cab with a lit-up sign on the roof made me rush a little faster.

I held up an arm. "Taxi!" I called out.

Then I promptly stumbled over my own two feet and almost face-planted right there on the concrete.

Okay. I admit I wasn't slightly smashed. I was totally drunk.

Here I'd been annoyed I couldn't catch a cab when I wasn't even far enough out on the sidewalk to hail one. Not to mention I was reciting an inner monologue all about my love for coffee, and I almost broke my face by tripping over air.

The second I was back in balance and sure I wasn't going to intimately meet the concrete, I noted the cab sailing right by without even so much as a thought to stop.

"I didn't want you to stop anyway!" I yelled after it.

About half a block away, a couple turned to stare. I waved at them.

I didn't want them to think I was insane.

"Ugh," I muttered. "Stupid shoes."

I was wearing high heels. Not the wedge kind or the kind with a nice platform either. I was wearing the full-on dangerous but sexy-as-hell stilettos.

They might be sexy, but my God, I was going to need to wear orthotics for a month after tonight. No wonder I drank so much. I had to dull the pain of these heinous death traps on my feet!

Enough was enough.

The first red pump came off and filled my hand. I stepped down and wobbled a little because now I was decidedly lopsided. The heels added a good four inches to my height.

I yanked off the other and gripped the pair in one hand while trying to talk myself out of throwing them in the nearby trashcan.

I wouldn't. But only because they cost me a butt load of money.

It seemed unfair and somehow barbaric to pay so much green for a pair of shoes that would leave me limping with feet full of Band-Aids the next day. I missed my Converse. And socks.

I liked socks; they were comfortable.

Another cab headed in my direction, and I forgot about how much I hated my shoes, loved socks, and tucked the red pumps under my arm and raced to the curb to lift a hand.

The couple up the block did the same, and the cab pulled over beside them.

Now I regretted waving. Maybe if I hadn't, they really would have thought I was nuts and let me have the cab.

Why was it whenever I needed a cab and tried to hail one, they never stopped? Yet when I didn't need one, they were always around?

After two more failed attempts, I considered going back in the pub where my friends were still enjoying another round, but in the end, I hefted my shoes a little higher and started walking.

I needed to sober up. Making coffee drunk would not be good for my little business.

I didn't get very far down the block when a car slid to the sidewalk. I glanced over, and the passenger window slid down.

"Need a cab?" the driver called out.

Anyone see the irony here?

The minute I *stopped* trying to get a cab was the minute one showed up.

"Yeah," I called out and muttered under my breath about the injustice of public transportation on my way over to the door.

The inside of the taxi looked like the hundreds of other cabs driving around this town. The bench seat was made of some fake leather material, and if I wasn't drunk, I'd cringe at having to put my butt on it. The carpet covering the floorboards was also black and needed a good vacuuming. It smelled like stale fast food, which made my vodka-saturated stomach lurch. If I wasn't so desperate to get home to my bed and shower, I'd get out and walk.

Walking wasn't safe anyway.

Raleigh, North Carolina, wasn't exactly the most dangerous place to be, but in my opinion (and if you don't agree, just watch the news), being out in the dark anywhere alone as a woman was hazardous to one's safety.

The second I was seated, my shoes hit my lap. Yeah, I know. I should have put them back on, but, ugh, my feet really freaking hurt.

The driver looked over his shoulder with a smile. "Long night?"

"Early morning," I quipped, still thinking ahead.

He chuckled and hit a button on the meter so it could start adding up my fare. "Where to?"

"Thirty-Five South Parker Street," I replied.

The car moved away from the curb and onto the fairly empty street. I glanced back at the pub and then leaned my forehead against the cold glass window. The tires jolted over what felt like a crater in the street, and my entire body jostled, my head smacking against the glass.

Ow. Pulling back, I straightened and glanced around at all the familiar stickers that littered many surfaces of the interior.

The cab is under surveillance. Buckle Up. Licensed driver number 509.

There should have been a sticker warning passengers that cabbies usually drove like lunatics.

"Night out with your friends?" His voice filtered to the backseat.

"Uh, yeah," I said. I wasn't a fan of talking to drivers. It was weird. I didn't know him. He didn't know me. I'd be in this cab for all of ten minutes, and then I'd never see him again.

It was actually a bizarre thing, riding in a cab.

I'd just been sitting here thinking how dangerous walking home would be. But wasn't this just as dangerous?

I was alone in a car with a man I didn't know anything about. I'd given him my home address, so not only would he know my face, but also where I lived.

Why is walking considered more dangerous…?

I glanced at the sticker disclosing the cab was under surveillance. That made me feel better. Usually, I wouldn't want to be watched or recorded, but this was good. It meant the driver couldn't do anything shady to me.

Right?

Besides, there was one of those thick Plexiglas partitions dividing the front seat from where I was in the back. Not all cabs had them, but this one did. The center panel was open so we could exchange directions, but I could see there was a panel that slid over it so we could be completely shut off from each other.

That feature was probably more to protect the driver than a passenger, but it still made me feel better. It also made me feel better to think about how the driver himself was sort of at risk. He might be a stranger to me, but I was just as much one to him. God only knew the kind of people who got in the back of his cab.

I shuddered at the thought.

Poor guy.

"So, uh, what do ya do?" the driver asked, breaking into my inner thoughts, which took away some of the pity I felt for him.

He was a chatty fellow.

"Why?" I asked suspiciously.

"You said you were worried about your early morning. Must have a job that has an early show time."

I blew out a breath and felt like the world's largest, paranoid idiot. He was just making conversation. Maybe he thought talking to me about stuff I'd said would make me feel more at ease during the ride.

Maybe I wasn't the only woman who ever started to freak out about being in a cab alone.

"I actually own a coffee truck," I replied. "I park it over by Raleigh Regional Hospital."

"Ah, so you gotta be up to make the coffee for all the doctors."

"They definitely like their caffeine," I said, glancing out the window. Just up ahead was my street, and I'd be home. My body relaxed back into the seat, and my fingers, which had been gripping my red pumps like my life depended on it, relented.

He made a sound. "Who can blame them?" He tossed the words over his shoulder. "Good stuff."

I felt my nose wrinkle. An odd sort of déjà vu moment hit me. I glanced over the seat at the driver. Why did it suddenly seem like he was familiar to me?

"Maybe you've been to it?" I asked, peering over the seat at him. "It's called Curbside Coffee. It's a light-green van."

I hated telling people it was a van. (Who wanted to buy coffee from the back of a van? Ew.) It was… But it wasn't. It was a Volkswagen Vanagon—a hybrid between a van and a bus. Think Mystery Machine in *Scooby Doo*. But mine wasn't for solving mysteries. It was modified for serving coffee. The best damn coffee in all of North Carolina.

"Don't think so," he said. "I don't get to that side of the metropolitan area very much. I drive mostly on this side."

That seemed a little odd. It wasn't that far away. But of course, most people didn't travel to the hospital by taxi.

He didn't look familiar, not at all. Not that I would remember every face to come to the truck; that would be impossible. I did have a lot of regulars, though. They made up a large percentage of my customers. After all, parking at the same place every day did kind of ensure that. This guy was definitely not a regular.

And now he not only knew what I looked like and my home address, but also where I worked.

Good going, Rose. You're on a roll tonight! Next time some friends asked me out for drinks, I was going to seriously consider staying home.

Speaking of… Shouldn't I be there by now?

A quick glance out the window had me straightening up like I'd been prodded with a hot poker.

"You missed my street!" I exclaimed, pointing out the back window to punctuate my words.

"What was that?" he said.

There was no way in hell he didn't hear me. I practically yelled.

I sprang forward, teetering on the edge of the seat, and pushed my face up to the window opening between the seats. "You missed my street. Turn around."

"Nah, I didn't miss your street," he mused. He wasn't concerned at all.

A feeling of creepy intuition started to unfold inside me. My pulse picked up. I felt it thudding with restrained dread as blood hammered through my veins. Low in my stomach, the muscles clenched tight, as if they were preparing for a fight, and the back of my neck tensed so quickly I felt like I was locked into place.

I blinked and scrutinized the back of his head and side of his face from this closer perspective. There wasn't anything special about him. He was ordinary, just another cabbie from the city. Not one thing about him screamed I should be afraid.

But I was.

Oh, I was.

"You did," I ground out, trying to unlock my jaw to speak without indicating how panicked I was becoming.

He laughed. A low, amused chuckle, the kind belaying I was missing some private joke only he was privy to.

The hair on the back of my neck stood up. "Pull over," I demanded, forgetting all about not wanting to sound freaked. "Pull over right now."

"I'm afraid I can't do that." The utterly calm and even tone to his voice scared me more than anything. He was totally in control.

Shoving back away from the glass, I reached for the handle to open the back door. Screw this. I'd just jump out!

My fingers ached I gripped the handle so tight and pulled.

Nothing happened.

I pulled again. And again.

The door was locked.

I threw my body across the seat and tried the other door. It was locked, too. My body shot up and my palm hit the glass right behind his head. "Stop the car!" I yelled.

He kept driving.

I beat on the glass, and it was like he suddenly forgot I was here. He acted as if he had no idea there was woman in the backseat of his cab, going ape shit.

There were no handles or buttons to roll down the windows. There was no button or way to unlock the doors. There was no way out. I was trapped.

Adrenaline and fear roared inside me, my hands shook, and my stomach rolled. My chest squeezed and my vision dimmed when I glanced out the window and noted the streets and buildings just flying right by.

Where was he taking me?

Oh my God. I was being kidnapped.

It was the middle of the night. It was dark. I was drunk, alone… completely at this taxi driver's whim.

NO. Hell no.

I wasn't going to let this happen. The more miles he drove, the more likely I would never go home again.

A sob ripped from my throat. I beat on the glass some more.

Searing anger rose up inside me. It eclipsed some of my fear and gave me some courage. My heels had fallen onto the floor in my attempts at getting free. I picked one up, wrapped my palms around the toe, and brandished like a weapon.

"I said stop this car!" I screamed and shoved my arm through the window between the seats. I pulled back my wrist and fired back down, smacking the heel into the side of his head.

He couldn't ignore that.

The driver's body flinched and he jerked away, the wheel of the car lurching with him. We swerved wildly on the road, and my body was tossed to the side. I cried out when the edge of the Plexiglas cut into the top of my arm as I fell.

I ignored the pain and quickly scrambled back up and hit him again. This time, the heel slammed down on the spot between his neck and shoulder.

"Son of a bitch!" he roared and turned toward me.

I lifted the shoe to hit him again, but he caught it and ripped away my weapon. He threw it on the passenger-side floorboard, out of reach, and snatched my wrist as I was pulling back for the other shoe.

I was yanked so hard my face hit the glass. I stifled a cry and twisted and fought to get my arm free. "Pull over!" I screamed.

The cab swerved again as we struggled. He was having a hard time driving with one arm while trying to fight me off with the other.

"Get back there!" he spat and shoved away my arm.

I retreated into the backseat, chest heaving, eyes watering, and wild panic clawing up my insides. Before I could do anything else, he slammed the window shut and locked it closed. I lurched forward and tried to open it anyway.

Of course it wouldn't budge.

"You're only making it worse for yourself." He acted like this was my fault. Like I asked to be kidnapped.

I was so enraged, so incredibly frightened that I was starting to go numb.

This wasn't happening.

I wasn't being kidnapped.

I hadn't just willingly stepped into a situation that was going to get me killed.

What does he want with me? What is he going to do?

Think! Get yourself out of this. Don't lie down and accept this fate. I could barely hear my thoughts because the feeling of terror was so strong, but I fought it back. I fought for even just a shred of sanity.

My phone! Of course!

An impatient sound ripped out of my throat, and I dove at my bag. The entire contents dumped out all over the floor in my haste to get the phone. I snatched it up as tears of relief blurred my vision.

I sat back and lit up the screen. On the dial pad, I hit 9-1-1 and pressed it tight against my ear. As I did, I watched the driver, prepared to fight him off so he couldn't take away my phone.

If he noticed what I was doing, he gave no indication.

This made me nervous… Why didn't he care I was calling the police?

The phone wasn't ringing. The call hadn't gone through.

"What?" I muttered and pulled it away to look at the screen.

Call failed. No service.

No, no, no. I dialed again. And again.

None of my calls went through.

Biting down on my lower lip and fighting back the keening sounds clawing out of my throat, I tried to send off a text.

I got a little red exclamation point indicating the text couldn't be sent.

Try again? the phone asked on the screen.

I tried again.

Five times.

I tried the call again, too.

It wasn't working. "Why aren't you working!" I shouted, frustrated.

In the front seat, the driver leaned forward, and my attention zeroed in on what he was doing. His hand patted something mounted to the dash beside the meter. "Scrambles the signal. Makes that fancy phone of yours completely useless." He seemed proud.

I slumped back, astonished. "Why are you doing this?"

When I thought he would say nothing, he spoke up. "Look at that." He gestured to the still-running meter. "You're gonna owe a hefty fair."

I blinked. He was insane. Completely and utterly psychotic. The phone slid out of my hand and dropped onto the seat.

"You like country music?" he called over his shoulder and reached for the radio. Sounds of a popular country song filled the interior of the cab.

He was kidnapping me, and he wanted to listen to music?

Something inside me snapped. Like a band that had long since turned brittle. With a battle cry, I picked up my other shoe and started beating on the window of the door closest to me. I knew the hope of me actually breaking this window was slim, but I could try.

This heel was pointy; I might have a chance. A chance was better than nothing. I beat on the glass over and over again. Pain radiated down my hand and up to my elbow. The harder I hit, the more it hurt, but I didn't care.

"It's useless," he said over my attempts.

It only made me try harder.

We were leaving the city; that much I could tell. I had to get out of here before we got any farther. By chance, I saw a couple of guys walking down the sidewalk. I threw myself against the window, beating on it and screaming.

"Help me!" I screamed. "Help!"

They glanced up. I beat on the glass some more.

The speed of the cab increased, and seconds later, we had passed.

I climbed into the back window, beating on it, my eyes never leaving the staring men.

Seconds later, the cab took a sharp turn, and my body flew away from the window, hit the bench seat, and flopped halfway onto the floor.

The car jerked to a stop, and my nails dug into the seat, trying to keep myself from falling any harder. God, my entire body hurt.

How long had I been at this guy's mercy?

Ten minutes? Twenty?

It felt like years.

It felt like I'd been fighting for days with no reprieve.

"Help!" I roared and lurched up, banging on the glass of the window. I stared out at the dark street, trying to decipher where we were, trying to memorize any detail I could.

It was hard. I was so beyond thought. I was beyond sight. My fight-or-flight response was so amped up I could barely even function.

Try! I demanded of myself.

"They saw me!" I told the driver. "Those guys back there. They've probably already called the police."

The car was idling at the curb. He turned slowly so he was facing me.

"Just let me go. Right here. Right now. I won't tell anyone anything about this," I begged.

"I didn't want to do this," he said, regret in his tone. "If only you'd just shut up."

"Just let me go. It will be over."

The man leaned down and lifted something from beneath the front seat. I swallowed thickly, watching him carefully, terribly afraid of what he might do next.

Horror, plain and simple, dawned over me as he pulled what he was holding over his head. It was a mask.

Like a gas mask… the kind that covered your entire face and had this huge protruding filter-looking thing at the mouth.

The lenses covering his eyes were dirty. They gave his face a yellow, jaundiced cast.

I shivered. My fingernails curled into my palms and bit into my flesh.

"What are you doing?" My voice shook, and I pressed back farther into the seat.

He stared at me, unspeaking, as he adjusted the strap at the back of his head.

I picked up my phone again, trying to call 9-1-1 once more. I knew it wouldn't work, but I'd try until I was dead.

Which might not be that long now...

A low sound filled the interior of the cab. I heard it even over the stupid country music. It sounded sort of like he'd turned the AC on full blast. Like something was blowing...

Noticeable mist started rising from beneath the front seat. Like steam off a cup of coffee, like water evaporating off a sidewalk on an ultra-hot day.

Gripping my phone so tight I was surprised it didn't shatter, I scrambled back and pressed into the corner of the seat as far away from the rising mist as I could get.

"What is that?" I demanded. "What are you doing?"

I started hyperventilating. I couldn't help it. The anxiety and fear was just too real. As my body fought for calm, my lungs searched for air. The only kind they could find was contaminated.

My eyes watered as even more of the mist filled the backseat of the car. I tried to hold my breath, but let's be real... A person could only do that for so long before the body automatically took over and sucked in.

The car pulled away from the empty, dark curb and onto the street. Drowsiness washed over me, and I fought it with all the valiance I could muster.

But I was no match for sleeping gas (or whatever this was). I was no match for the driver with a mask strapped to his face.

My body melted against the seat as I fought for consciousness.

I didn't want to pass out. I wasn't sure if I'd ever wake up.

It was a losing battle.

The last thought I had before completely succumbing was, *I'm not ready to die.*

2

Rose

I wasn't dead.

Well, unless I *was* and only thought I was alive. It happened on TV all the time. You know when people die and then wake up as ghosts and don't really know they're dead until they walk through a wall or try and have a conversation with their best friend and get no reply.

Hey, at this point, I was willing to believe anything was possible. After being kidnapped by a taxi driver and drugged, I was pretty sure I could argue a good case that the tooth fairy existed.

Clearly, I was still a little drunk. Or maybe whatever filled up my lungs was still in my system and it was some sort of hallucinogen.

Either way, I wasn't dead.

I guess that made up for the ridiculous thoughts crowding my pounding head.

Ow. It felt like someone took a hammer to my skull and got in a couple really good knocks. I started to lift a hand up to my head, the small action bringing in a wealth of reality.

Flashes of the taxi ride, the man wearing a mask, and the bone-chilling fear I'd felt earlier assailed me. I wasn't just having a drunken bad dream or a hangover from hell. This was really happening. Instantly, my hand went slack against the ground, and I fought the urge in my muscles to tense up.

Look asleep, I told myself. *Don't let him know you're awake.*

Just the thought of that man made me want to cry. Was he still here? Was he somewhere nearby watching me, just waiting for me to open my eyes?

I forced back the sounds bubbling up in my chest. They were so distraught and so full of sorrow it was physically painful to keep them inside.

But this pain was no match for the pain I knew was waiting if my kidnapper realized I was awake. True, I had no idea what he wanted with me, but it wasn't good.

Nothing good would come of this.

Keeping my breathing even and my face muscles relaxed, I listened and tried to assimilate as much as I could about my surroundings.

The floor was cold and hard, like concrete. I was lying on it without any kind of cushion or blanket, and I could feel every pressure point lying on the impenetrable surface. I must have been here a while because I was stiff and my shoulder blades hurt like they'd been supporting my weight for a while.

My fingers and toes were cold. Almost icy. That seemed a little odd because it was summer and summer's in the South made it almost impossible to have icy anything.

Was I in a freezer?

That thought was freaky, and I had to remind myself to calm down. I definitely wasn't in a freezer; it wasn't that cold.

I was still wearing all my clothes, minus my shoes. I'd probably never see those things again. Funny, even though I'd just been complaining about them, now I was sorry. My legs were bare and it felt like my skirt had ridden up, because there was a bit of a draft.

My teeth sank into my lower lip before I could think better of it.

Was I raped? The thought was like an icepick shoved into my stomach.

I wouldn't have to be naked for that to have happened, especially since I was wearing a skirt… *No*. It didn't feel like I'd been violated that way. I searched every corner of my foggy mind, trying to recall anything—a sound, a touch… a feeling that would indicate my body had been violated in some horrible way.

The only memories were of what happened in the taxi and now waking up here. I was probably only feeling a draft because I was sprawled out on some hard, cold floor.

I didn't have much hope right now, not much relief, but realizing I wasn't sexually abused did make me feel a little bit stronger.

With a little more boldness, I continued taking mental stock of my surroundings and my body.

There was something around my wrist. Just the left one. It was heavy and cool, kind of like metal. But my other wrist was bare.

I wanted to open my eyes. I wanted to know what I was dealing with. First, I listened. I *really* listened. It wasn't easy because as it turns out, when you're scared for your life, it's incredibly hard to calm the mind enough to listen. All I could hear was the sound of my own heartbeat; all I could think about was questioning if every heartbeat was unique.

If my heart stopped beating, would there ever be a sound just like it ever again?

What if heartbeats were like fingerprints, exclusive to the person? Identifying in ways no one had yet to discover?

I was beginning to think my brain had ADD. I could never seem to just focus.

Focus.

I was finally able to quiet and search out the sounds of breathing, voices, or footsteps. The sound of cars or a radio… anything. Anything at all.

It was silent.

I heard nothing.

In my mind, I counted to three. *One, two… three.* Slowly, I cracked open my eyes. Even as I warned myself not to, I did it. I made a face, like a wince—you know, like when you screw up your face as a scary movie plays on TV and you just know something's lurking, ready to jump out.

I just knew someone was there, hovering nearby, waiting to do heinous and unspeakable things to me.

The second my eyes opened fully, they slammed shut again, as if I suddenly changed my mind. Even in the split second they opened, I saw no one.

I pried them open again and stared up. When no one shouted and came rushing over, I turned my head and looked around the room. My fingers and lip trembled as I stared around, anxiously searching the large, open space.

I saw no one.

A heavy breath exhaled from my chest, and I pushed myself up into a sitting position. I swear my body creaked. For a woman who was only twenty-four, my body was betraying me. It took an excessive amount of time to move and flex just to sit up.

I didn't dare call out, but I did do another thorough inspection of the room. It looked like I was in a warehouse of some kind. The walls were made of metal or tin. The roof the same. I was toward the back of the building, off to the side near one of the walls.

The lighting was dim; there were no windows. There was a light of some kind up near the front. I couldn't tell what kind but it must have been pretty bright to give enough illumination back here.

As I stared at some of the stuff I was currently sharing the space with, I thought maybe it wasn't a warehouse after all, but some kind of barn or shed. A couple very large tractors were parked inside. One was very dirty and worn-looking, and the other was in better shape but definitely had been used.

The entire place smelled sort of like earth, grass, and hay.

Maybe this was some kind of farm? I knew there were farmlands outside of Raleigh somewhere… It was possible I was at one. I had no idea what time it was or how long I'd been in the taxi.

Oh God, what if I'm not even in North Carolina anymore?

I moved to press a hand to my chest because it was suddenly tight and uncomfortable. The rattling of chains made me freeze.

I looked down.

Numbly, I stared at my new bracelet. I always thought maybe I was a jewelry girl.

I was pretty sure I'd just changed my mind.

A wide metal cuff wrapped around my wrist, attached to a short length of chain. The chain was thick and heavy, and it wrapped around some type of thick metal pipe or pole.

I was chained up. Like an animal. A prisoner.

Swift and fierce rage swept through me. A sound that could only be described as desperation filled my ears when I lurched to my feet. The weight of the chain was heavy, and it tried to pull me down. I was unrelenting and shoved back to throw all my weight into trying to break free of the leash.

Of course, I was no match for the chain.

I tugged and fought against it. I shoved at the pipe, kicked and yanked until my chest heaved and my chilled fingers were no longer cold.

Refusing to give up, I started searching around for something nearby I could use to cut the chain with. I had no idea what kind of tool could even do that, but I'd try a puny pair of scissors if given the chance.

I had maybe five feet of chain to move around with. I used to think five feet was a respectable distance. Now?

Now it seemed like I used longer pieces of floss to clean my teeth.

A vast sense of hopelessness welled up inside me. The urge to sink down and cry was so strong I swayed on my feet. But I would not give in. Not until I was dead.

Not ever.

I went back to searching for something—anything I could use as a weapon or a tool. The radius in which I was chained was swept clear of anything. It was literally me and my restraints.

A laugh bubbled up.

I was in the center of some kind of tractor shed, chained to a pipe in the shadows, with bare feet. I was dressed in clothes I rarely ever wore—a flouncy skirt with wide white and navy horizontal stripes and a white button-up shirt that was now only half tucked in.

I was dirty and cold. My mouth felt dry and my throat hurt, probably from all the screaming I did in the cab. I was thirsty, too.

But I was alive. I would figure out a way home. I would never let this kidnapper bring me down.

The loud and shiver-inducing sound of metal scraping against metal had me jolting as if I were electrocuted. Hushed voices and footsteps made the floor seem mighty appealing, and I dropped like I had an anvil tied around my waist.

Yes. Yes, I saw the irony here. I just declared I wouldn't let him bring me down, and now here I was lying on the ground.

But I had to lie here so he wouldn't know I was awake. I needed to buy myself some time.

Besides, I wasn't speaking literally. It was figuratively.

"She's still out!" someone hissed from a distance away.

It took everything inside me not to cower or flinch away from that voice.

"How much goddamn gas did you give her!" he demanded.

I listened intently, thankful they weren't right beside me but wishing they were just a little closer so I could be certain to hear everything. Knowledge was power after all.

"Not that much," another voice replied. "She's probably just faking."

Well, shit.

Shit for two reasons:

1.) I was hoping my kidnapper was stupid and wouldn't think about me "faking" being asleep. I was hoping he'd just let me lie here as long as I pretended.

And

2.) There was more than one kidnapper. I'd just heard two different voices.

"She's not very big. You could have overdosed her. Then she'll be useless to us!" the man snapped back.

I was pretty sure the one doing most of the talking wasn't the one from the taxi, but it sounded like he was in charge. Made sense (if kidnapping ever made sense). If I was going to be a dirty criminal, I'd get someone to do all my dirty work (i.e. the actual abducting) and sit back and call the shots. That way I could have some deniability.

That meant the guy who was driving was probably a lackey.

It gave me low self-esteem and pretty much kicked me when I was already so down to know I couldn't even get away from a lackey.

You were taken off guard. I reminded myself. *They don't have the element of surprise anymore.*

"I didn't OD her," the one who I was pretty sure was in the taxi muttered. "I'll wake her up."

The sound of a ringing phone made my breath catch. I wanted to call out. I wanted to whimper. That telephone represented a lot to me in the moment. It was my salvation, a lifeline. My phone was long gone… but if I could get ahold of that one…

"It's them," the boss said. "Deal with her."

He answered with a generic greeting, and then his voice faded away, like he was leaving. If it wasn't for this stupid chain, I'd rush them both and take my chances in a physical battle for that phone.

There was some brief movement, then silence. A few seconds later, I heard what sounded like the whisper of running water, but I couldn't be sure. I took a chance, cracked one eye open, and peered around. I was alone again.

Fear rendered me useless. I felt my limbs begin to shake. Not the timid little shakes either, the kind that felt violent, the kind that jerked your whole body. I fought the urge to meltdown right there.

In my mind, I envisioned a line, maybe one drawn with chalk or paint. On one side was a dark, black well of endless terror. If stepped over there, I would fall deep into that hole of inky horror, and I might not find my way out. On the other side was a well of resolve. There was solid ground here, maybe a little cracked but still strong enough to stand on. Even though the line between the two was thin, even though it appeared tenuous at best, I still had to maintain my grip.

My life literally depended on it.

The scuffle of feet announced he was back. My fingernails bit into my palms as I worked for calm, working to relax my limbs against the cold, unforgiving floor, and tilted my head just slightly away from my captor, as if it had naturally fallen that way in sleep.

I felt his presence more than heard it. Some people just gave off an ugly energy. Their vibes disrupted the very air. It was like that now, like there were ripples in the atmosphere around me because he was approaching.

I just wanted him to go away.

I wanted to go home.

The sound of something metal clanging had me on high alert. Was he going to chain me up more? What was he doing?

A heavy downpour of freezing-cold water assuaged me. I'd never jumped off a high-dive before. But I imagined the feeling you got when your skin slapped into a wall of water was a lot like what this felt like right now.

It never occurred to me water could be violent, yet that was the only way I could describe this.

The blast of freezing liquid, flung down on my prone form, stunned my body but at the same time put it in flight mode. My lungs seized the second I was hit. The water hit me as one solid form on first contact. The second it slammed into me, it shattered into a million tiny drops that felt like shards of ice cutting into my skin.

I gasped and bolted up. The only thought my shocked body and mind could form was, *Run!*

In a way, it was like waking from the worst dream you could ever have. Only I'd never had a dream this horrible before—like even my subconscious couldn't have imagined this.

My chest burned when I sucked in gulps of air and tried to catch my breath. Water soaked me, sliding over my skin, dragging at my hair and plastering my clothes against me. My fingers stung with cold. Having already been chilled, the frigid temp of the water only magnified the lack of heat.

Gooseflesh erupted across my body, and I shuddered. I scrambled backward, dragging the chain around my wrist with me. It was heavy, like an anvil around my ankle, dragging me down into a pitch-black body of water just waiting to swallow me whole. I fought the weight, wanting as much space between me and the man as humanly possible.

As I rushed back, I blinked furiously, trying to get the water out of my vision so I could see clearly. When it didn't work, I swiped at my face and hair with my hands.

It was him. The taxi driver.

The mask he wore was gone, and he was facing me. It was the first full-on view I got of him since he took me. He was dressed in a pair of grey slacks and a white polo tucked in. His waist was soft and a little pudgy, his face round, and his eyes brown. The hair on his head was brown, sort of thin at the top and cut into a short, ordinary men's style.

He didn't have a beard or any visible tattoos.

If I saw him on the street, I'd not think twice about him. That's what made him so incredibly scary. How many times had I passed by someone just as evil as him on the street and not known?

How many "ordinary" depraved people like him walked around every single day and no one knew?

My stomach heaved, and I fought the urge to vomit right there. I lurched back, up off my knees, and into a crouching position. The chained wrist was still heavy and dragged my arm down. I left it hanging, there was no point in wasting my strength trying to hold it up when it wasn't absolutely necessary.

My free arm wrapped around my middle, an automatic and protective gesture. Cold water dripped down my cheeks and over my lips. I parted them ever so slightly because the beckoning of water was just a little too strong. My God, I was thirsty. So much so I had a brief thought of pulling the drenched strands of my hair into my mouth to ring out the water.

He dropped the metal bucket at his feet, the handle clanging against the side. "That's what you get for faking."

I wasn't admitting to anything. I stared at him warily, willing my brain to come up with something, anything I could do to get the hell out of here.

"Nothing to say?" he asked, raking his eyes over me in a way that made me feel like I'd never be clean again. "You sure did plenty of yelling and screaming last night."

It's morning? "Would anyone hear me if I screamed?" I asked. The husky, low tone of my voice alarmed me.

He smirked. "Nope. But you're welcome to try."

He was a liar and a criminal. I didn't believe a word out of his mouth, but I knew screaming right now would be useless. That, too, seemed like a waste of energy.

"What do you want with me?" I asked, moving until my back hit the pole I was chained to.

"Lots of things," he replied, looking down my body and then back up.

I bit down on my lower lip so I wouldn't cry. I'd never give this animal the satisfaction.

Besides, if all he wanted was to rape me, he would have done it by now.

He took a step forward, and my body locked up, ready to fight. But that's as far as he got because the man I assumed was his boss appeared, tucking a cell into his pocket.

"There's been a new development," he said.

The taxi driver glanced over his shoulder. "What is it?"

He gestured with his head to come away from me. With a lingering look that made my skin crawl, my captor swiveled around and walked across the large area toward his partner.

The other man grabbed him by his elbow and towed him a little farther away. "…opportunity for more…"

I strained to hear, not even pretending not to listen. They knew I was awake. I glanced down at my soaked clothing. Hell, they made sure I was awake. If they didn't want me listening, they shouldn't have kidnapped me.

I only caught snippets of the hushed conversation, which was extremely frustrating.

"What!" the taxi man exclaimed loudly. Then he started shaking his head insistently, like he didn't like what the other man was telling him.

That earned him a stealthy jab to his chest with a thick, stubby finger. His lips moved, but I couldn't hear what he was saying. "…Tonight…" he finished before stepping back.

"That wasn't part of the deal," Taxi Man argued.

"The deal changed," his boss intoned.

"How much?"

The boss glanced at me, and our eyes locked. He looked back and stepped closer and whispered something.

Taxi Man's eyes widened. "Fine."

"Let's go." The boss clapped him on the back, and they turned away from me. "We have plans to make."

"What about her?" Taxi Man motioned behind him at me.

Was it so much to ask I just be forgotten about?

"Leave her. She's not our problem right now. She's his."

Whose?

Taxi Man glanced back at me before they turned out of sight. "See ya soon."

I shuddered.

They left, the heavy scraping of metal against metal their departing sound. It looked like some huge sliding door at the front of the building. When they were gone, I collapsed back against the pole in relief.

It seemed as though I was granted some kind of reprieve. Still, it didn't feel like much of a gift—more of a prolonging of torture.

Or maybe… just maybe it was an opportunity to figure out a way the hell out of here.

3

Derek

It's a damn good thing I liked my job.

Because some days it really sucked donkey balls.

Sometimes it was a fine balance between passion and exhaustion. Some days I forget why I did what I did. Some days I wondered what kept me going.

I lost a patient today.

A patient I'd been fighting with for a very long time. We felt like a team, this patient and I. It was hard not to get invested in patients—in people—when you saw them on such a regular basis. When she first started coming to see me, there was a lot of hope. Her case wasn't that severe, and I thought we'd be able to beat it. I'd bought her a lot of time over the past several years.

Unfortunately, her condition deteriorated faster than I'd wanted.

We slowed it as much as humanly possible.

That's the thing about being human.

Humanity has its limits. There's only so much a man can do before it all rests on fate and a higher power.

This wasn't the first time I'd seen a patient die. It wasn't going to be the last.

I saved far more than I lost.

But that didn't matter to the ones I failed. To the ones I wasn't able to save, my successes probably felt like a gross amount of luck I'd stumbled into.

I couldn't even blame them for that. Hell, sometimes I found myself wallowing in agreement. When I would walk into their room for rounds to ask invasive questions and ascertain how things were progressing, sometimes I would see the acceptance in their eyes.

I would see the death. It had a filmy kind of existence in their stare, like a layer of fat that needed skimmed off a container of gravy.

Sometimes I was haunted by that look. By the accusation accompanying it.

You're letting me die.

Why can't you do something?

Help me.

So yeah, sometimes I really fucking hated my career choice.

I wasn't equipped to play God, though I admit sometimes that's what I felt like I was doing.

A lot of people often said doctors had God complexes. Well, I wasn't one of those doctors. To me, the life and death of a patient was something I wished I had no control over at all.

It was days like this when I felt like I was dumb for wishing that.

In truth, I did have some control over it. I had the ability to add years, decades even, to people's time on this earth. I had the ability to drastically change the quality of a person's life.

Medicine wasn't a miracle, though. It was a science. Not even an exact one. Maybe some would disagree, but I begged to differ. The thing about medicine— specifically the kind I practiced— was it depended a lot on the person. The body. The subject. Sure, there was a damn good baseline on how to treat illness and disease. There were surefire ways to prolong the life and use of organs in a person's body.

But nothing was absolute.

The only thing in this entire world that I knew of as absolute was death.

So while I could fight it as valiantly and aggressively as I could, sometimes death won. The hard truth was there just weren't enough viable organs for people who needed them.

Currently, in the United States, more than one hundred and twenty-three thousand people needed an organ transplant. Over one hundred thousand of those were people who needed kidneys.

Though I did many different kind of transplants, I specialized in kidneys.

To put those numbers into a little perspective, roughly only twenty-eight thousand people get the transplant they need to survive every year.

That's a lot of people who don't get what they need.

That's a lot of death.

Eighteen people die every day in this country, waiting for a transplant.

Today, one of those eighteen people was mine.

Watching a patient covered somberly by a sheet as the time of death is being called and knowing it could have been avoided if only they'd gotten what they needed was… difficult.

I tried to remain detached as much as possible, but the thing that made a man a good doctor was his humanity. His empathy. Not being a robot. Not looking through a patient instead of at them.

I was a good doctor.

So days like today made me feel like a failure.

I pushed into the doctors' lounge as I rubbed a hand over the back of my neck. God, today had been fucking endless. I felt like I'd aged about ten years, and if I were a cat, I'd only have seven lives left.

The room was empty and quiet, thank fuck.

I needed a few minutes of breather time. Even the sound of my scrubs rubbing together annoyed me as I walked.

I dropped onto the brown leather couch and slumped into the cushions, whipping off my stethoscope and dropping it beside me. The cool temperature of the leather pressed into the back of my neck when I rested my head against it.

My eyes closed, and I went about the usual "talking to" I think most doctors probably had to give themselves in some form on a regular basis. *This wasn't your fault. There is only so much you can do. You aren't a miracle worker. If there isn't an organ available, there just isn't one available.*

I knew all those statements were true.

Knowing something and allowing yourself to believe it were two different things. It was hard to fight against the heavy weight of death. Especially after a helluva long day at the hospital.

I'd earned the right to sit here in private and be sad for a few minutes. I'd even earned the pissed-off frustration that was giving the sadness quite an ass kicking.

Sometimes it was hard to accept being just a man.

Sometimes it was hard to know I couldn't save them all.

I wanted to.

I'm not sure how long I sat there with my eyes closed, but they opened when someone pushed into the lounge behind me.

"Ah, Dr. Kelley," spoke a familiar voice.

"Hey, Reggie, how's it going?"

A tall blonde with her hair pinned neatly behind her head stopped beside the couch and looked down. "I heard."

News traveled fast in a hospital. It was like its own contained soap opera. I couldn't even say I didn't understand. I did. Doctors worked a lot of hours. We spent lots and lots of time at this hospital. Our co-workers saw more of us than our families. Gossip was kind of like the icing on a long-day cupcake.

Not that I liked gossip.

Unless it was when someone was whispering about a nurse and doctor getting it on in the janitor's closet.

Oh yeah, that shit happened. And it was entertaining as hell.

Note: I'd never done it. I'd thought about it, though.

I grunted. "Can't save them all." Pushing up from the couch, I grabbed the stethoscope and flung it around the back of my neck.

"That's true." Reggie agreed, reaching for my wrist and encircling it lightly with her fingers. "Still sucks."

I half smiled and turned back. "Yeah."

I knew she understood. She'd been there.

She released my wrist to step close and hug me. Her arms looped up around my neck as her body pressed close. She had a nice rack. I liked the way it kind of squished against my chest.

I'm a guy. Did you really think I wouldn't notice the way it felt when a woman's breasts rubbed against me?

Fine. She wasn't rubbing them against me, but I felt them. Same difference.

Reggie was tall, not much shorter than me, and I was six feet. She had an athletic body. It was obvious she took care of herself. She was single, like me, and I knew it was likely because of her job. Both of us were fairly young and dedicated to our careers, which didn't leave much time for anything else.

I wrapped an arm around her waist, returning the hug. After a moment, I eased away, and she pulled back to smile. "You done for the day?"

"Thank God," I said.

She smiled. She was a pretty woman with blond hair and brown eyes. "Get some rest. You earned it."

"That's the plan, right after I hit the gym." There was no way I could just go home right now and expect to get some sleep. I needed to work off some of the frustration of the day.

"What's your schedule like this weekend?" she asked casually.

I wandered over to my locker and entered the combination into the lock. She was going to ask me out.

We'd kinda been dancing around this for a while now. In fact, we'd actually had a date planned once, about a month ago. But I got called in for a transplant and couldn't make it. She hadn't been upset; she knew the drill. But after that, I never made an attempt to reschedule.

I had a feeling she'd been waiting, though, wondering why I hadn't.

I'd been the one to ask her out in the first place. She'd put out interested signals almost since the day we met. We were a good fit. A natural fit. Both of us were hella busy. We both worked long hours and were committed to our jobs. Those things made it hard to hold on to a relationship.

Hell, I'd had more than one woman dump me because of it.

Those break-ups never really bothered me. I didn't miss a beat. Those women were better off, obviously. If I didn't even notice they'd vacated my life, then they didn't belong there anyway.

I was pretty sure Reggie had a called-off engagement under her belt. I heard some gossip about it. But that's all I knew. Honestly, I tried to stay out of the drama going around (unless of course they were talking about people having sex), so when I heard the whispers, I made myself busy.

Our failed romances was another reason we would work. Expectations wouldn't be very high and the understanding that work came first would be a given.

So why hadn't I rescheduled our date?

She was hot. Had good tits.

Side bar: I was pretty sure they were fake. I wasn't hating. In fact, fake meant they'd always stay nice and perky.

And of course, we had similar careers and could see each other at work to make up for when we didn't see each other outside of work.

Because dating someone who would "work" doesn't seem like a good enough reason to date.

"I'm on call, but hopefully I'll be off," I said ruefully, digging around in my locker for my gym clothes.

Aaand, I just gave her an opening. I had to give her props. She was tired of waiting for me to set something up so she was gonna do it herself. It was another reason to like her.

I had a sudden craving for coffee.

I never drank coffee until a couple months ago. I didn't even like the shit. Until I was bewitched by a barista I was convinced poured something addictive into the cup before she handed it over.

I liked her coffee.

Almost as much as I liked her red hair and freckles.

It probably wouldn't work with her (dating I mean). Hell, it was the reason I only flirted and never asked her out.

Even though an invite for a movie or dinner… or sex was always on the tip of my tongue when I stepped up to her coffee truck.

I wouldn't actually invite her to have sex; that would guarantee I wouldn't get any. But damn, how could I not think about it when I'd see her round ass bouncing around inside her café on wheels?

"I'm off this weekend, too," Reggie said, and I was almost startled. I'd forgotten she was still there.

I spun from the locker, my gym bag and car keys in hand. "Yeah?" I echoed. What the fuck was she talking about?

"So since we are both off…" She started.

Fuck. I wasn't up for this right now.

I couldn't say no because it might make things awkward at work. But if I said yes and we went out and I wished I'd said no, it would make things awkward at work.

Double jeopardy. That's what women were.

Damned if I did. Damned if I didn't.

The lounge door flung open, and we both looked up.

Saved! I mentally fist pumped in the air.

"Dr. Kelley!" A nurse rushed in, looking around.

"Yeah, Beth?" I replied, instantly alert.

Shit, not another emergency tonight. Not another patient failing.

"You have a phone call."

I felt myself relax. Then I stiffened again. "Why the urgency?"

Her eyes rounded; her reply was breathless. "It's from the national registry list. I think it's for him."

I left my locker ajar, dumped the shit I was holding in my hands on the floor, and rushed for the door.

"Good luck!" Reggie called behind me.

I didn't even look back.

This was it. The call I'd been waiting for. The only thing in the entire world that could turn this shitty day around.

4

Derek

The phone on the desk was probably a dinosaur.

Hell, these days, if a phone didn't fit in your pocket, explore the web, and literally talk back when you asked it a question, it was practically ancient.

This particular phone was large, square, and had a twisty black cord. About thirty buttons adorned the square, flat surface, and there were about ten little blinking lights all going off that made me feel bad for the nurses.

"Line two," Beth called as I skidded around the counter and picked up the black receiver.

"Doctor Kelley," I said briskly into the line. My heart was hammering. Anticipation and hope tingled my fingers and made my chest tight.

If this was a false alarm or not for him… there was a bottle of whiskey collecting dust in my kitchen that just might have to be introduced to the back of my throat.

"Dr. Kelley, this is Stacey from the national donor registry list."

"Yes," I said, mentally shouting for her to hurry the hell up.

"We are calling to let you know we have matched an organ for one of your patients. It will be ready for transport tomorrow and only take a few hours to arrive at your hospital."

"Which patient?" I asked.

There was a pause. "Rocco Kelley."

My whole body jerked, and I exhaled loudly. "Best news I've gotten all day."

"Will you be available tomorrow evening for the transplant?" The woman went on like she didn't just change my life.

"Of course," I said. "Don't you need me to fly to the organ and either remove it or pick it up for transport?"

I did that a lot, and I fully expected to do that for this kidney.

"It isn't necessary at this time. We have a transplant team already onsite. The organ is being harvested from a donor who is being removed from life support. There will be several removed during the procedure."

"What about transport?" I pressed.

"That is also already taken care of."

"By who?" I demanded. This was important. I needed to be sure it was done right. Transplanting an organ wasn't like delivering a bouquet of flowers.

"An organ from the same donor is being picked up and delivered to St. Vincent's via a chopper at the same time. The pilot said he would touch down to deliver the kidney to your hospital on his way."

St. Vincent's was another very large hospital about four hours from here. "So a doctor from St. Vincent's will be overseeing the transport?"

"Yes."

"Who?" I asked.

"I'm sorry?"

"Which doctor?" I pressed. I knew them all over there. They had a large transplant wing, and sometimes we worked together. "Dr. Ross, Dr. Peter…?" I asked, impatient.

"Dr. Ross."

I nodded. He was a good doctor. I could trust him with the organ.

"You're sure this kidney is a match?"

"Positive."

I smiled, so ready to celebrate.

We talked a few more details, and then I hung up the phone. Beth, a regular nurse on this floor, was right behind me when I turned.

"Well?" she asked, anxious.

"It's a match!"

She grinned, and we hugged quickly.

"Best news I've had all week!" she exclaimed.

"I gotta go tell them." I pulled back, grinning.

"When will it be here?" she asked as I was rushing away.

"Tomorrow!" I called out. "Clear my schedule!"

"With pleasure!"

I ran down the hall, my sneakers making an obnoxious squeaking sound against the buffed linoleum. I'd been rushing so fast I'd overshot the doorway all the way at the end of the hall, and on my way past, I grabbed the doorframe to slow me down.

My sister, Laura, jerked up from her chair when she saw my antics.

"Derek?" she said, alarmed. "What is it? The tests…" A look of absolute fear screwed up her face, and I watched her try and hide it.

I glanced at the bed, where my nephew Rocco was sleeping.

I grabbed up my sister and hugged her tight. "Derek," she insisted against my chest.

I pulled her back, holding on to her shoulders. "There's a match."

She gasped. "Are you sure?"

"I just got off the phone with the registry."

Her eyes filled with tears. "Oh my God."

I nodded.

"And it's a match?"

"Yes," I said, hugging her again.

She sobbed into my chest, and I glanced again at the kid in the bed.

At ten years old, my nephew Rocco was small for his age. From the time he'd turned three, he'd been sick. It didn't take long to realize both his kidneys were on a steady decline and he was going to need a transplant.

His illness was an incredible blow for my entire family. The sun rose and set with Rocco. He was the only grandchild, my sister's only, and my best friend.

Even though he'd been sick most of his life, he was still an amazing kid. I liked him better than almost every adult I knew. He was bright, funny, and played a mean game of poker.

It wasn't fair he was plagued with bad kidneys. It wasn't fair he was restrained to a hospital bed more and more as the years passed.

He'd been on the list for a kidney for years now. The odds of finding one to match his rare blood type and the fact he was a kid (a smaller organ was ideal) made it that much harder.

In the past six months, his health had been on a steady decline. I'd done everything I could. I researched alternative therapies, tried traditional ones. Called in consults from doctors with more experience and man hours. I even typed myself to see if I could give him one of my kidneys.

The entire family did. No one was viable.

His prick of a father left when he was one. No one could find him. He literally drove away one day and never came back. He might be a match… but he was nowhere.

I'd hired private investigators. I'd email and called every place he'd been seen or spotted. If he knew his son desperately needed a transplant, he didn't care. He was the shittiest human being I'd ever had the displeasure of meeting.

I'd become more of a father figure to Rocco than an uncle. I was his doctor, too. He'd been admitted in this hospital for over two weeks now.

Things were looking pretty grim.

I spent my off time researching, looking for anything that might buy him time.

If he… if died before we could get the transplant he needed… I was afraid of who I'd become. I knew it would change me in the core of who I was.

The change wouldn't be a good one.

"You're one hundred percent sure?" Laura asked again, pulling away and swiping at her eyes.

"They have an entire process of making sure." I assured her. "You know this."

She nodded. She knew almost as much as I did about transplants now. The only person who was more desperate than me to make sure Rocco lived was her.

"When?" She glanced over at his dark head on the pillow.

"Tomorrow night. They have a team bringing the organ to me."

"You'll be here for the surgery?"

I was offended she had to ask. "Wild animals couldn't keep me away," I vowed. I'd do this surgery half dead.

"My team will start getting him prepped. I'll get some stuff going tonight. Then I'm going to go home, shower, and try and get some sleep. I want to be on top of my game tomorrow when his kidney gets here."

She nodded. "Of course. You need to go home. Rest."

I was so tempted to wake the kid and tell him the good news. I wanted to so badly my fingers trembled. But I held back. He needed his sleep. He needed all his strength for tomorrow.

"I'll get the ball rolling. I'll be here in the morning."

"Thank you, Derek," Laura whispered, tears welling again.

I hugged her one last time before retreating to the door. Renewed energy coursed through my system. This was why I loved my job. Because even though I lost some good people, I got to save some, too.

Rocco was going to have a full and healthy life after tomorrow. I'd make sure of it.

"Derek?" Laura whispered as I was leaving.

I turned back.

"It's going to be okay, right?"

I retreated back to her side and looked into her eyes. "He's going to be just fine. This is exactly everything we've been praying for."

She nodded, seeming to steel herself. Even though he was getting what he needed, he still had a surgery to get through. That was enough to worry any mother.

I'd be worried, too, if I wasn't going to be the one in the operating room with him.

"No one will take better care of him than you," she said as if she read my thoughts.

"Damn straight." I agreed and smiled.

The sense of relief I felt was incredible. It was like a two-thousand-ton weight had been lifted off my shoulders. A weight I'd been burdened with for years. The fact that I couldn't find my nephew a kidney—me, a goddamned transplant doctor—kept me up at night.

But transplant doctors don't get head-of-the-line privileges. It doesn't work that way. It was a heaping dose of learning what my patients went through.

I hated it.

"Maybe I should just fly to where the kidney is, just in case," I said, almost to myself.

"What?" she asked.

"They said they had a skilled transplant team in place already and a doctor who would bring it. I know the doctor. He's a good surgeon. But this is Rocco… I want to oversee the harvesting. Get a look at the kidney."

"But then you won't be rested for the surgery."

"I can sleep on the plane."

She frowned. "You said you trust the doctor overseeing it?"

I nodded. "He's from St. Vincent's."

She nodded immediately. She knew the hospital. Rocco had been seen there several times.

"The doctors there know him. They will take care of his kidney. I really think you need to go home, rest."

She was right… I'd just come off a double shift. I was exhausted and beaten down from today. A night of sleep would be ideal for the surgery tomorrow.

Laura stepped up. "Derek, I know you've done everything humanly possible for Rocco. I wouldn't trust anyone else with his surgery, but you need to rest. This has been just as hard on you as the rest of us. Please. I'll worry."

I relented. Dr. Ross was a good doctor. I knew he'd handle this well.

"Yeah, okay," I said, running my fingers through my hair. "I'll see you in the morning." I leaned down and kissed her on the cheek.

She smiled, looking more relaxed already.

"Once he's recovered, we're going to Disneyland," I announced.

She nodded. "He will love it."

I spent a while getting the ball rolling on the surgery and calling my team to let them know. After everyone had their instructions, I went back into the lounge to pick up the bag I'd left on the floor. It wasn't lying out anymore. Everything was back in the locker, the door was closed, the lock on.

Quickly, I opened it up and glanced inside. There was a yellow sticky note almost at my eye level stuck to the front of the metal shelf inside.

Sending good thoughts your way!—Reg

I smiled, left the note where it was and grabbed my shit.

Reggie was definitely good people. Maybe I should give her a chance.

She isn't the one you want and you know it, a voice in the back of my mind declared.

I couldn't even argue.

It was true.

5

Rose

A chain is a formidable opponent.

It is entirely maddening to see an escape route, to know you're alone and could make a legit attempt at freedom before anyone came back, only to have the knowledge taunt you mercilessly.

I struggled.

No. What I was doing went beyond struggling. I had no idea where I was, why I'd been kidnapped, or how long I was going to be alone until they came back. I didn't know if I would ever see my home again, my coffee truck… my family.

Everything as I knew it, *life* as I knew it, could be over.

I was emotionally battered, and now because of the stupid and barbaric chain around my wrist, I was becoming physically battered as well.

The second my captors left me here alone, I got to work. I tugged and yanked. I pulled and fought with this chain. It was impervious to my attempts at somehow yanking it off the pipe it was wrapped around. When my arms were literally shaking from effort and my fingertips red and raw from gripping the chain, I sank onto the still damp concrete floor and dropped my face into my hands.

I allowed myself about a minute of pity. Then I shut it down.

If my arms and legs were too weak to keep fighting against these stupid yet impossibly strong inanimate objects, I would change course.

The metal cuff around my wrist wasn't loose. I tried to push it down over my hand in several different ways. When it was locked around my skin, it was done so tightly my wrist was already becoming raw. Even just sitting here would likely make it rub because they'd placed it on so snug.

Why couldn't I have been kidnapped by dumb criminals? You know, ones who attach things with a little give… enough I could manipulate and squeeze my hand out?

Why couldn't the chain be brittle and rusty? Why couldn't there be a tool nearby I could use to help?

I dropped my hands into my lap, pulled my legs in close, and stared down.

It was incredibly hard to hold on to hope when all seemed so hopeless. I wasn't sure how long I'd been fighting to get free, but I knew it had been hours. My wrist was scraped and bleeding. The skin felt tender and raw. My throat was dry and felt swollen. Blood welled and smeared on my fingertips. The effort of fighting against the chain and cuff had literally torn at my skin.

Taking my skirt, I wrapped my fingers in the fabric, bunching it around the wounds without a second thought to how ruined this outfit was.

It didn't matter.

Nothing mattered anymore but living.

The beating of my heart and the oxygen filling my lungs became the most basic elements needed for survival. It was almost amazing how fast a life and necessities could be condensed when death stared you in the face.

I gripped the skirt and hunched in on myself as I thought about all the things I never got to do. The things I never said and the plans I would never get to follow through on.

A tear fell and slid haphazardly down to the corner of my lip. I caught it with my tongue and drew it into my mouth. The salty flavor seemed to jar me out of what I was going to refer to as a "woe as me" moment.

Sitting here like I was just going to accept my fate, as if I were done fighting, was not acceptable.

I might have still been chained. I might have still had to sit here and know there was a door so close, but I didn't have to give up.

If I couldn't get free, maybe I could think of something else.

The man had a phone earlier. I would bet almost anything the taxi driver had one, too. Everyone had a phone these days—hell, even some six-year-olds.

If I could get ahold of one of those, I could call for help.

Not far from where I was slumped on the ground was the bucket the man used to give me an impromptu shower.

I was still damp, by the way. It might be hot here in the South, but inside this shaded metal building was kinda cool, which I supposed I should have been thankful for, but it certainly didn't help me get dry. I was soggy, my undergarments were so very uncomfortable, my shirt was still plastered to my chest, and my hair felt cold and clumpy to the touch.

But there was a bucket. It was the only thing within reaching distance. I wasn't sure what I could do with it, but desperate times called for desperate measures.

I scooted across the cement, inching my way until the chain was taut and refused to let me go any farther. My wrist hit the pavement, and I spun so my feet were facing the bucket. I lay down, my cuffed arm over my head, and stretched my body as long as I could toward the bucket.

My bare foot kicked out, just catching the top edge, and it fell over with a loud clattering sound. When it rolled toward me and not in the opposite direction, I collapsed against the ground like I'd just run ten miles.

Seconds later, I stretched out again and used my toes to attempt grasp the handle. Several tries later, the bucket made a dragging sound as I brought it in closer.

"Yes!" I exclaimed, scrambling up and grabbing the metal handle. I hugged it close to my chest like it was something far better than it was.

What did one do with a bucket when it was the only weapon they had?

I couldn't even think about how pathetic it was this old rusty thing was my only hope, because it was more than I had five minutes ago.

I studied the gray metal, simple handle, and ordinary shape as if it were a long-lost piece of the Titanic. It was so quiet in here… I never did mind the quiet or my own company. In fact, I rather liked it. It was one of the reasons I worked for myself. I didn't like being told what to do or punching a timeclock set by someone else.

But the quiet right now was unnerving. It felt like a death sentence.

Shuddering, I banged the bucket down between my legs and listened to the sound that filled the space. The handle clattered against the side when I slammed it down. I stared at it, lifting it with one of my raw fingertips and letting it drop.

This bucket was sort of old school. You know, it had a metal handle where the ends stuck through a drilled hole on each side of the top. To keep it in place, the metal folded in on itself so it couldn't slip back through the hole.

Well, I guess it was old school. I really didn't know how buckets were made…

Anyway, it seemed like maybe if I could get the handle off and bend it to be a little less curved, then maybe, just maybe, I could use it as some wort of weapon. It might not be a knife with a razor-sharp end, but I could still do some damage with it. That's the thing about the human body… It isn't impenetrable. In fact, it's sort of vulnerable that way.

I got to work. One side looked like it might be a little easier to get loose because it was slightly dented, and I was hoping the hole would be a little distorted.

The flesh on my fingers screamed as I worked, but I ignored it just as I tried to ignore the red slicking my skin. I'd rather rip all the flesh off my hands than be sitting here without anything at all when those men came back.

They'd probably be back soon. I had no idea where they'd gone, what they were up to… It was something I tried not to dwell on. I couldn't stop what they were doing, at least not right now. My concentration needed to be fully focused on defending myself.

I don't know how long it took to work the handle free, but I managed.

When at last the metal sprang free and fell into my lap, I actually cried. I didn't feel embarrassed either because I was so incredibly grateful I'd managed to do something, even if it was something small.

Exhaustion clung to me the same way the water had clung to my clothes. I ached all over; even my bones felt sore. Sitting on a hard, cold ground for hours wasn't comfortable. It was even less so when sitting after physically fighting with a pipe and chain.

My lips felt dry, to the point when I moved my mouth into any kind of facial expression, I could feel them stretch like they wanted to crack.

I wasn't sure what time it was… but I was likely coming up on twenty-four hours without any water. I could go longer, but being taken while I was drunk only dehydrated me more. The little bit of water I'd stooped so low to suck out of my hair (hey, don't judge) did nothing but make my thirst worse.

My stomach growled, my body hungry. The thought of food made my nose wrinkle up in disgust, but I knew that was just a mental reaction. I was anxious and under a lot of stress right now. Hell, I lost my appetite when I ran out of coffee filters and the flavor packets everyone liked so much at the coffee car.

I laughed. The sound echoed around me.

That seemed so stupid now, to get stressed about my stock. Mentally, I told myself I shouldn't degrade the feelings I'd had before I was kidnapped. Being stressed about something like a job wasn't anything to be ashamed of.

I wasn't dumb for being a human.

I was just scared right now.

If food were suddenly presented to me, I'd eat it. Even if I had to shove it past my gag reflex. My body needed all the strength it could get. My God, I was already so incredibly drained. I felt weak and foggy after struggling all day.

What would I be like in another twenty-four hours?

The sharp edge of my teeth sank into my lip, and the metallic, warm sensation of blood hit my tongue. I pulled back to dab at my lower lip with my finger. The cracked and thin skin had obviously had enough.

I picked up the now handle-less bucket and carried it over to place it behind the pipe. I wasn't sure what else I would do with it, but I wasn't about to let it go.

Once it was behind me, I sat, leaning against the pipe. It felt cold against my cheek. The joints in my knuckles stung. I realized it was because of the force with which I griped the metal handle. With effort, I forced my body to relax enough so maybe, just maybe, I would stop hurting for a few minutes.

I needed to straighten the handle out a little. And maybe I could rub it against the concrete enough that it would sharpen into more of a point on one end.

Just the thought of getting to work on that had fresh tears spilling over my cheeks. I rubbed at my face and tugged on the tangled ends of hair falling over my shoulder.

A few minutes of rest wouldn't be a bad idea. It wouldn't be weak. Getting some strength back was just as necessary as fighting to get free.

Giving in, I lay on the hard, cold floor and tucked an arm under my head. My other hand kept hold on the weapon I'd managed to secure and pulled it in close against my chest.

I lay there staring out over the space, studying the shadows and tractors until my eyes grew too heavy to keep open.

6

Derek

I went to the gym.

Yeah, I was exhausted, but I was also wired. I was fucking ecstatic Rocco was getting a kidney, but even that didn't make me forget about the woman I lost today.

The thing I learned about being a transplant doctor was all lives were equal.

It didn't matter your race, religion, social status, or what was in your bank account.

Organs could fail anyone.

Disease didn't discriminate.

Death didn't either.

The life that was lost today wasn't worth any less than Rocco's.

My heart denied that statement. It denied it with every fiber in my being. Rocco's life was beyond valuable to me. He was worth everything.

Because he was my nephew.

Of course I wanted to save him. Of course I wanted all the time in the world I could get.

But the woman who died today? Her family wanted the same things.

And that right there was why I didn't have a God complex.

I didn't get to decide. When it came right down to it, we were all equal.

We were all at the mercy of the universe.

I drove directly from the hospital to a twenty-four-hour gym where I had a monthly membership. I liked working out late at night because no one was ever here. I had the place to myself.

It made for a faster workout because I didn't have to wait for equipment or get sidetracked by people wanting to talk.

I went in, did my time, and walked out.

I kept it simple tonight, opting for a run on a treadmill at a challenging pace. When that was done I did some upper body work and headed back into the locker room for my stuff.

I'd just shower at home. Having the gym to myself was cool, but it was still a public shower.

No thanks.

I'd seen too many pictures and actual cases of fungus at the hospital to last me a lifetime.

On the way home, exhaustion fully settled into my muscles and body. I knew I'd be able to sleep the second I lay down. I planned on getting a full eight hours. Then I'd get up, fuel up, and head to the hospital. It was going to be another long day, but it was one I was looking forward to.

I smiled. Maybe on the way in, I'd stop for a coffee. The caffeine might give me an extra boost in the operating room.

Or maybe the girl serving it would.

She was like a breath of fresh air. Hell, I liked her. I liked her a whole hell of a lot. *Maybe I should just suck it up and ask her out.*

Chicks dug doctors.

Until the reality of dating one sank in.

I was going to be busy in the coming weeks. Rocco would need a lot of care. When I wasn't at work, I'd be with him.

It was shitty timing to date. Even if she did make an appearance in my thoughts at least once a day. It really wouldn't be fair to ask her out and then be unavailable.

Dooo it.

That voice in the back of my head was a persistent asshole. He seemed to like trouble, too.

Something told me Rose would be a lot of trouble.

Hell, maybe I was just horny.

Maybe I should make a date with Reggie and we could have one of those friends with benefits relationships because we were too busy for more.

Or maybe I just needed a one-night stand.

I pulled onto the street where my three-bedroom house sat and drove slowly past all the houses of similar style. I bought the place about a year ago; it was a good investment.

It was still half empty because I was never home to fill it up, but someday I'd get around to it. It had all the shit I needed for now. Like a bed, a shower, and a TV.

It was a newer construction, with the usual vinyl siding and concrete driveway. The siding was a blue-gray shade, and the shutters and front door were black. There was an attached garage, which was a definite plus, so I hit the opener as I pulled close.

The light from the overhead spilled out into the driveway as the door slowly opened, and I pulled up the concrete to wait for it to open completely.

All the lights inside were off. I hadn't been home in almost a full twenty-four hours.

I needed to check the mail, too; I hadn't done it in a while. The mailman was probably getting pissed. The last time I went too long without checking it, I got a note taped to my front door.

Once my Land Rover was parked inside, I left the door up, grabbed my keys, phone, and got out. Now was as good a time as any to get the mail. I'd be too busy tomorrow anyway.

I jogged down the driveway toward the mailbox. I surveyed the grass to make sure it wasn't time to mow it again. Grass here didn't grow as fast because it was hot as hell.

On the road, I grabbed an armload of the mail with a grimace. Yeah, it'd been a while since I got it. Hell, probably ninety percent of this shit would go right in the trash without even being opened.

Junk mail was just as annoying as trying to piss with a boner.

Halfway up the driveway, I heard the sound of an engine but didn't bother to turn around. It was probably just a neighbor or car passing by.

When I stepped into the garage, headlights bounced over the pavement and glinted off the taillights of my SUV.

"What the fuck?" I muttered and swung around.

I squinted against the imposing headlights, annoyance ripping through me.

It was a cab.

The bright-yellow paint and little sign on the roof was unmistakable. The lights dimmed so there were just the fog lights, and my eyes adjusted.

A hand came out the window, followed by part of a head.

"Hey, buddy, you got a minute?"

"What?" I called.

"Can you give me some directions?"

Didn't cabs have GPS in them?

Fuck if I knew. I never took cabs. Never had to. Last time I went out with some friends, one of them was the DD.

"Sure," I replied and dumped the mail on a nearby workbench.

I started down the driveway toward him. The cabbie pushed open his door and got out.

I stopped several feet away. "Where you headed?"

"You're the first guy I've seen in miles. I'm not use to driving in this residential area, and all these damn streets look the same," he bitched.

I chuckled. "Yeah, there's not much originality around here."

"So I'm looking for Pender Street," he said.

I frowned. "I'm not familiar with it." In fact, I'd never heard of it. "It must be on the other side of town."

He muttered some colorful curse words. "The call said it was near Irongate Drive. This is it, ain't it?"

I nodded. "Yeah. Maybe drive a couple streets over."

He pushed away from his car and came closer. His hands were shoved into the pockets of his jacket.

It was summer. Why was he wearing a jacket?

"That way?" He pulled one hand out and pointed off in one direction.

"Yeah." I lied. I had no fucking clue. There was something off about this guy. "I'll catch you later, man," I said and moved toward the garage.

"Hey," he called out. "One more thing."

"What?" I looked back, then did a double take.

He was pointing a gun at me.

"I'm really not in the mood for this." I warned him.

"Get in the car, nice and slow."

I laughed.

He jabbed the gun in my direction, an angry look on his face. "I said get in the car!"

"No."

He seemed surprised I didn't rush to do it. I guess when faced with a gun, most people complied.

I wasn't most people.

"I will shoot you right here and now," he vowed.

"Hope you got a silencer on that, then. My neighbor's a real nosy bitch," I drawled. My neighbor wasn't nosy. That gun didn't have a silencer on it. I couldn't make out what kind of gun it was exactly; it was too dark.

But it most definitely didn't have a silencer.

Instead of shooting, he rushed me.

Stupid.

I swung around and clocked him immediately. He fell backward like he was shocked. I enjoyed the way my fist smacked against his face.

Anger lit through me. Anger I didn't even know was there.

It was fucking insane scum like him walked around healthy and free while other people died daily—good people—because their bodies failed them.

I lunged forward and hit him again, this time in the midsection. He bent, and I reached down to relieve him of his weapon, but he wrenched away.

I grabbed the back of his jacket and yanked him back, reaching for it again.

He elbowed me in the side, and all the breath whooshed out of me. I released him for a split second, only to recover and punch him again.

He fell onto the driveway, hitting his back like a two-dollar hooker, and rolled.

I reached into my pocket for my phone to get the cops over here so they could deal with his rotten ass. I didn't have time for this bullshit.

Fucking wanker.

He saw me pull out my phone and made a sound. He was still on the ground when the gun came up. I'd been so focused on the phone I hadn't noticed his movements until it was one second too late.

He got off a shot.

Something sharp and piercing hit my side.

Almost like I'd been bit by some giant mosquito.

I glanced down.

A thin, metal-looking dart was sticking out of my stomach. A yellow tail quivered in the night air.

What the shit was this?

I yanked it out and stared down at it. Then I glanced back up.

The cabbie watched me warily.

I threw the dart on the ground and rushed him. "You son of a bitch!" I yelled.

He jumped up and scurried back. My hand closed around the fabric between his shoulder blades, and I yanked him back.

The world around me tilted.

I blinked.

Everything grew fuzzy.

"What the fuck did you do to me?" I asked, my voice sounding so far away, even to my own ears.

The grip I had on the man slipped, and I wilted to my knees. I looked up at him, trying to fight whatever the hell he'd shot me with. The world was so blurry… My limbs were so heavy.

"Nighty-night," the man said and wagged his fingers at me.

I moved to lunge at him, but I fell instead.

The last thing I remembered was the sound of the taxi's engine as everything around me went black.

7

Rose

Fear is a powerful thing.

I could even argue it is one of the most influential motivators of life. I'm not talking about the kind of fear that makes you jump back from a giant spider or a snake slithering across the road. Not the fear you feel when you awaken from a bad dream in the middle of the night.

I learned real fast there are two kinds of fear in life: perceived and literal.

The literal kind is a much smaller category; the margin for this kind of fear is reserved. Reserved for unfortunate people like me who find themselves in life-or-death situations.

It is this kind of fear that eclipses all else. It shapes every thought, every breath, every single beat of a heart.

Everything I did now was through an automatic defense mechanism I didn't even know I had.

No amount of body-numbing exhaustion would ever be enough to make me forget that fear. Even half dead, I would feel it, know it, and react to it.

The quiet was pierced with the now familiar groan of metal upon metal. I came awake violently, on red alert instantly. The chain rattled a bit when I sat up abruptly, my fingers clutching the metal handle as if my life depended on it.

It probably did.

The sound of scuffling feet and a few grunts echoed toward me.

They were back. They were coming.

What would they do to me?

Alarmed, I looked at the handle clutched in my fingers. I needed to hide it. It wasn't much, but it was all I had. Maybe the men would laugh when they saw it and not care I'd literally broken skin on my hands to pry it off the bucket.

I wasn't going to give them the chance to laugh. To take it away.

They'd taken enough from me already.

Quickly, I tucked the metal into the wide waistband of my skirt and pulled the white button-down to cover it up. I liked the feeling of it against the small of my back. The cold temperature of the smooth, narrow rod was comforting. It gave me a sensation of strength when I was literally the weakest I'd ever been.

As the sounds of the men approaching drew closer, I crab-crawled back until my back hit the pipe I was chained to. My hands griped it, and I pressed my legs together, waiting for my kidnappers to show themselves.

Inside my chest, the erratic beating of my heart made me feel out of control and panicked. I didn't like the feeling, but I didn't know how to calm myself.

"Bastard is heavy," a voice grunted from the other side of the oldest tractor.

With keen eyes, I watched, and with persistent ears, I listened. Their feet shuffled more than they had before. It was almost as if they were struggling or trying to move something heavy.

The urge to scream assailed me.

What if they were hauling in some sort of cage to put me in? Or maybe they were bringing in some kind of torture chair to strap me in while they did unspeakable and vile things to my body.

I didn't want to have my fingernails pulled off and my tongue stretched out until it was deformed and partially falling out of my mouth.

Get a grip, Rose!

Apparently, literal fear also came with a heaping side of irrational thought.

But what if…?

I shut it down and forced my attention to the here and now. That's all that mattered, what was happening right now. From here on out, I didn't live for what might happen in the upcoming minutes. I focused on this second.

The man from the taxi and his boss came into view. They were carrying something so big it took both of them to haul it. At first, all I saw was the back of the taxi man. He was still in the same pants and white dress shirt from before. His back muscles seemed to strain with the weight of whatever he was holding.

His heavy breathing reached my ears, and I had a moment's thought that he seemed out of shape, something I could use to my advantage.

The closer they came, the more I was able to see the entire picture of what was happening.

The other man was facing me. He, too, was holding something in front of him that he seemed to find bulky. His face was pinched, and the veins in his neck bulged with effort. He was a little more in shape than the taxi man, but honestly, he wasn't exactly going to be in the Olympics anytime soon.

Or ever.

The almost-white hair on his head was mussed, and the tie around his neck was loosened and askew.

He glanced up and saw me staring. I averted my gaze immediately. I'd rather not draw attention to myself any more than necessary. That thought was fleeting, though, a barely formed sentence in the back of my mind.

Because I saw what they were doing. What they were carrying… rather *who* they were carrying.

I gasped and pushed to my feet, using the pipe as support for my still, bone-weary frame. It was a man. A rather large one… From where I was standing, I could see his shoulder and length down his side. Taxi Man was holding him under his armpits, and one long, bulky arm fell straight toward the floor. In fact, if the men carrying him did any worse of a job, his knuckles would likely be dragged across the cement.

The other man was holding him by the ankles. My eyes went to his feet. They were dressed in Nikes, a really nice pair actually. And they were big.

"You sure you wanna put him by her?" Taxi man grunted.

"Area's already clear. Just do it."

I stared like the unfolding scene was the most interesting thing I'd ever witnessed as the two men lugged the man closer.

His head was covered. They'd put a bag or pillow case over it. I wondered if they'd done the same thing to me when they brought me in. I couldn't remember. I was glad. I didn't want the memory of having my sight cut off by something that could be used to suffocate me.

The newest victim seemed like dead weight. He wasn't putting up a fight at all. Judging by his size, I would surmise that was good for the kidnappers, because this guy was bigger than both of them and he probably could have fought his way free.

They'd knocked him out, too.

Just like they'd done to me.

I wondered if the poor guy was someone who'd mistakenly gotten into the back of the wrong cab and was now the number two candidate for the twelve o'clock news.

Naturally, I was the number one candidate.

I'd been kidnapped longer. And I was a lady. Ladies first.

"Here's good," the boss declared, and they literally just dropped him on the ground.

I whimpered when his body hit the pavement. Even though he was close to the ground already, it still made a sick slapping sound. And his head… what if he'd hit it?

I didn't know this man. I hadn't even seen his face. It didn't matter. He and I were kindred now. We'd both been kidnapped by insane people and were now in a fight for our lives.

"Watch it," the boss hissed at his accomplice. "We need him uninjured."

"Bastard's fine," Taxi Man rebutted. "He had it coming anyway for the fight he put up earlier."

So he'd put up a fight? That was good. It meant he wasn't going to take this lying down. It meant I had an ally.

The white-haired man made a sound that might have been a laugh, but who's to say? Maybe he had a pack-a-day habit and he needed to cough. "I'm impressed he gave you that shiner before you managed to dart him."

Dart him?

Taxi Man muttered something I didn't hear and swung to face me. I recoiled from the cold look in his eyes and from the waves of anger he exuded. His eye was definitely blackened, a dark ring around it. Just under the eye was a pudgy-looking pouch where the area was swelling.

Immense satisfaction filled me at the sight of it.

His lip was swollen, too, and there was a smear of red beneath it like he'd been bleeding.

Good. I hope you bleed some more.

I didn't back down from his appraisal of my body. I stared straight at him, almost in challenge. An ugly glint came into his stare, and I lifted my chin.

I wasn't going to cower, even though my body and mind begged me to.

He took a step toward me, and I was glad I was against the pipe so I couldn't step back.

"Here," the man behind him drawled, and the familiar rattling of chain filled the space.

An identical metal cuff was placed around the man's wrist. The length of chain affixed to it was longer than what I got, but that was only because he was lying a little farther away.

Taxi Man took the end of the chain and glanced back. Stalking toward me, he knelt near my feet and worked to tie the chain around the pipe, just above mine.

My body shuddered with his nearness, and he seemed to get off on it. Lifting one hand off the chain, he wrapped it around my ankle and began to slide his clammy palm up my calf.

I made a sound of distress and wrenched away so quickly I stumbled, but instead of allowing it to slow me, I kept moving. Impulsively, I struck out, using the very foot he'd been trying to feel, catching him in the jaw.

With a cry, his body fell back, unbalanced, landing on his hip.

I leapt forward and grabbed the chain he was trying to secure and worked to unwrap it from the pipe. He lunged at me, and we grappled over the chain. Taxi Man grabbed me around the hips and tackled me. I fell over, my knee hit the pavement, and pain exploded down my leg. I screamed but kept fighting, trying to claw at his face and neck with my nails.

"Stupid bitch!" he roared and rolled.

I ended up pinned on the hard floor, panting, with him straddling my body, staring down with flared nostrils.

I would never give in.

My hand reared back and I punched out, hitting him right in the balls. His eyes went wide as I scrambled to buck him off. Despite the white tone to his skin and the grimace pulling his lips, he didn't move. Instead, he grabbed my hands and squeezed both my wrists together, limiting my movement. He reared his other arm back, and even though I tried to move, there was nowhere I could go.

The punch rocked my head on my shoulders. Pain bloomed across my cheekbone and rang in my ear. The back of my head hurt from rubbing along the cement, and my vision dimmed out for long seconds.

"Hold her!" Taxi Man demanded as I fought for clarity.

Hands beneath my armpits were rough and unforgiving when they towed me back. The sound of the chain dragging along with me was depressing, and then an unwanted arm wrapped around my body from behind and held firm.

I watched through blurred vision as Taxi Man secured the new prisoner's chain, essentially sentencing that man to the same fate I was already living.

I tried to help you, I thought, glancing at the man who still had a bag over his head. *But how will I help you when I can't even help myself?*

When he was done, he stalked over in front of me. I didn't quiver, though I wanted to. "I like a woman with some attitude. Makes it so much more satisfying when I show them who's in charge."

Terror was raw inside me, but instead of crying, I spit in his face.

His eyes flared and he drew his pudgy, unattractive form up to its full height. I wished he weren't bigger than me. I wished I were bigger. Stronger. Something.

One hand shot out and grabbed my jaw. Fingers squeezed the bone until I tried to pull back in pain. The man holding me refused to budge. I was essentially pinned between two lunatics, one who I was pretty sure would try and rape me before all was said and done.

His nails dug into my flesh low on my cheek, and I thought about reaching around into my waistband and grabbing for the bucket handle.

"I think you need a little lesson in obedience," he growled.

"We don't have time for this," the man holding me intoned. "We need to go."

Taxi Man glanced down at the figure still sprawled out on the floor and then back to one the restraining me. "Go. I'll be along in a few."

"Just remember I need her unharmed," the voice spoke near my ear. And then he was gone. He just let go of me and walked away. The silent way he moved was unnerving. And so was the way he seemed to care not at all about leaving me with this animal.

I glanced over my shoulder, wanting to call him back even though I knew he would offer no protection.

"He won't help you," Taxi Man said, reading my thoughts. "No one is going to help you now."

His fingers were tight like a vise when wrapped around my throat. I made a panicked, choking sound and begin to claw at his hand with both of mine. But it seemed the harder I fought, the tighter he squeezed.

I gasped, trying to draw in precious air, but it was becoming more and more difficult.

He yanked me forward, and I fell, scraping my big toe over the floor. His face filled my vision. His hot breath was horrid. It smelled like the end of life.

I was suddenly sincerely sorry I'd tried to fight him at all.

His lips were like two fleshy, damp worms when they pressed and squirmed against mine. I gagged, physically revolted by him. That seemed to make him more incensed. He shoved hard. I fell back onto the ground as I sucked in air past the burning sensation in my throat.

A heavy body landed on top of me. I screamed and began to fight. The chain on my wrist made it hard to hit as fast and forcefully as I wanted. A sob taunted the back of my throat as I scrapped with him, and he laughed.

My wrists were pinned above my head, pressing into the stone-cold concrete, and his other hand snaked up beneath my skirt.

"No!" I screamed. I screamed so loud my voice broke. "Get off me!"

"I'm gonna get off on you." He corrected as his finger found the center of my panties.

I started crying. But even as I cried, I struggled and fought. If he was going to rape me, it wasn't going to be easy for him.

I thrashed my head around, trying to get ahold of the arm pinning me so I could bite him.

"He said not to hurt me!" I screamed, trying to think of anything I could to deter him.

"I won't hurt you. Not much anyway," he drawled, poking at me with his finger.

I gagged again.

He was totally erect. I couldn't not notice the bulge in his ugly gray pants. How could any man be turned on by a woman who was practically vomiting at his closeness?

My mind raced for a way to escape.

I thought of the metal handle, and I began fighting to get my hand free with even more haste.

His finger left my panties and reached for his belt buckle.

I sobbed louder and started screaming again. "Help me!" I screeched. "Help!"

"No one's gonna hear you," he taunted, his pants falling open.

My eyes squeezed shut, and I turned my face away.

A muffled shout filled the space, and suddenly the weight holding me down was gone. The hands forcing my wrists over my head were no longer there. Without even wondering, I scrambled up, pulling my skirt down as far over me as I could, and leapt to my feet.

Before even straightening, I yanked the metal handle out of my waistband and gripped it tight.

The sound of flesh hitting flesh pulled me back from intense internal panic. I glanced up and gasped.

The other captive was awake!

And he was pissed!

Taxi Man was half sprawled on the ground with his lower half straddled. My fellow hostage's bulging arm was pulled back and slammed down like a jury delivering a final ruling. The fist smashed into my kidnapper, and his head snapped back.

He hit him again, and blood spurted out of his nose and all over his face.

The distinct sound of a gun cocking put pause on everything.

The man in the chain looked up. So did I.

It took a minute to search out the sound, but when I did, my hopes fell. Standing behind the tractor, as if he needed protection, was Taxi Man's boss. There was a rather large and capable-looking gun (I think it was a rifle) resting on the dirty metal of the machine and pointing right at the two men.

"Let him go." a hushed, hoarse voice commanded.

I wrinkled my nose.

"Go ahead and shoot me," my new roommate declared and raised his fist again.

"No!" I gasped and rushed forward.

The next thing I knew, the gun swung to me and with it came a red dot that centered right over my chest.

I made a choked sound.

"It's not you we'll shoot," Taxi Man spat.

I stared down at the red mark, shaking. *Would I die instantly, or would there be pain?*

The next thing I knew, Taxi Man was scrambling away and rushed behind the tractor. The gun pointing at me disappeared, taking with it that terrifying red dot.

I stared aptly at where the men disappeared to, waiting for them to come back, waiting for a shot to be fired… anything. My body was so tight I might snap at any given moment.

They left. The sound of the stupid heavy door was proof.

Once I was sure they were gone, I whimpered and slid down the pipe until my butt hit the floor. My body shook so uncontrollably my teeth began to chatter. It hurt… It hurt to shake, to move, to breathe.

Most of all, it hurt to think.

Chains rattled and dragged when the new man turned to face me. "Are you okay?"

I started to laugh—an unbalanced and scary sound. *Am I okay?*

I was about as okay as a bad case of Ebola.

A low curse filled the space, and he came closer and crouched in front of me. I tensed up and scrambled back.

"Okay, hey," he said quiet and gentle. Like he was trying to coax a kitten away from its mother. "It's okay. I won't hurt you."

I sure liked his voice… It was familiar. Despite my chattering teeth and trembling body, I glanced up.

Dark, kind eyes met mine. Olive-toned skin, a strong nose, and a jaw full of dark scruff filled my vision. His coffee-colored hair was mussed and kinda long on top so it fell down over his forehead and into his eyes.

Oh. My. God.

I knew him.

8

Derek

Recognition was instantaneous.

The second her pale eyes lifted to mine, I knew her.

"Rose?" I said quietly, a shocked note in my question.

Her lower lip trembled. "You recognize me?"

I'd recognize you anywhere.

"Are you kidding? I'd know my coffee fairy anywhere," I said with a teasing, light tone.

Her trembling lips paused long enough to pull up in a semi smile. I'd take it. I'd worked with worse.

"You recognize me?" I asked.

She nodded.

I made a relieved sound and pressed a hand to my chest. "Good thing. For a second there, I was thinking I wasn't as good at flirting as I thought."

She gave me another half attempt at a smile but then shivered.

I moved toward her and reached out my hand, causing her to tense and pull back. I reminded myself to move slow, that she was terrified.

It was hard. Hard not to grab her up and survey the damage I could had been done. My stomach clenched when I thought about the piercing sound of her scream that brought me out of whatever the hell was in the dart that made me pass out.

I'd ripped the rag off my head and glanced around to see some man trying to rape a woman… just feet from where I lay.

My surroundings didn't register; I didn't really even think. One second, I was lying there groggy, and the next, I was burying my fist into some guy's face. I would have killed him. I wanted to. Hell, I would have taken a bullet just to wrap the chain around his neck and squeeze until he life faded from his eyes.

What I didn't want was a poor defenseless woman being shot and killed because of something I'd done.

That was before I'd realized it was Rose. Now that I did…

The urge to kill that asshole was even stronger. But it was the right decision. Clearly, she was already traumatized enough without me killing some guy and then getting us both shot for it.

Still, I really hoped not killing him wasn't something that came back to bite me in the ass.

"How badly are you hurt?" I asked, dropping my hands. A chain rattled, and I looked down.

I was chained up, something I hadn't fully processed until just this minute. A quick glance at her and I noted she was, too.

"I… I'm not sure." Her voice shook.

"Your hands are bleeding," I said gently. "Can I look at them?"

I reached for one, focused on the red smears of fresh blood marring her pale skin. Just before I could grasp it, she pulled it up and into her chest. That's when I noticed she was clutching something I knew she would die for before giving it up.

I glanced at it, not trying to reach out again. It was some kind of piece of metal or something… "You find a weapon?"

She nodded.

"Good thinking." Between us, I stretched out my hand, palm up. "You hold on to that. We might need it. Will you show me your hand?"

She swallowed, a process I noted seemed difficult and painful. Her lips were dry and cracked. Her face had clearly been hit recently.

How long had she been here like this?

I tried to remember the last time I saw her. My days often ran together, so it was hard to say. Two days? Three?

Even though I was distracted by my own thoughts, I stayed in tune with her. A few moments after I made no move to take her weapon, or grab her in any way, she decided to let me see her hand once the weapon was transferred into the opposite fist.

A rush of tenderness filled me. She was obviously terrified, beaten and in pain. Someone just literally tried to rape her and then pointed a gun at her chest.

Still…

She was trusting me.

Even if only a little. The small gesture of allowing me to look at her wounds seemed not so small. It seemed monumental as we sat crouched on the cold floor in the impeding darkness.

I wanted so badly in that moment to take even just a fraction of her fear. A tablespoon of her pain. Anything at all that would give her just the slightest amount of comfort.

The hand I still held out between us moved slowly, cautiously toward hers. I cupped her hand in mine and pulled it closer to me, keeping my fingers gentle and my facial expression neutral.

I was used to blood. I was used to wounds, cuts, stitches. I was used to far worse things than the broken and torn skin on her fingers.

None of those far worse things affected me the way these superficial wounds did right now.

The pad of my thumb grazed over them. I stared down intently. "Did they give you any water?" I asked, thinking these definitely needed to be cleaned and wrapped. They would be more painful if they got infected or continued to rip.

When she didn't answer, I glanced up. Her eyes were overfull with fresh tears.

"It's okay." I soothed. "We don't need water."

Improvising, my hand delved beneath the unzipped the hoodie I was wearing over an old t-shirt and ripped off a strip from the hem.

"Dr. Kelley!" Rose gasped, hoarse. "What are you doing?"

I glanced up, the fabric forgotten in my hand. One of my eyebrows lifted. *"Dr. Kelley?"*

She blushed.

I fucking loved when the skin beneath the splattering of freckles on her cheeks turned a bright shade of pink. Seeing her blush was honestly one of the highlights of my day. I'd been telling her since I first stepped up to her coffee truck not to call me that. She wasn't my patient. I wasn't her doctor.

Well, I guess maybe right now I was. No. This didn't count.

She always said it was more professional to call me that. We were at my workplace after all.

I didn't consider her coffee truck outside the hospital my workplace, but I kinda liked arguing with her about it on almost a daily basis.

"Derek." She conceded softly.

I liked the way my name sounded when she said it. Almost like I was a secret she'd been keeping for a long time. "Ah, I was beginning to think you didn't even know my first name."

A ghost of a smile appeared on her exhausted face. "Oh, I remember."

"Rose…" I gasped playfully and glanced back down at her hand and what I was doing. "Are you flirting with me?"

"I can't believe you're here," she whispered. Her hand, which was back to being cradled in my palm, flexed a little.

So much for trying to distract her.

Using my teeth, I ripped the torn piece of my shirt in half. I was pretty fucking shocked I was here, too. Being kidnapped in the driveway of my own damn house wasn't on my bucket list. Hell, it wasn't even on my radar.

Maybe if I were a more suspicious bastard, this wouldn't have happened.

But if I was, she'd still be here alone. If there was ever a reason to be shot with some kind of tranquilizer dart and shoved into the back of a phony taxicab and carted off to Bumfuck Egypt, that was pretty much it.

Never in a million years would I have fathomed this. One thing was for sure. I'd never look at another cab the same way again.

"How long have you been here, Rose?" I asked softly. Honestly, I hadn't wanted to get into it all right away. So many questions chewed at me. I was confused, slightly groggy from that shit I was shot with, pissed off… and maybe a little alarmed at the situation. Fine, I wasn't a little alarmed. I was kinda flipping the fuck out inside. I had no clue where I was or what the hell was going on.

The shadows in her eyes trumped it all.

The second I saw her, *recognized her*, and noted the blood and ragged appearance, there was nothing I wanted more than to make sure she was okay. Once I knew that, everything else would come.

Besides, I had a feeling I had some time to ask questions.

I don't have time.

Rocco needs me.

A lump formed in my throat, and I swallowed it down. I needed to stay calm and cool. I would figure a way out of this in time. I would.

Anything less is unacceptable.

"What day is it?" she asked.

"Sunday," I replied. "Might be Monday by now. Not sure how long it took to get here."

"They had a bag over your head." Her voice wobbled.

"At least that way I didn't have to make conversation." I tried to joke.

Neither of us laughed.

I took a torn piece of fabric and dabbed at the open wounds on her fingers. She stiffened but said nothing. I worked as carefully and quickly as I could. The light in here sucked. If it weren't for some kind of lamp or something way up front, it would be completely dark.

"Were you trying to get free?" I asked as I worked.

"I wasn't able to."

"At least you tried."

"I've been here a little over twenty-four hours," Rose said, her voice void.

I paused in my ministrations. Twenty-four hours wasn't a huge amount of time, but I bet to her, it felt like a lifetime. An ache formed in the pit of my stomach. I didn't bother trying to push it away. I knew it wasn't going anywhere.

Twenty-four hours of sitting here, chained up like a dog. No food. No water. No help. They clearly abused her… I cleared my throat and tied the cloth around the cleaned-up hand.

"Next hand," I instructed. I was angry, so angry someone would do this to her. To me.

Why?

After laying the metal piece in her lap, she held out her other hand.

"Is that from the bucket behind you?" I asked as I began to clean her wounds.

"Yes," she said. "I pried it off."

That explained some of the damage to her hands. I'd bet almost anything the rest of the damage was from trying to get the chain off.

"Smart," I said, not looking at her. I was afraid if I did, she'd see the anger simmering just beneath the surface.

"It was the best I could do. There is literally nothing else within reach. They even took the bag over your head," she said, forlorn. The fact she noticed the bag was gone said a lot about her. She was alert, committed to saving her life and paying attention to every detail she could.

I finished wiping away as much blood as I could and tied the fabric around her hand. "Definitely not surgeon quality, but it should help," I said, laying my other hand over hers so it was sandwiched between mine.

Her fingers felt like ice.

"You cold?" I asked, noting the skirt and thin-looking shirt she wore. Her knee was skinned, and her hair looked damp.

She shrugged. "I won't freeze. It's summer."

True, she wouldn't freeze. But being cold was hard on the body. Her body was fighting so much right now it seemed like a terrible waste to make it also fight to try and keep her warm. Not to mention, I wouldn't be surprised if she was in shock.

"Here," I said, stripping off the zippered hoodie I was wearing. It was navy blue and worn so it was extra soft.

"Oh, no." She protested, drawing back. "Keep it on. You'll need it."

"I have on more clothes than you." I pointed out and slowly stretched forward to wrap it around her back.

The second the fabric folded around her shoulders, her body seemed to melt toward the shirt and an involuntary shudder shook her shoulders.

My palms settled on her, steadying her. "Feels good, huh?"

She glanced up, sheepish. "It's still warm from your body."

"Soak it up," I instructed and went back to tucking it around her.

Giving in, Rose pushed her arms through the sleeves but stopped partway through the action and let out a cry. "What?" I asked gently, my arms automatically lifted, hands hovering around her so I could fix whatever was bothering her.

"The stupid chain." She shook her arm, and the chain rattled.

Ah. She couldn't put her arm through the sleeve without pulling the chain with it. More fury erupted. I could even make her comfortable because of a stupid fucking chain.

I shut down the anger, for now anyway. "We'll just tuck this side around you," I offered, pulling the front together and zipping it up around her. The arm with the chain was folded against her middle. The silver links fell out from beneath it and draped over her waist. Before pulling back completely, I reached around for the hood, which was partially folded in on itself, and adjusted the fabric, pulling it close around the back of her neck, giving her a little extra warmth.

"Thank you, Derek," she whispered.

My stomach clenched. I moved from the fabric to her face, gently cupping her jaw. "We're going to get out of here, Rose."

Our faces were so close our noses almost touched. Her eyes were filled with doubt and exhaustion, never a good combination.

"Do you know what they want?" she asked, a spark of hope in her voice.

Goddamn, I wish I knew. I wish I had an answer for every question she could ever think of. But I had no idea. "It doesn't matter," I told her, confidence in my tone. "We aren't staying."

"I'm really scared." Her voice broke.

My thumb caressed her jaw. "Yeah, sweetheart, I know."

A tear fell down her cheek. The weight of it dragged the drop of liquid all the way down to my fingers. I brushed it away and pulled back.

When I stood, the chain hung down from my wrist, making a trail to the concrete floor. Rose gripped the bucket handle and looked up at me warily. All traces of the fear and vulnerability she showed just seconds ago were gone.

That look gave me a good glimpse at how she'd gotten this far. She was tough and determined to save herself. I admired that so goddamned much.

"I'm gonna touch you again. Maybe don't stab me with your shank." I added a little wink with the last part.

Before she could say or do anything, I reached down and slid one arm behind her knees and the other around her back. I lifted her, thinking about how light she seemed and how much I hated that.

I wished she were bigger. Seemed a bigger body would offer more protection.

"What are you doing?" She worried.

"Relax," I whispered, tucking her against my chest and sitting down. "I'm just getting comfortable."

She made a sound. "Well, I have it on good authority this floor is not comfortable."

I fought a smile. "Good thing you aren't sitting on the floor, then."

I leaned back against the pipe we were chained to and shifted Rose in my lap. Her eyes widened as if she just realized where she was.

"I can't sit on your lap." She protested and tried to scramble away.

I didn't restrain her. I was afraid, after what she'd been through, she'd panic.

"Best seat in the house," I drawled, catching her hand and motioning for her to come back.

"This is not a house. It's a cage." Her voice was flat.

"Have you had any sleep since you got here?" I asked gently.

"A little." She hedged. "I was out for a long time when they brought me here."

"They shoot you with a tranq, too?" I asked.

"A tranq?"

I nodded. "A dart with stuff in it that puts you to sleep."

"They did that to you?" Her eyes widened a little and some anger crept in.

I liked that look a lot better than the void one she sometimes wore.

I nodded.

She slumped, drained.

"Come here." I cajoled. "I got some extra body heat for ya."

Her teeth sank into her lower lip as she thought about it. I opened my arms and legs, making a space for her against my chest.

Rose crawled over, fit herself between my legs, and leaned her side and cheek all along my front. After adjusting the hoodie around her again, I used both arms to fold her close.

I felt her slow exhale.

She rubbed her cheek against the soft T-shirt I was wearing as if she were trying to burrow closer. "You smell good," she whispered.

"I'd just come from the gym. I probably stink."

"I was out with some friends, at that popular pub in downtown Raleigh." She began. I nodded even though I knew she couldn't see me. "It was late, and I was drunk."

Already, I hated this story. Probably because I knew it ended with her here.

"I couldn't get a cab to stop. They never stop for me. So I started walking home. I didn't want to wait for everyone else because I had to get up to early…" Her voice trailed away. "I should have just waited."

My arms tightened around her. I tucked her a little bit closer and rested my chin on the top of her head.

"He pulled to the curb in a cab, the same kind I ride in all the time. I thought it was safer than walking, so I got in."

"I thought it was a real cab, too," I confided, hoping that made her feel better.

"You were in it?" she questioned.

"Yeah, he pulled into my driveway to ask for directions."

Against me, she nodded. "I gave him my address, but he didn't drive me home. Instead, he…" I felt her begin to tremble. "He put on what I now know was a gas mask and filled the backseat with some kind of gas that knocked me out."

How long had she been trapped in the backseat of that cab, wondering what was happening to her? How long had she stared at the passing streets, knowing she had no control and looking up to see a man in a mask in the driver's seat?

Holy fucking shit, I couldn't even have made this up.

"When I woke up, I was chained to this pipe."

"Rose…" I began, one of my hands slowly rubbing her back. "How bad have they hurt you?"

"Not too bad. You stopped him before he could…" She shivered.

Yeah. It was official. I was pissed at myself I hadn't just killed him when I had the chance.

"I'm here now. I'll protect you from him," I vowed.

She made a sound and pulled back to look at me. "You can't. You're just as much a prisoner now as I am."

I drew her back to my chest and said nothing.

"Why is your hair damp, Rose?" I murmured a little while later.

"He dumped a bucket of water on me."

The muscles in my jaw clenched. "You're exhausted. Why don't you try and get some sleep?"

"I can't."

I gave her a gentle squeeze. "Yes, you can. I'll watch over you, wake you up if they come back."

"Aren't you tired?"

"Nah, I got some extra sleep last night." I lied. Truth was I'd just come off a double shift. Besides the four hours of sleep I'd grabbed in the doctor's lounge at the hospital, I hadn't had any.

Rose needed the rest way more than I did. Besides, I wouldn't be able to sleep right now even if I tried. I had too much to think through and surroundings to study.

She did that little movement with her cheek again, pressing closer. My heart constricted. Tucking my legs in close and my arms farther around her, I made sure she was tightly surrounded by me.

It was the best I could offer right now in the way of making her situation a little better.

"Maybe just a few minutes." Her voice was muffled against my chest.

I smiled over her head. "I'm pretty comfortable, huh?"

Her head lifted, sincere wide eyes looking up at me. It was very dim in here, but I knew their color. Her eyes were a beautiful muted shade of green that contrasted to perfection against her light-red hair.

"I'm so sorry you're here, Derek." She began. "But at the same time, I'm so glad."

"I know, sweetheart," I whispered, pushing her head back into my chest. "I feel the same way."

Within minutes, her body relaxed into mine and her breathing turned deep. Without thought, I brushed a kiss along the top of her head.

What were the odds I'd be kidnapped and chained up beside a woman I'd developed a serious coffee habit just so I could see?

I hadn't even liked coffee until I passed by her truck one morning and heard her light laugh float to my ears the same way the scent of her freshly ground coffee beans wafted to my nose. The second my eyes found her standing behind the counter, making lattes and handing out muffins, I'd been enamored.

I flirted with her every chance I got.

I'd been wanting to spend more time with her.

This wasn't what I had in mind.

Why her? Why me?

What in the hell was going on?

9

Rose

Was fate laughing at me?

Was I being Punked? The second I opened my eyes, I began looking around for a celebrity who was going to jump out and tell us we were on candid camera.

I didn't see any celebrities.

I didn't even think *Punked* was on TV anymore.

Honestly, I didn't even look around that good. I didn't want to lift my head. I liked it where it was, pressed into Derek's chest. His shirt was soft against my cheek, and his body heat was nothing short of delicious. He'd totally been right when he said he was the best seat in the house.

It was no small feat to make someone feel comfortable in a circumstance like ours.

My eyes squeezed shut with the thought. I wasn't ready to face reality again just yet. For the first time since climbing into the back of that cab, I'd been able to relax. My body didn't hurt from being so tense. My fingers and toes weren't stinging with cold. I wasn't lying here wondering how much time I had left before I died.

And he smelled good.

Strong. I never would have thought strong had a scent, but now I knew. Maybe he was right. Maybe he was stinky from the gym. Still, his sweat wasn't smelly, and it didn't make me wrinkle my nose. I caught myself more than once, since allowing myself to relax into him, inhaling just a little bit deeper.

I was a little less scared with him here. I felt now there was definite hope of escaping. He exuded strength. When I first woke up in this place, I was totally freaked out, but not Derek. He was calm and confident, like he knew this was only temporary and we'd be able to get away.

His confidence inspired me to hold on to my own.

Would anyone else have been able to make me feel this way in such grim circumstances?

I doubted it. I knew Derek. He was familiar to me.

Not long after I started parking Curbside Coffee at the hospital, I caught my first glimpse of him. Derek had the kind of presence people noticed. Just walking across the campus of the hospital drew eyes his way. At first, I watched him out of fascination; he was incredibly good-looking.

His hair was the color of coffee, deep and rich. When the sun hit it, a burnished chestnut color reflected off the strands. He wore it longer than most doctors there. It wasn't cropped close to his head or buzzed into a nonexistent style. Instead, it was long on the top, a little floppy, which I found totally adorable.

Oftentimes, when he would smile at me or flirt, it would fall over his forehead and into his deep-brown eyes.

Sometimes I'd see him stop to talk to people as he was on his way in, and he'd grin, the white of his teeth contrasting immensely against the dark, neatly trimmed beard. He'd always laugh and push his hand through his hair.

If he knew how much his presence affected others, he never acted like it. There was an unpretentious air always about him. He was always smiling like he was a genuinely happy person. I bet he had one hell of a bedside manner.

As if his outgoing, easy personality and model good looks weren't enough, he was also a doctor. Not just a doctor, but a surgeon.

He wasn't the type of guy to just introduce himself as such. I knew because I heard people talk about him. I wasn't the only woman who would stop what she was doing to stare. All the nurses and hospital staff would, too. I eavesdropped on more than one conversation at the coffee truck, just to learn a little more about him.

Derek was well liked among his colleagues, and from what else I could gather, he was also a workaholic, totally dedicated to his patients. The nurses all speculated that's why he was single. His job, which made him even hotter, ironically, was also his one fatal flaw.

Apparently, most women didn't want to compete with his career for attention.

I totally had him pegged as a non-coffee drinker (which frankly *I* thought was his one fatal flaw) because I'd seen him for weeks walking to and from the buildings, and not once did he carry a coffee cup.

Most doctors lived on the juice. Hell, almost everyone that worked at the hospital did. It was why Curbside Coffee had literally become a permanent fixture there. I had a steady flow of customers on a daily basis. I never had to look around for anyone in need of coffee. I never had to worry about where to park the truck.

I parked in the same spot every day, and everyone came to me.

I'd worried at first the hospital would get angry with me for being here. Maybe there was some kind of café inside I was taking business from. So I marched into the admin offices and asked for permission.

I got it. In fact, they told me they'd like it if I'd make my truck an everyday occurrence.

I'd always loved the mobility of my truck, and I still did. But I loved working at the hospital. I loved the faces I saw on a daily basis, and I loved seeing new ones passing through as well.

Derek wasn't a new face, but the first time he stepped up to my truck, it took everything in me not to gape in surprise.

"You drink coffee?" I'd practically gasped the second I saw him.

He'd laughed, adjusted the gray backpack on his shoulder (he always carried a backpack to and from work), and replied, "Doesn't everybody?"

I heard angels sing and wedding chimes in the air that day.

Okay, I didn't. But there were butterflies in my belly.

After that, he came to my truck almost every day. I looked for his face in every customer that approached.

At first, we'd just exchange pleasantries and generic comments about the weather.

I didn't care. Hell, I'd talk with him about anything and it would be amazing.

Gradually, we started talking for real. He'd mention his patients (no names or specifics of course) or the long hours he was set to work. I'd talk about coffee and whatever I was up to that day. He started flirting with me. I flirted back.

He always ordered the same thing, black coffee with cream, but it never seemed like his type of drink. One day I told him that. He laughed, a kind of sheepish look in his eyes. I'd wondered about it, but before I could ask, he challenged me to make him something I thought he would like.

I made him a cinnamon cappuccino with extra foam and a hint of maple syrup instead of sugar.

I made good coffee. No. I made damn good coffee. The best. But handing over that drink that day made me want to chew off all my nails in anxiety.

I'd watched him aptly as he took the first sip.

His eyes turned thoughtful, and I knew the second the flavors burst across his tongue and the heat of the drink slid down to his belly.

"Are you a witch?" he'd asked, a twinkle in his eyes. "No," he said before I could answer. "You're too beautiful to be a witch."

I blushed. I always blushed around him.

"You're a fairy A coffee fairy." He'd held up the mug. "This is the best damn coffee I've ever had."

I'd been high on that complement the rest of the week. Now, whenever I saw him approach, it was that drink I made him.

Now we were here.

What were the odds? Why him? Why me?

I'd always hoped he'd ask me out. I didn't care what the gossips at my cart said about his hectic schedule. Any time I got to spend with him seemed like it would be worth it.

Being kidnapped was not a date.

Being held by him right now was not because it wasn't romantic (even though part of me was totally squeeing with glee).

We were thrown together, both victims of something criminal I still didn't understand.

Derek must have sensed the change in me. His palm rubbed up the side of my arm. "Doing okay?" he murmured.

"How long was I asleep?" I asked, lifting my head.

"A while." His eyes swept over my features.

My gaze dropped to his mouth. His lips were full and soft-looking. I loved to watch him talk because I would imagine what it was like for those lips to move against mine.

I shook off the thought. Now wasn't the time to be thinking of kissing. Now was the time to be thinking about surviving.

"Did you recognize the man who kidnapped you?" he asked, still rubbing my arm.

I shook my head. "I've never seen either of them before."

"So there are only two?"

I nodded. "Only the one was in the cab, the one you… um, pulled off me." His eyes narrowed and his lips drew into a line. I hurried on to say, "But there was the other one here. He's the one that pointed the gun at us."

"You get a good look at him?"

I nodded. "I didn't recognize him either."

"Have they said anything to you? Anything at all?"

He was trying to find a reason. Some kind of explanation or link as to why this was happening. I knew what he was going through. I'd been wracking my brain since I got here, but I was no closer now than before.

I pulled my hands into my lap and let the sleeves of the sweatshirt fall over my fingers. Still in the center of his legs, I straightened so we were facing each other. "They haven't said much. I pretended to be asleep when I first got here so they would leave me alone. I heard them arguing, but it didn't tell me anything. Then one got a phone call—I think he might be in charge—and they left."

"How long were they gone?" he asked.

"Almost the entire day. When they came back, they were carrying you in the room." I fell silent but then remembered. "They seem concerned about our well-being."

He laughed, and I scowled at him. "I mean, the boss told the taxi man to be careful with you. He said he needed you uninjured."

"What else?" he pressed, somehow sensing I still had more to say.

"The boss said he needed me unharmed, too."

"Why would you kidnap two people if you didn't want to harm them?" Derek mulled over the words as if he'd been talking to himself.

"They said something else I thought was odd." I recalled.

"Tell me," Derek murmured and tucked a long, tangled strand of hair behind my ear.

I pushed my face closer to his hand, and his palm flattened. I never realized how big his hands were until one rested against my cheek. "That's some wingspan you got there," I mused.

With one stroke against my cheekbone, he pulled back, holding the same hand between us. "I have hands of a surgeon, you know," he confided. It was the first time he'd ever actually sounded a little arrogant.

It was kind of a turn-on.

"What's so special about that?" I asked.

"A surgeon's hands are very skilled."

I rolled my eyes. "Is that so?"

He nodded once and picked up my wrapped fingers. The pad of his thumb brushed over the back of my hand while his fingers caressed the exposed part of my palm. "Steady, too."

"Is that why you haven't been freaking out yet? Because you're skilled and steady?"

"No, darlin'," he drawled. I didn't notice a Southern drawl much anymore because I was surrounded by them on a daily basis. But oh my word. I heard it just then, and it put me in danger of swooning. "My hands are skilled and steady, but the rest of me is all man."

Little shivers raced up my spine. He was so enticing.

"Then why aren't you scared?"

"I am. But just like you, I'm not going to let fear disable me."

Not only were his hands skilled and steady, but so was his tongue.

With words. His tongue was skilled with words.

Geesh. Get your minds out of the gutter.

Although, I'd be a big fat liar if I said the other skills he might possess didn't cross my mind.

Bringing my mind back to the matter at hand and the fact I had something to tell him, I refocused, trying not to think too much about what it felt like to have my fingers enclosed by his.

"When they were talking earlier, before they showed up with you, the boss said something I thought was a little strange."

Derek nodded, encouraging.

"He said plans had changed. Then he said I was *his* problem now."

"His who?" He frowned.

"That's what I didn't understand. They acted like someone else was involved."

"Can you remember anything else?"

I shook my head slowly. "No. I've mostly been here alone."

"You're not alone anymore," he replied and pulled me close again.

My arms slipped around his waist to hug him close, enjoying the feel and comfort of him for a few seconds more before sitting back and straightening. As much as I wanted to bury my face against him and pretend this was a bad dream, I wouldn't.

We had work to do.

I was glad to not be alone. Maybe between the both of us, we could figure a way out of here.

10

Derek

I had to get out of here.

Time was not on my side. On Rocco's side.

A harvested organ was only viable for so long. The clock was ticking.

If I didn't find a way out of here soon, the promise I'd made to my sister, to my nephew, and to myself would be broken. We'd been waiting years for a match.

What if I didn't make it?

What if they couldn't find another surgeon to take on the surgery?

There were two other transplant doctors in Raleigh. Both were great doctors. One was currently out of the country on his honeymoon.

The other was just as swamped as me.

I had to be there. If I didn't make it and Rocco didn't get the transplant… I'd never forgive myself.

Too many hours had passed. We'd been sitting here, and I couldn't just sit around anymore.

When I was first brought here, all my focus went to Rose. The second I saw her huddled against the pipe, with wet clothes, a punched face, and a void look in her eyes, I knew fear for the first time since waking up.

Of course I was concerned for myself but more so for her.

That told me a whole hell of a lot about how much I cared about her.

My main focus became making sure she wasn't seriously injured. Making sure she hadn't been physically violated. She needed to get warm, and that scary empty look in her eyes needed to find somewhere else to live.

Now that she rested for a while and we'd compared notes, we had to get of here.

But how?

"The way I see it…" I began, watching Rose scrape the metal handle against the hard floor. Back and forth. Back and forth. The concrete already had a slight path in it; scrape marks from her repeated movement. It was working, though. Gradually, the end of the handle was becoming a little sharper. "It's two against two. We can take them."

"They have a gun." She pointed out.

"They want us unharmed. They aren't going to shoot us." I countered. If I'd known that little tidbit when they pointed the gun at her earlier, I wouldn't have given in so readily.

She fell silent, the only sound the scraping of the metal.

I'd been trying to get the metal cuff from around my wrist for a while. Basically, the only way I was going to get it off would be to break my hand so I could slide it through.

If I broke my hand, I wouldn't be able to do the surgery on Rocco.

On anyone.

A surgeon's hands were his bread and butter.

Frustration smacked me in the face. A growl erupted out of my throat, and I snatched her hand away from the floor. Her fingers curled around the makeshift weapon so she didn't drop it, but otherwise, my sudden movement didn't startle her.

It was that act of complete trust that pulled me back. My fingers gentled, and the upset erupting inside me moved out like the tide on a beach. Rose didn't flinch away from me.

"I didn't scare you," I said. It was a real asshole thing to sound kind of in awe about that. My tone implied I'd wanted to scare her.

I didn't.

Rose knew.

"I trust you."

So simple.

So incredible.

"Why?"

She smiled, rueful. "You don't think I should?"

"Under these circumstances, absolutely."

Her brow puzzled. "So there is a circumstance when I shouldn't?"

"Oh, definitely," I drawled, scooting a little closer. I released her hand to play with the ends of her long light-cinnamon strands.

Her breathing increased. If I felt her pulse, it would probably be elevated, too.

I affected her.

Good.

"If we were somewhere I didn't have to be on high alert for your safety and mine…" My words trailed off because I noticed the way she stared at my mouth when I whispered.

Frankly, it was the ~~worst~~ best kind of distraction.

"Yes?" Her voice was breathless.

"I would take advantage of you, Rose. Your body would betray you when it handed over its loyalty to me."

"You can't take advantage of me."

"No?" I raised an eyebrow. Was she doubting my skills of seduction?

Slowly, her head shook, the tip of her tongue jutting out to wet her lips. "You can't take what I'm already willing to give."

Hot damn.

My stomach muscles bunched with anticipation. Apparently, I wasn't the only one with skill.

"It's a damn shame, fairy." I sighed regretfully.

Rose drew back at my words. She misconstrued their meaning. Well, not really. She just thought I was replying to her blatant admittance of attraction.

I wasn't.

Before I could lose her completely, I yanked her back into the moment.

"It's a damn shame it took being kidnapped and chained to a pipe for me to finally get some alone time with you."

Her lips pulled into a smile, relief lighting her eyes.

I couldn't help but notice the dryness in her usually luscious lips. The way they were cracking from lack of moisture.

"You could have just asked me out."

"How about it, Rose? How about some pizza, maybe a movie, a totally boring and mundane date with me?"

Her white teeth flashed. The reply was rueful. "Something tells me nothing with you would ever be boring."

"Is that a yes?"

Her eyes skittered away from mine to take in our surroundings. I saw awareness flood back in. The bleak reality we were stuck in threatened to ruin the moment I'd managed to create with her.

I wasn't ready to let go yet.

"On second thought." I spoke up. Her eyes came back. "I'd like to suspend that invitation."

She laughed. "I think that's the fastest any man has ever run away from me."

I chuckled. "No one's ever run from you."

"I eat, sleep, and breathe my business. It's not exactly a turn-on."

"You always smell like coffee," I murmured, scooting closer to brush the hair back behind her shoulder. Even now, the rich scent clung to her, even though she'd been prisoner for over a day.

Rose shrugged. "Hazard of the job."

"I want to kiss you."

Her breath caught. Then a shaky laugh exhaled. "I have enough injuries already without adding the whiplash you're giving me."

"Not whiplash," I murmured, stroking the pad of my thumb over her lower lip. "Bad timing. Worst circumstances ever for a first kiss." I allowed.

"But..." she murmured, turning her face into my touch.

"But I still want to taste you. I want to lick across those chapped lips and soothe some of the dry. If you and I can get lost in each other here, now, then that invitation for a date… it's going to turn into a demand."

Her sigh was the only reply I needed.

Her skin was smooth and cool to the touch when I cupped her jaw. Using gentle pressure with my thumbs, I tilted her face up because absolute full access was what I desired. At the base of her neck, my fingertips burrowed into her hair, and her eyes fluttered closed.

The first taste hit my senses when I licked across her lips. Every single taste bud clamored for more; once just wasn't enough to satisfy. My tongue dragged gently over the fullness of her mouth, eradicating the worst of the dryness to give way to a hot trail of want.

With a sigh, her mouth opened, and like a puzzle, my lips fit into hers the exact way they should. I couldn't stop moving; my body took complete control. With gentle ferocity, I attacked her mouth. She moaned, and her tongue slipped past my teeth to seek out mine.

We tangled together, fused as one. Needing even more, I grasped her around the waist, lifting her into my lap. The chains binding us made a rattling sound, but we ignored them.

I was lost. Lost to a world that was infinitely better than reality.

Rose grabbed me, the pads of her fingers kneading the back of my head and mussing my hair. I loved the way she kissed. She didn't hold back, didn't give in.

When I licked, she licked. When I moved, so did she. Her fingers were like vises, anchoring me in place, and the sounds erupting from her throat… made me desperate to get her beneath me.

A sound in the distance interrupted. Both of us stilled but didn't pull apart. Even an imminent threat couldn't keep us from fusing together. It would have to be absolute to break the bond. Our lips rested on each other's as we listened for signs we were no longer alone.

I felt the weight of her stare and opened my eyes.

I stared back, noting the golden flecks accenting the green of her irises. Neither of us moved, but my hands tightened on her back. The instinct to swiftly tuck her behind me was fierce. The second I heard another sound or voice, it wouldn't even be a thought, just an action.

Long beats passed.

I felt the rise and fall of her chest against mine. Our breath mingled as we listened.

No one was here.

We were still alone.

Leaving my eyes trained on hers, I kissed her softly one last time. Her pupils flared, and it pulled my mouth into a smile. I lifted my head, noting how much less dry her lips appeared.

Rose surprised me and swiped her thumb under the swell of my lower lip. It did nothing for my rock-hard cock when the tongue that just slaughtered my mouth came out and licked across the area.

I thought about attacking her again. God, I wanted to.

Even as I had the thought, she ducked her head into the space between my neck and shoulder as if she were suddenly shy.

I liked the juxtaposition of her spice with a little bit of sweet. She sure could keep a man busy for a long, long time.

Like forever.

What the fuck?

Did I hit my head when they kidnapped me? Was there some kind of hallucinogen in that dart? One kiss in the middle of a literal cage and I was thinking about forever?

I was going mental. Now was not the time. If there was ever a time I needed to keep a clear head, it was now.

She shifted. By the way she moved, I was given the distinct impression something was hurting her.

"What is it?" I asked.

"This chain is heavy." She grimaced. The fingers in my hair slid away, and her shackled wrist dropped onto my shoulder with a thump.

"I'm sorry," she rushed out. "My arm's tired. I didn't mean to drop it like that."

The chains were thick and heavy, the metal cuff bulky and tight. I was larger than her, wider, and it was uncomfortable on me. I could only imagine the exertion it took for her to hold up her arm.

"Don't try to fight the weight," I replied. Gently, I lifted her hand and wrist, supporting the weight and bringing it down to rest between our bodies.

"We're tangled together." She pointed to the chain.

The impromptu kissing session certainly did tangle us up in more than one way. The knots in the metal were only increasing the tugging on her wrist.

"I'll fix it," I whispered and got to work.

It took me a while to work the chains apart. When I was done, my own wrist stung with raw skin, and the paleness in her cheeks told me all I needed to know about her.

I stood, bringing her with me. The muscles in my body screamed. I worked out a lot. I took good care of myself to help offset the busy schedule I constantly worked. But being chained up and left on a concrete floor was enough to make any man a little sore.

Not to mention I'd supported the majority of Rose's weight while she slept.

I bent, sitting her down so she was supported by the pipe. Once I made sure our chains really were untangled, I paced away to work some blood flow through my limbs and work out some of the soreness.

Rose watched me. I could tell by the way she sank against the pipe she was fading fast. Over twenty-four hours without any hydration was taking its toll. I looked around for the hundredth time as I stretched, hoping I'd see something I'd overlooked.

"I have to pee," Rose announced.

"Have you gone at all since you've been here?" I asked, entering doctor mode.

"No."

"You're dehydrated," I intoned darkly.

"I should get up and move around, too. Maybe it would help with the soreness." She pushed away from the pipe, then slumped back. Her shackled wrist landed on the floor, boneless.

"Stay there," I ordered.

I ripped off more of my shirt and crouched in front of her.

Neither of us said anything when I lifted her wrist and rested it on my thigh. The skin beneath the cuff was raw and swollen. I was sure beneath the metal, it was bleeding. I pretended not to notice, but her muscles quivered. They were so exhausted they quaked.

"This might hurt," I told her. "I'm sorry."

She nodded.

Working as quickly as I could without being too rough, I pushed the edge of the fabric beneath the cuff. Rose stiffened and hissed a breath but otherwise said nothing.

"I know it hurts, sweetheart," I whispered. "But putting this between your skin and the metal will help."

"I know," she whispered.

It took a few minutes to work it around and beneath as much as I could. Her toes curled in on themselves and her knees pressed together… The skin I couldn't see was definitely in rough condition.

"When do you think they're going to come back?" she asked as I finished.

I sat back on my haunches, noticed the fabric I tied around her hands was coming loose, and reached to fix it. "Probably soon." I paused. "I wish I knew what time it was."

"It's probably morning. It seems less dark in here than when they brought you in."

I thought about Rocco, about the dwindling hours until his surgery. A low swear permeated the space around us.

"What?"

"I'm supposed to be somewhere."

"The hospital?" she asked.

I nodded.

"Well, when you don't show up, maybe they'll know something's wrong." Her tone was hopeful.

"Oh, they'll know," I muttered. "But if we don't get out of here soon, it's going to be too late."

The ominous tone in which I said the words scared her. She thought I was implying we were going to die.

I sighed. "My nephew has been on a waiting list for a kidney for years. He's really sick."

She made a sound, and her free hand covered my leg.

"I've never said it out loud." I hedged. "I've barely allowed myself to think it…"

"What is it, Derek?"

"He's been worsening over the past year. I've… I was beginning to think we were out of time." Every single patient I lost in recent months was especially hard because my mind would morbidly wander to Rocco and if next time it would be him I'd lose.

"I'm so sorry," she said gently, giving my thigh a squeeze. "How old is he?"

"Ten." I felt my mouth kick up. "He's my best friend."

"Really?"

I nodded. "You think it's lame my best friend is ten?"

"It makes me like you more."

Dread and anxiety pressed in on me. The emotion was so much heavier than the chain weighing on my wrist. "I got a call yesterday. They matched him with a kidney. It's being transported in today. I'm supposed to do the surgery this evening… It's his only chance at survival."

Rose gasped. "Will another surgeon be able to step in… just in case you don't make it?"

"I sure as hell hope so." I worried. If I couldn't be there, I wouldn't want Rocco to suffer. I'd rather him have a chance than none at all.

"I promised him I'd be there. I promised my sister."

"I was literally sleeping on you when I should have been helping you get out." The guilt in her tone was unacceptable.

I shook my head adamantly. "No. None of this is your doing. Taking on even a margin of blame for anything is not allowed."

Her chin jutted out and a stubborn glint not only crossed her eyes, but her entire body.

"Ah, so you do have some of that redhead heat in you," I mused.

"Yes," she rebuked. "So arguing with me is futile."

I stood up, pacing away again. "You needed some decompression time. Your body was about to give out on you, Rose," I said quietly. "I know what that looks like."

She didn't say anything, probably because she could feel the intensity coming off me. You ever notice that? How sometimes feelings were so much louder than words?

Vibes, the physical weight of our body's invisible energy was a powerful thing.

That's why when people said *mind over matter*, I believed it.

I spoke quietly. "Sometimes our bodies need a break. Sometimes our minds do, too. I needed to sit there with you just as much as you needed that break."

"Why?" Her quiet tone matched mine.

I swung around, the chains an ever constant sound to remind us we no longer had the freedom we'd always taken for granted.

"Because you're important."

Our eyes locked. I hoped she understood. Understood everything I didn't say.

I should have asked you out when I first followed the sound of your laugh. It shouldn't have taken a literal kidnapping to make me see you're inevitable. This isn't a tease to what could have been. It's a prelude to what will be.

Even from several feet away, I saw her swallow thickly. Yes, I knew her throat was dry, but I liked to think it was partly a reaction to what was swirling around between us.

"I feel stronger now." The hand without the shackle flattened on the pipe firmly planted into the floor, and she hoisted herself up.

The weight of the chain seemed to drag her body sideways, I hurried to her side and slipped an arm around her waist, supporting and lifting her into place.

Rose didn't act like the fact I had to help her stand was anything that would hold her back. Her shoulders squared as she stepped back and held up the handle. "Even if I ground this against the floor the rest of the day, I still don't think it would be the right size to pick the locks on the cuffs."

I agreed.

"While you slept, I did some recon with the pipe. I'm pretty sure it goes deep underground. I can't knock it over or even displace it enough to remove the chains," I said.

"So we fight. Two on two. Like you said, we can take them."

I hated taking that chance with her life like that. Just because they said they didn't want us hurt didn't mean if push came to shove they wouldn't.

"If I crush the bones in my hand, I can pull it out." I reasoned. "Then I'm sure I could find something in here to free you."

I hated that was our best plan. But it was. Breaking my hand and slipping lose didn't require us to physically fight. Rose was determined, but she was weak. She was in no condition to be fighting against a grown man.

If I did this, we could hopefully escape before they even came back.

She gasped. "Would that work?"

I nodded.

Her eyes flared with hope, then dimmed. "But your hand. You need it for surgery."

"I won't be doing any surgeries if I'm dead." Harsh? You bet. The truth? Unfortunately.

Besides, Rose wasn't the type of girl I had to mince words around. It was frankly refreshing.

She shook her head like it was filled with water and she was trying to knock it out. "I'll break mine instead."

"No," I said, flat.

She made a huffing sound and put both hands on her hips to glare at me. "Why is it okay for you to break your hand but not me?"

"You've been through enough," I replied, gruff. It was beyond ridiculous if she thought I would let her cause physical harm to herself to save my ass.

But what about Rocco…? Would you risk her for him?

"I can still oversee Rocco's surgery. I can assist another surgeon. At least I'll be there to make sure the operation goes as scheduled."

"His name is Rocco?"

I nodded.

She smiled. The next thing I knew, she had the metal bucket in her hand, extending it to me. "Use this.

You'll be able to use more force because you can swing it down from a better angle."

I took the bucket because it was shaking in her grasp.

My eyes widened when she sat on the floor and placed her cuffed hand palm down on the concrete and spread her fingers wide.

"Do it."

She really thought I would just slam a bucket down on her hand? A hand that was already damaged and bleeding. Not to mention her wrist…

"No."

"You're wasting time. We have no idea when they're going to be back."

I stared at her incredulously.

"This isn't just for you," she noted. "This is for me, too. I want out of here just as badly."

Pain pierced my heart. "I know, sweetheart."

"Then do it."

The bucket hit the stone beside my feet with a loud clatter. I wasn't going to crush all the bones in her hand.

She made a frustrated sound and all but growled my name. "Derek."

I ignored her and tried to think of which way would most effectively and most simply break my hand. She wouldn't do it, so I was going to have to do it to myself.

Muttering, Rose pushed to her feet. I hated the way one side of her body was pulled down so she appeared lopsided. She didn't seem to notice, though.

I was about to get a lecture. The kind women give when they're all riled up.

It was actually a good motivator to break my hand much faster so I could get the hell away.

We didn't get the chance to lock horns. I didn't get the chance to hear a lecture. And my hand stayed intact.

All our plans were interrupted by the earsplitting sound of metal rubbing against metal.

Rose's breath hissed between her lips. "They're back!"

11

Rose

A girl knows she's in trouble when two things happen:

1.) When a guy keeps kissing you, like kissing you *really good*, even when you know your breath is worse than dirty socks.

And

2.) He tells you you're important. (Not only that, but he says it with a Southern drawl and his voice is deep and throaty.)

If you need me, I'll be over here swooning. On the floor. Tell my kidnappers.

I couldn't even be pissed off Derek refused to break my hand. What kind of sexist crap is that? My hand was just as capable of being broken as his.

I could do my job with one hand. He could not.

But he kissed me.

Apparently, his tongue and soft lips that consumed me completely also ate away at valuable brain tissue. I wanted to be mad, but it was hard when he was so adorably stubborn, with dark hair falling into his eyes and towering close by with his strong body quite literally dripping in chain.

How come it didn't make him look like a lopsided hunchback like me?

And did you hear that sound?

I'm positive it was my ovaries exploding. He was best friends with his nephew. Who's ten.

But all that could wait.

The worry in his soulful eyes and the grim set to his kissable mouth was more important. He had a life to save. He shouldn't have been here.

I shouldn't have been here either.

Just when I thought we were going to get out of here, Taxi Man and his gun-toting boss showed up.

Some of the bravado I was feeling disappeared. These men scared me. This entire situation scared me. Derek had been a nice distraction—a very capable one at that—but distractions weren't welcome right now. We needed to work together and get out of here.

Fast.

"Good, you're up," Taxi Man said to both of us, dividing his gaze.

Okay, fine. He was less watchful of me.

Probably because of the pretty shiners and busted nose he was sporting courteous of Derek.

Seeing Taxi Man brought back memories of him on top of me. I shuddered.

Even though Derek wasn't looking at me, he noticed my reaction and slowly moved a few steps to angle his body in front of mine.

Taxi Man folded his arms over his chest, keeping far enough back so Derek couldn't reach him. "You're being moved," he announced.

"To where?" Derek demanded.

The sound of a gun being cocked drew my eyes. Boss Man was standing there with that fancy rifle in his hands and a pistol tucked into the front of his dress pants.

"Try anything fucked up and we'll kill you."

"Thought you didn't want us hurt." Derek's voice was calm, like he wasn't even threatened.

My palms were slick with sweat, and I gripped at the bucket handle behind my back, ready to swing it around at a moment's notice.

"We don't. Not yet anyway. Doesn't mean we won't do what we gotta do."

"What do you want with us?" I half snapped. Either they wanted us unharmed or didn't care. They couldn't have it both ways.

Frankly, even scared, I was getting tired of the threats.

Both sets of eyes turned on me. However, Derek didn't turn. His stare stayed locked on the men threatening us. The muscles in his back bunched, which told me he might prefer if I didn't talk and draw attention my way.

I'd prefer I wasn't chained to a pipe.

We don't always get what we want.

Speaking of chain, I noted without looking the way Derek was slowly pulling a length of chain into his palm. Guess my question was a good distraction.

"We was just going to show you," Taxi Man replied. I hated the sound of his voice. He acted like he was being all accommodating and giving me what I wanted by telling me.

Gee. Excuse me if I didn't vote for him as person of the year.

Dumbass.

And he had terrible grammar.

"We aren't going anywhere with you," Derek intoned.

"Look," Taxi Man said, like he was put out and tired of us. "The faster you do what we want, the faster we can let you go."

Derek laughed, incredulous. "You're going to let us go."

We were met with stony silence. Something about it made my skin crawl and a terrible feeling worm low into my belly.

Taxi Man glanced at me. The way his eyes shifted over and then away was not confidence inspiring.

They aren't going to let me go.

Derek, maybe. But not me.

They're going to kill me.

But why? Why me and not him? Why did it feel like he was less disposable than me?

Taxi Man took a step forward and reached behind him. Instantly, I went on high alert and so did Derek. He shifted backward closer to me.

"Don't try nothing funny." Taxi Man spoke. The distinct sound of clattering keys filled the air as he produced them from his back pocket.

To accentuate his demand, Boss Man took several steps closer, brandishing his weapon like he knew how to use it.

I thought at first they would unchain Derek, but Taxi man turned and came at me. I refused to flinch or step back. I refused to cower at all. I lifted my chin and gripped my homemade weapon.

When he got close, I was going to stab him.

He must have seen the anger or maybe disgust in my eyes, because he stopped short and motioned for his backup.

Derek stepped menacingly toward us, as if warning the men to back off.

"Relax, tough guy," Boss Man remarked. "We aren't going to hurt her unless you do something that forces us."

"Nope. That pleasure is going to be all yours," Taxi Man added.

My eyes flew up to Derek. He frowned like he too heard the remark but had no idea what it could mean.

The end of the rifle met my temple. The metal was hard and unforgiving. He pressed in so hard against my skin I could feel my heart thumping against the nose.

I rocked on my feet, a little waver meant to steady me so I could throw all my force into my attack.

Gun or no gun, I was fighting.

I'd go for the one with the gun. Maybe upon injury, he'd drop it and I could take it and shoot them both.

Oh yes. I would shoot.

Mark my words.

The sound of dragging chain had everyone near me stiffening. I glanced up.

"Come any closer and I'll shoot her right now," Boss Man vowed.

The arm with the cuff around it was snatched up, and I bit back a yelp. The skin was so tender, the jarring, sudden movement hurt.

I spared a glance at Derek, rocking on my feet again. He shook his head imperceptibly.

I frowned.

He repeated the action.

Slowly and carefully, I slipped the metal into the waistband of my skirt.

Neither man noticed because the one with the gun was too involved watching Derek, and the other was unlocking my chain.

The cuff around my wrist clattered against the floor. My arm screamed with relief. The muscles all the way up to my shoulder vibrated with exhaustion and felt like a cup of Jell-O. It was like I'd just lifted four times my body weight and did way, way too many reps.

I lurched to the side, away from the gun and the men.

Taxi Man seemed to be expecting it, and his hand locked around my wrist. The one that was raw.

"Oww!" I howled in pain as he jerked me back around.

"Son of a bitch!" Derek roared and lunged forward. The chain he'd been holding found its way around Taxi Man's throat, and his eyes bulged.

He released me to claw at the chain as it tightened and cut off his air supply.

"Run, Rose!" Derek ordered as he squeezed.

The way his biceps bulged beneath the T-shirt was almost mesmerizing. He was powerful enough to kill this guy.

I hoped he did.

I turned to flee as wheezing filled the room.

The sound of a scuffle behind me erupted, and my steps faltered. Something heavy and hard smacked into my back, just between my shoulder blades.

Pain exploded up my back and down the backs of my arms. I cried out and plunged forward, landing in a heap on the ground.

My hands stung from the fall, but I ignored it and rolled. My back hurt terribly, but I had to keep moving.

"Don't move," a deadly voice whispered. The nose of the gun pressed right between my eyes with such force it pinched my head against the concrete.

The boss stared down at me, his eyes glittering with anger and his white hair ruffled.

"Was it too much to ask that you just be civilized?" he asked.

I'm thinking if anyone needed a course in manners, it was him.

I tried to glance off to the side, to see if Derek was okay, but he wouldn't let me turn my head. Instead, I was trapped, lying prone, with this man towering over me and what could be my cause of death pressed to my head.

Someone off to my side was sucking in great gulps of air, and it sounded like it was painful. I figured that was probably Taxi Man… Derek must have let go.

"Derek?" I called out, not caring if I got in trouble. I had to know if he was okay.

He'd been trying to give me a chance to get out of here.

"He's indisposed." Boss Man smirked.

I grabbed the gun's barrel with both hands and tried to push it free. What I got for my effort was the man over me all but lying on it to keep it in place.

I whimpered.

It hurt.

Pain shot through my skull. I stopped fighting, but I didn't let go of the barrel.

"Unchain him," Boss Man called over his shoulder.

Taxi Man's breathing was still labored when I heard the jangle of the keys. What felt like hours later, but was probably only seconds, the sick sound of flesh hitting flesh made me gag.

Derek made a low sound, and I started struggling again.

Boss Man looked down, his eyes cold and knowing. "Don't waste too much energy trying to save him. In the end, he won't do the same for you."

I paused, and our eyes collided.

He nodded emphatically.

"Rose," Derek said, his voice low, "I'm okay."

He didn't sound okay.

"Let me up," I demanded.

To my intense surprise, the gun lifted off my head, and the man stepped back a mere fraction.

"Don't try anything." He warned.

I scrambled back, my eyes seeking out Derek.

He was getting to his feet. When he looked at me, I noted there was a mark on the side of his face, already swelling and turning an ugly shade of blue.

I made a sound and rushed toward him. The man with the gun made a tsking sound and stuck out his foot to trip me.

I halted, but it was too late. I ran right into him and stumbled forward.

I braced myself for the landing. I already knew what this floor felt like very intimately, so it wasn't hard to image what was coming.

Before I hit, Derek scooped me up. One arm wrapped around my waist and pulled. I sagged forward, all the air leaving my lungs in great whoosh.

"Back off," he growled over my head. It was totally intimidating, and the hairs on my arms lifted.

I craned my neck. Taxi Man stood there with an ominous welt around his neck, looking like he was ready to kill.

"Leave them," Boss Man ordered. "It doesn't matter anyway."

He pulled the gun out of the front of his pants and held it out to Taxi Man. Then he looked back at us.

"We're taking a walk. Don't try anything."

Derek nodded. His hand curled around my upper arm. We were motioned to walk ahead while the men and their guns took up residence right behind us.

As we walked toward the wide-open door, I squinted against the harsh sunlight shining inside. It felt like years since I'd seen the sun. Since I'd seen anything other than a dark and dingy space.

"Keep walking," Boss Man ordered and hit the center of Derek's back with the gun just hard enough to make him stumble.

Even though he faltered, he didn't let go of me. His grip remained sure and steady.

Out of the corner of my eyes, I glanced over at him. He met my stare with a sidelong glance of his own.

"Get ready," he mouthed. To punctuate the words, he squeezed my arm.

Outside, the sun was hot and unrelenting. There wasn't a single cloud in the bright-blue sky that seemed to stretch on for miles. I glanced around hungrily, looking for anything or anyone I could signal for help.

There was no one.

We were in the center of a very large field. A farm to be exact.

Off to my right was a green expanse of grass that stretched as far as I could see. It was tall and dry as if it had been left untended for the entire season.

Straight ahead was a corn field. All the stalks were taller than me, and the browning leaves swayed gently in the air. I knew right away that's where we would head. We could find concealment in the crop, and it would hopefully shield us as we ran.

We were instructed to move, turning so we were walking parallel with the crops. I glanced to the other side, suddenly realizing where we'd been kept all this time.

Silos.

Right here beside us was a group of three huge metal silos.

They looked old, weathered, and kinda creepy. You know how old buildings take on that sort of haunted look when they're no longer in use. That's how these appeared. Abandoned and unwanted.

Whoever's farm this was probably didn't even know their silos were being used for debauchery. Looking around, I had to wonder if they would even care.

Derek's fingers squeezed my arm, and I pulled my attention from our surroundings and glanced up at him.

All of the sudden, he shoved me away. A sound of surprise ripped from my throat. He'd put all his weight into it, and I went flying across the grass.

I stumbled and then fell onto my side. Strands of hair fell over my face, and I pushed them back and stared at Derek incredulously.

But he wasn't looking at me. He was charging the man with the rifle, knocking it aside and delivering a swift uppercut to his jaw.

Recovering, I scrambled up and started to run. Taxi Man once again grabbed me by the wrist, and I howled.

God! Why couldn't he ever grab the other one?

I swung around to face him, yanked the metal handle free of my waistband, and plunged it down into his shoulder. The makeshift weapon did its job and broke the skin, plunging in and drawing blood.

"You little bitch!" he screeched. Without letting go of his gun, he reached for the piece of metal sticking out of his arm.

As much as I loved that little weapon, I had to go.

I started running as fast as I could.

I heard Derek's pounding footsteps behind me.

"The corn," he rushed out, and I increased my speed.

I'd never thought a field of corn would ever look like salvation. I never thought the idea of getting lost in a field sounded like a good idea.

As I ran, the thundering of my heart was the only sound I could hear, and my chest squeezed with effort as I sprinted with everything I had. In those seconds, corn represented everything. Hope. Survival. A chance.

Right beside me, dirt exploded. Little granules sprayed my legs and arms. I stumbled but kept going.

"Run faster!" Derek demanded. His legs were longer, his stride surer. He sped up past me but grabbed my hand to spur me along.

"They're shooting at us!" I gasped as even more dirt exploded around us.

I winced when another shot went off, and I cowered, expecting dirt to fly at me, peppering my clothes and skin with grittiness.

No dirt exploded this time.

Instead, I felt the slamming, sharp pain of something hammering into my leg with intense force.

I tripped.

A burning sensation tingled up the back of my leg as I hit the ground, hard.

"Rose!" Derek bit out. All at once, he stopped running and turned back for me.

"Go!" I yelled, urging him on. "Go get help."

"I'm not leaving you," he vowed, rushing to my side.

I tried to get up, managing to get as far as my knees. Then I made the mistake of looking down.

Fresh, dark-red blood slicked my pale skin. It was everywhere.

I glanced up at Derek. "I've been shot."

Getting shot hurt. I wouldn't recommend it.

"Hang on, fairy." He urged. "We're almost there."

More dirt exploded around us, and I screamed.

Derek hunched down, shielding me with his own body. I was lifted into his arms, and he started running again.

I glanced at the corn field, a beacon in my dimming vision.

It seemed farther than ever even, though we were closer now than before.

Derek's body jerked. I glanced up. His eyes went wide.

A string of curses flew out of his mouth. "Are you fucking shitting me right now? Goddamn it. I'm gonna kill those son of a bitches."

Oh my.

"Derek?"

He grunted and kept running.

Vaguely, I heard shouts behind us.

Derek's stride slowed. He swayed a little. His eyes collided with mine, glassy and far away.

"I'm sorry, Rose," he slurred.

I grabbed him by the face as he sank to his knees. I don't know how, but carefully, he placed me on the ground.

Promptly after, he passed out.

12

Derek

I was really starting to get pissed off.

They shot Rose.

Then they tranquilized me again.

What the fuck?

And there was something else. When they were shooting the real bullets and exploding the earth around us, it was Rose they aimed at.

Not me.

Again, I ask what the fuck?

I tried to run even after I felt the dart sink into my back. I *did* run. Until I fell the fuck over.

You'll have to excuse my language. I tend to have the mouth of a sailor when someone's trying to kill me.

It's not you they want to kill.

My eyes sprang open. Everything in front of me was blurry. I blinked, trying to get our surroundings back into focus.

Rose!

This time my eyes flew open. I didn't pay attention to the fuzziness. I glanced to my side, only to find it empty. I glanced to the other side.

She wasn't there.

Panic delivered a nice uppercut to my chin. Where was she? God, had they shot her again when I was out?

Was she bleeding out somewhere?

Is she already dead?

The idea was intolerable. Physically excruciating. If she died while I was lying here passed out…

I shook off the thought. I couldn't allow it in my head. It would mess with me. It would cripple me. Right now, the surgeon needed to come out. The cool, compartmentalized man I was when I did surgery even in the grimmest of situations was exactly who I needed to be right now.

This wasn't the time to be taunted by thoughts of death.

Blinking hard and shaking my head, I glanced around. It appeared I was back in a silo. But not the one I'd been in before. This one was different.

There were no tractors or any kind of equipment. It was bare, so bare I could make out the rounded shape to the walls. They were metal just like the other room. This one had a skylight in the tip of the roof. From it, rays from the sun shone downward, giving the place more illumination.

It made it easier to see Rose wasn't beside me.

I pushed up, a familiar weight and rattling sound making me look down.

I was chained up again.

This was the kind of shit that made men have bruised egos. I should have been able to take those men. I should have been able to strangle one, then go for the other.

They used Rose against me. Like a lovesick fool, I allowed it.

No. Not lovesick.

I wasn't in love with Rose. She was my coffee fairy. A spark in a tiring day. She was someone I planned on seeing way, way more of.

If she's still alive.

I shook off that thought, too.

I wasn't in love with her. But she was someone I could fall for.

That made her a weakness.

Seeing a gun pointed at her head caused me to relent far faster than I would otherwise. Hell, I'd even felt bad when I shoved her away, trying to give her as much distance when she started to run.

There was no room for weakness right now. There was no room for guilt.

If she was dead… I'd bring this place down. I'd take a bullet. I'd take more than one. I'd find that dart gun and shove it so far up their asses they'd walk funny the rest of their lives.

Which wouldn't be long.

The dart.

It was perfectly clear now what Rose told me was right. They didn't want us harmed. Well, me anyway. If they didn't care, they would have shot me with a gun like they did her.

Why was I so valuable? What was it about me they needed?

Instead of thinking of my weaknesses, I thought of my strengths. What was my greatest strength?

Horror dawned.

No way.

No goddamn way.

You've been briefed on this. You've been schooled.

Sure, I'd listened to the lectures. I'd even read the material. Well, some of it. The problem with possibilities is that's all they are.

You never think something like that would happen—until you're sitting in the middle of a silo with a chain slapped around your wrist.

My body protested when I forced myself into an erect sitting position. I was stiff and sore. It didn't matter, though.

Inhaling and exhaling, my fingers shoved back my hair, then rubbed at my eyes.

When I looked up, I noticed something I hadn't before.

Across the wide, round silo was a curtain. A familiar-looking curtain.

My leg muscles stretched as I stood cautiously, glancing around, half expecting one of the assholes who put me here to jump out. Next time I saw them, I was going to fight.

Even if it was to the death.

But first…

First, I wanted to see what was behind that curtain, because the thoughts in my mind were anything but happy.

I took a step and noticed something else.

Yeah, I was a little slow on the uptake today.

I blamed the drugs, the lack of water and sleep… the general pissiness of my entire mood.

The chain attached to the cuff around my wrist stretched out across the concrete floor. It was like a trail that snaked away from me and disappeared underneath the curtain.

"Rose?" I called out. I couldn't take not knowing where she was anymore.

I couldn't take the thoughts swirling in my head and the implications of those thoughts.

She didn't answer.

Even though I wanted to run, I didn't. I walked with equal parts caution and dread.

Please don't let her be dead behind that curtain.

Please don't let it be worse than death.

But if what I was thinking was correct... nothing happened.

Not yet anyway.

The room was eerily silent, except of course for the dragging chain. It was ominous and unwelcome, but at the same time, I was glad for it.

It was better than absolute quiet.

The curtain came closer. The pit in my stomach threatened to open up and swallow everything around it. The fabric was familiar to my touch. The slightly stiff texture from too much starch warred with the fact it was soft from being laundered so many times.

It was exactly like the curtains I pushed back on a daily basis as I did rounds. Sometimes they hung by while I did surgery.

My fingers dug into the material, and impatience kicked me. Without hesitation, I ripped the curtain back.

The sound the metal hooks made sliding over the makeshift rod was also unnervingly familiar.

My vision was no longer blurred, the edges of sight no longer vague.

I saw everything with complete and utter clarity.

Everything was exactly as I suspected.
No.
It was worse.

13

Rose

There was a bullet in my leg.

Hot, metal ammunition burrowed below the surface of my skin. It didn't belong there. It was a foreign object of mass destruction, and my body knew this.

My body screamed at me to get it out.

Problem was I couldn't.

I thought I was scared before.

Now?

I'd give anything to go back to several hours ago when I was being distracted by Derek's kiss. At the time, it was unavoidable, getting caught up in his eyes. I'd felt a little guilty for that. For letting myself feel something other than extreme fear in our situation.

But I'd had some time to think.

It's all I'd done.

Mostly about the situation. I'd conjured up so many conspiracy theories, from aliens to superheroes to odd scientific experiments. I'd thought of *Silence of the Lambs* and comforted myself that I wasn't being rubbed down with lotion.

I brainstormed ways to get the hell out of here and plotted the death of the men who kidnapped me.

In between the morose and morbid thoughts, I thought of him. How could I not? He would be the last person to see me alive. He would also be my last regret.

I regretted not having a chance with him. Not getting to feel his lips anywhere but on my lips.

Most of all, I regretted not getting to know him, because really, he seemed like someone I would really like.

And I liked it when he called me fairy.

He wasn't dead.

I consoled myself with that thought more than once. The second he face-planted in the field, I'd seen the dart sticking out of his back. I'd pulled it out and tossed it aside. Not that it helped at all.

Seconds later, I was "put out," but a lot less politely than with a dart.

Boss Man hit me in the side of the head with the butt of his gun. Next thing I knew… I was here.

A place I thought only existed in really good horror movies.

Through all my mental torture, I cried. I couldn't *not* cry. I was past that point of self-control. All I had left now was pain and fear… and the pure stubbornness to refuse to let them hear.

I might be crying big, fat tears and soundless sobs might be ripping up my insides like a 10.0 earthquake, but those bastards would never get the satisfaction of hearing me.

Plus, there was the fact my mouth was taped shut.

Not only that, but there was cotton or something shoved in my mouth.

I tried not to think about it because when I did, a panic attack threatened to take over my body.

What if I choke?

Gah, just the feeling of something pressed against my tongue, not being able to swallow the way I was used to doing…

Shut it down.

No more of that.

But for the record, even if my mouth weren't duct taped shut, I would still refuse to let them hear my cry.

I'm not sure how long I sat like this, but it was a long time. Beneath my leg, blood oozed. The idiots did tie something around it, something they seemed to glean a lot of pleasure from doing. They tied it extra tight.

To help stop the blood flow, you know.

Right. 'Cause they cared about that shit.

If they cared that much, they might have gotten the bullet out of my body. Or wait… *Maybe never shot me at all.*

I was bleeding through the cloth. I could feel it. Blood was heavy and sticky as it soaked into fabric. It also itched and burned.

Honestly?

I was starting to get numb.

Numb inside and out.

Fatigue clung to me like a well-worn blanket, molding around every curve. Between fear, blood loss, and dehydration, I knew it was only a matter of time. I was going to slip away to unconsciousness, and I might never wake.

On and off, I think I dozed. Or maybe I passed out and came to. I really didn't know.

The sounds of rattling chains and movement where I couldn't see brought me out of the haze I existed in. I tried to turn and look.

I couldn't.

This was likely it.

The only comfort I would know in death was that I wouldn't have to live another second of this cruelty.

"Rose." Derek's voice was an echo in my head. Far away but close. I clung to that sound, hanging on to my last moments of comfort and marveling at the ability my mind had to conjure up his voice.

The violent sound of a curtain being ripped away followed by a cry of distress made my eyes snap open.

I turned my head as much as I could, and Derek filled my vision. Sounds gathered in my throat, which wanted so badly to escape. The relief of just seeing his face was like being given a drink of water.

(Seriously. I could have gone for like a gallon of water.)

"Rose, sweetheart," Derek crooned. His hands hovered over me, around me, like he didn't know what to do.

I made another sound, more desperate and loud. Derek was like a jolt of espresso to me, waking me and giving me a burst of energy.

"What the fuck did they do to you?" His voice was hoarse and gruff.

Deftly, his fingers worked at the tape on my mouth while my eyes begged him to rip it away.

"One, two… three!" he said and ripped it off like it was a giant Band-Aid.

My skin screamed in agony, but I ignored it. The second the tape was gone, I spit out the cotton, letting it fall over my chin.

He made a sound and pulled the rest out. I gasped and sucked in air. Relief poured over me like warm water.

"Derek." My voice broke.

I was tied down, ankles and wrists. There was even something holding my head down.

Do you know what it's like to be strapped to a table, prone, at the mercy of someone else? Someone who was most definitely not a friend.

I did.

I think I'd rather take another bullet.

Derek ripped the band off my head. It sounded like Velcro when he pulled.

"Where are they?" I gasped, looking around, trying to see everything around us.

"Don't know," he grunted as he undid my wrists. When my hands were free, he helped me sit up. I wobbled a little. I felt so woozy.

But I pushed past it and reached for an ankle. Derek made fast work of one of the buckles, then gently pushed my hand away and undid the other.

"Shit." His hand encircled my ankle, the leg with the bullet wound. "I'm gonna take care of this right now."

"Derek," I whimpered.

Damn my voice. Damn my shaking insides.

His eyes flashed up. Hell, his entire body jerked when I said his name. Not even one second ticked by and I was swept against the hard wall of his chest.

I nuzzled into his neck and tried to make myself as small as I could get. If I could have crawled inside him, I would have. His hand stroked the back of my head, soothing, sure. My body shook and quivered.

I didn't cry. Honestly, I don't think I had any tears left.

"It's all right now, fairy," he murmured. The brush of his lips against my hair made me shiver.

He held me only a moment. Long enough to give me a dose of comfort and strength. Too soon, he pulled back, keeping his hands on my shoulders. "Let's clean up your leg."

The table I'd been strapped to was stainless steel. No more comfortable than the concrete. Gently, Derek slid my body back so my leg was resting on the surface.

I'd been ready to leap off, but I knew I couldn't just yet.

I hated this table.

"Guess I don't need to ask where you're gonna get the supplies." I tried to joke. It didn't come off as snarky or fun.

I was out of sarcasm like I was tears.

He didn't say anything as he moved around the makeshift doctor's cubicle. This entire place was creepy as hell. They'd turned the silo into a medical room. Large operating table, large overhead lights. Small rolling trays filled with shiny and sharp-looking instruments. An IV pole with a bag of fluid (hell, maybe poison) already hanging from it. There were monitors and stuff I didn't recognize. Scrubs and caps lay folded nearby.

The whole place was constructed with a lot of care.

It was clean. I would almost argue it was sterile, but I knew better. I was in the middle of a farm in a makeshift operating room… Sterile was not the word I would use to describe it.

One of the pieces in here looked like a large rolling toolbox made of stainless steel. Derek was digging around in it, piling most of what he needed on top.

He looked almost comfortable here. He worked and moved as if he knew where everything was.

It made this odd feeling of panic claw its way up the back of my throat again.

"You still with me?" Derek said, glancing over his shoulder.

I just stared at him.

"Rose." He turned around more fully, scrutinizing me with a watchful eye.

I nodded once. He frowned and turned back, adding a few more things to the top, then wheeled the whole thing down by my feet.

"I found some local anesthetic that should help with some of the pain," he told me and reached for the cloth tied around my leg.

"Does your leg feel hot?" he asked.

I stared at him.

"Do you feel sick?"

When I continued to not answer, he glanced up.

"You know where everything is," I said, hollow.

Derek's eyes widened, then narrowed. He seemed a little shocked, but he didn't say it out loud.

I wanted to tell him I was sorry, but I couldn't.

Sorry was saved for when you weren't in a fight for your life.

Slowly Derek raised both hands. They were already smeared with my blood. He put them palms out, like he was surrendering, and took a step away from me.

"Look at me, Rose," he commanded, low.

I did. My eyes never left his.

"I have nothing to do with this. Nothing. I think I might know what's going on…" He swallowed, and his face actually took on an ashen hue for a few long seconds. "I would never hurt you."

They all say that.

"I know where everything is because this room is set up just like an OR. An operating room," he clarified.

"I know what an OR is," I said.

He nodded, still holding up his hands.

"Natural instinct kicked in. I'm in an OR. A creepy-as-fuck OR, and you're hurt. You need help. This is what I do."

I had no way of knowing if he was telling the truth. I'd never seen the inside of an OR. Except on all those doctor drama shows on TV.

Wait.

I trusted him.

This was the same guy who not long ago refused to leave me behind when I was shot. He came back, picked me up, and literally ran with me in his arms. He kept running even after he was shot with a tranq.

He tended to my fingers and held me while I slept.

Derek didn't do this to me. He couldn't.

My lower lip wobbled.

"I just want to help you. But I won't unless you give me permission."

I nodded.

"I'm going to take that cloth off your leg, give you a shot, and then try to pull out the bullet. It's going to hurt like a bitch. You can bite me, hit me, yell at me… whatever you want."

I felt my dry lips pull upward.

It hurt.

"I'm thirsty," I said.

"I'm gonna try and find some water," he said, lowering his hands, cautious. He behaved like I had a gun, like he couldn't overpower me with practically one finger.

I trusted him.

Derek practically ransacked the room, looking for water. I saw him look at the IV bag and pole, a thoughtful look on his face. But then he abandoned it and kept searching. I definitely didn't have time to sit here stuck with an IV to rehydrate.

A minute later, a satisfied grunt filled the space. "Fucking right."

Next thing I knew, there was a gallon of water being held up to my lips. I drank it down greedily. He cautioned me to slow down, but I couldn't. My body was desperate.

When I pulled back, it barely seemed I'd made a dent in the fluid, but regardless, I knew I had. My body was already sighing in relief; already asking for more. I reached for the jug, and he surrendered it to me.

"Got it?" he asked, still holding the bottom, supporting some of the weight. I would have been offended, but I was pretty weak. Considering this was my only opportunity for water, it only made sense he was concerned I might not be able to heft it up to my lips and hold it there.

"I'm good," I said, trying to steady my shaking hand.

Slowly, he pulled back. Closely, he watched, making sure I wasn't about to fumble and ready to swoop in if I did.

My heart swelled. The way he watched me, how obvious it was he was truly concerned. How had I ever had even a second of doubt?

"How about it?" he asked, motioning to my leg.

I nodded and drained some more water. It was distilled. I didn't care. It was wet, which was good enough for me.

Even with the numbing medicine, I still felt him dig the metal out of my leg. It hit the top of the table with an audible *ting*. In between sips of water, I bit my lip and averted my gaze.

"I have no idea how you do this for a living," I muttered.

"I don't normally retrieve bullets." His tone was dark. "Believe me. I hope I never do this again."

"Do you like surgery?" I asked, mostly to distract myself from him cleaning out the wound and prepping it for stitches.

Yep. Stitches.

I was totally appalled the kidnappers had this place. It was clearly for something diabolical. But at the same time, it was coming in handy.

"I do," he said as he worked. I could tell he was completely in his element. I imagined it to be like athletes when they got in the zone. "It's different almost every day. And saving people is rewarding."

"You ever lose anyone?"

"Too often." He glanced up. "Lost one the night I got kidnapped."

"I'm sure that's very hard." I laid a hand on his shoulder. He paused in what he was doing, seemingly pulled out of his "zone" long enough to cover my hand with his.

"Every single time."

A heartbeat passed.

Derek pulled his hand away, and so did I. "I don't know how much time we have. But you need stitches. I'll try and do it fast."

The first poke of the needle through my tender, inflamed skin was brutal. I jerked, not meaning to, but my body naturally tried to get away.

"Sorry," I said through gritted teeth and pushed my leg toward him.

"It's gonna hurt, fairy." He warned. "The shot I gave you hasn't had enough time to take full effect. We can't wait."

"Do it." My fingers curled around the edges of the table and squeezed until I thought my knuckles might snap. The stab of the needle and tug of the stitch was probably the worst pain I'd ever felt. But I submitted to it.

If I could get through being kidnapped, chained up, strapped down, and shot, I could get through this, too.

"You said before you thought you know what's going on here." To say my voice was strained was an understatement.

He kept working. He was right. His hands were skilled.

"It's not good."

"Can't be any worse than the thoughts I was having while strapped to this table." I reminded him.

"When they come back, I'm going to kill them." He sounded like he was asking me to pass the gravy at Christmas dinner or reading me the choices off a takeout menu.

What was stranger? His matter-of-fact tone or hearing my response matched his to a T?

"Good."

"There." He sat back and admired the work. "Not my best, but considering I rushed and your leg is vibrating from pain, I'd say we did all right."

My leg was numb now. Of course it was, because the worst of it was over. The black thread looked garish against my marshmallow-white skin. The X's lining my calf made me look like some kind of freaky doll, the kind that came alive in the middle of the night.

Around the wound was red and splotchy, with a couple smears of fresh blood. There was also some light bruising and, of course, a lot of swelling.

Derek tied a knot in the thread, trimmed the excess, and tossed his tools down. Using his teeth, he ripped open some kind of wipe and carefully cleaned the area around it. Once that was done, he leaned close and blew out his breath to help dry it.

My skin tingled. Not my leg, though; that part was numb. My chest. My fingers. The back of my neck, and the base of my spine.

Even now he affected me.

His dark eyes shifted up to mine as his gentle breath caressed my aggrieved skin. He was exhausted and bruised on the side of his face from being hit. I'd felt a fine tremor in his fingers when he'd been working on my leg.

Still, he was strong. Still, he made my well-being a priority.

It reminded me of his nephew.

I gasped. The action hurt my throat, and my fingers splayed out across my neck without meaning to. "What time is it?" I worried. "You need to get out of here."

His lips thinned, cheeks paled. "I don't think I'm going to make it."

"We will," I said, firm. I moved to jump down off the table. His hand on my hip stopped me.

"Wait," he murmured. He picked up something else off his pile of supplies and ripped it open to draw out a large bandage. "This will keep the area protected. You need antibiotics, but I can't do anything about that now."

I sat long enough for him to smooth it over my leg. It was such a large bandage, it wrapped almost completely around my calf.

When he pulled back, I pushed off the table.

He caught me. "Easy now," he murmured. "That leg isn't going to be able to take any weight."

"Well, it's going to have to get with the program, 'cause I'm not crawling."

A ghost of a smile flirted with his lips.

He was still holding me. I felt the brush of the metal at his wrist.

"What are you chained to?" I asked.

I was lowered to the ground. On one solid foot, just using the other for balance, I gripped the table while he glanced at the chain. At the same time, we followed its length. There was pipe behind all the medical equipment. This wasn't the same kind as in the other silo. This one stuck up from the ground only about three feet.

At first, that seemed ideal, because we could slide the chain around it up and off. Of course, it wasn't that easy. The entire three feet was wrapped in it. Even if we managed to unwind it all, it would take us forever.

Abruptly, he spun away from the pipe. "You need to get out of here. Head for the corn fields. Find a road and get help."

"I'm not leaving you."

"You have to." He glanced around like he was afraid someone would walk in any second.

It made my skin crawl. The urge to listen and run poked at me. I wanted out of here so incredibly bad.

But Derek didn't leave me behind, and I would do the same for him.

"Put your hand on the table," I said, moving as fast as I could back into the nasty OR.

"Why?"

I was looking around, searching for anything heavy and large. Nearby, there was a big black-and-white cooler with a large plastic handle on top. I lifted it. The weight was pretty hefty.

I carried it over to the table.

"We're going to have to break your hand. It's the only way."

He laid his hand on the table, palm flat on the metal surface. His skin turned ghostly pale as he moved.

I thought about how he used his hands to fix me. How he said a surgeon had skillful fingers. This could change his career.

"Are there any tools in here that might be able to break the chain?" I asked, suddenly hesitant.

"No." His voice was resolved. "Do it."

I swallowed.

"Slam it down once, then do it again right after. Do it as hard as you can."

"I don't want to do this," I told him even as I lifted my arm.

Understanding lit his eyes. "Go without me. It's you they really need."

I didn't know what that meant, but it scared me.

"Well, I need you." I admitted. Before, those words would have gotten caught in my throat. How nervous it would have made me to admit how much I liked him.

How quickly life comes into perspective when you're faced without a life at all.

Without another word, I hefted the cooler high above my head and prepared to swing it down. Derek's hand flexed against the table in anticipation.

"Stop!" a familiar voice yelled, rushing into the space.

Both of us turned and looked.

It was our kidnappers.

Derek moved fast, rushed around the table, and shoved me behind him.

"I'm not going to do it," he announced, not one ounce of give in his voice.

Do what?

"So you figured it out, did you?" Boss Man mused.

"You're a pair of sick fucks," he spat.

"Soon to be very rich sick fucks." Taxi Man corrected.

It was always about money, wasn't it?

Derek slammed his hand back on the table. "Now, Rose." He urged.

I brought the cooler up.

"I wouldn't do that if I were you," Boss Man intoned.

"I'm pretty sure you're the last person in this entire universe I would ever ask for advice," I snapped.

"You're going to need that hand," he said again, completely ignoring me to remain focused solely on Derek.

"I'm not doing your dirty work!" Derek growled and gave me a nod.

"Not even to save someone you love?"

I brought the cooler down as hard as I could. It slammed into the stainless top. The impact vibrated my bones and caused my teeth to knock together. I bounced back from the force, and the cooler clattered to the floor while the top of the table hummed.

I would have fallen if not for Derek. He caught me around the waist and pulled me into his side.

"You moved. Why did you move?"

Against my side, Derek's hand clenched.

"Got your attention now, don't I?" Boss Man mused. Nearby, Taxi Man looked smug.

I seriously wanted to kick him.

In the balls.

"What are you talking about?" Derek asked, his chest heaved.

"Use that surgeon's brain to figure it out." Taxi man taunted.

"What's going on?" I spoke quietly, to Derek only.

Taxi Man laughed. "I told you he wasn't going to save you. He's not here to help you. In fact, he's the reason you're even here."

I didn't want to believe it. Everything inside me screamed no.

Yet there was this one voice.

A voice so quiet it shouldn't have been heard over all the other protests in my head. Sometimes the quiet ones were the wisest.

Yes.

Swallowing back the bile filling my throat, I looked at Derek. I felt the desperation in my gaze.

Tell me it's not true.

His own eyes held a plea. I wasn't sure what it meant, though.

"They want your organs, Rose." He spoke, his voice hoarse. "They kidnapped me to cut them out."

I swayed on my feet. Of all the things... *this* had never even crossed my mind.

"They want my organs?" I echoed, wrapping an arm across my waist.

Derek nodded once. "They want to sell them on the black market."

Black market organs?

Holy shit.

14

Derek

Mind games.

I knew they were being played. I knew I was a victim.

It was sort of like watching a train wreck, being part of it even. Everything progressed at agonizingly slow speed, and all I could do was stand here, watch, and know shit was about to hit the fan.

Black market organs were not just urban tales. It happened all over the world. Most people didn't realize it happened closer to home and wasn't reserved for third world countries. I admit even I was guilty of that.

Being a transplant surgeon, of course I heard rumors. I read the news reports. I even heard whispers. I knew what people went through when their bodies were failing them. How they stared at the phone, at their doctors and nurses, day after day, with the same question in their eyes.

Will I get what I need today?

When will the waiting—the slow, tormenting, dying of pieces of me be replaced?

I empathized with loved ones who also waited on an organ. Watching someone you loved die was almost as bad as being the one in the hospital bed.

Those people were desperate. *No.* Beyond desperate.

There was a point at which desperation crossed over into something else.

Obsession.

When their entire lives were consumed with finding an organ, a match, a way to save a life and logical reasoning went out the window. So did regard for just about everything else. I'd come close to that obsession border many times myself when I looked at Rocco this past year.

People like the men who kidnapped Rose and me preyed on people. Used their obsession, fear, even the love they had for the people who were dying against them.

How far would you go to save someone you loved?

How much would you pay?

Would you value a faceless stranger's life over someone you knew and loved?

Is it even possible to think clearly when you've crossed over into the gray matter of obsession?

It happened more and more. The list of people waiting was far too long, the rate of death far too steep. People ended up in negotiation with black market organ dealers, and they paid exorbitant amounts of cash.

Here in the US, a black market organ could fetch over two hundred thousand dollars.

A steep price.

But if it saved the life of someone you couldn't live without… would you pay it?

In other countries, it was a lot easier. Desperate people would walk into illegal hospitals and sell an organ for as little as five thousand dollars. Other people, people like Rose, were taken and had them cut out of their body.

Some people were left to die. Some were stitched back up. A lot of those people probably died, too.

You could have heard a pin drop in the center of the makeshift operating room. My stomach was queasy. I had so many questions.

So many fears.

Not even to save someone you love? What did that mean?

Rose yanked away from me. She pulled back so hard she stumbled. I lunged sideways and caught her even though it was me she was trying to escape from.

She was weak, looked like hell, and was obviously horrified.

Hell. When I saw this room, I was, too.

She doubted me, but I couldn't be mad. I'd been brought here to literally cut out pieces of her body.

"I'm fine," she insisted, straightening.

I pulled back but didn't move away. I stayed close for two reasons:

1.) In case she fell over.

And

2.) Because I was going to protect her.

"You want to cut out my organs?" Her voice wobbled.

Boss man pointed at me. "He does."

I stiffened. "No," I argued harshly. What the fuck? Why was he acting like this was all my plan?

Rose ignored me. It cut deep down.

"Which one?" she asked, still staring at the boss.

Her question was morbid. I glanced at her face. Her eyes were glassy. That wasn't a good thing.

"It doesn't matter." I made a slashing movement with my hand. "I'm not doing it."

Taxi Man laughed. His shirt was sweat stained and partially untucked. "You will."

His confidence pissed me off.

"You might as well kill me right now," I spat. "There is no way in hell I'm cutting her open."

"The clock is ticking." The man with white hair glanced at his watch to punctuate his words. "We need to get started."

I planted my feet and crossed my arms. I didn't know what kind of person they thought they kidnapped, but I was not him. I didn't cut up innocent people for criminals. I didn't perform illegal surgeries just to save my own life.

Like they'd let me live anyway. The second they got what they wanted, I'd get a bullet in the brain.

"What if I told you the call you got at the hospital yesterday was a phony?"

Stillness came over me. My heartrate slowed like hypothermia was setting in.

"I get a lot of calls," I replied after a full beat of silence.

"You know what call I'm talking about." The level, smug way his eyes trained on mine made it hard to breathe.

"It wasn't a fake."

Behind me, Rose shifted as she listened aptly.

"It was." Boss Man promised. "Know how I know?"

I didn't say anything.

He pulled a cellphone out of his dress pants and held it up. After a couple taps on the screen, some audio played through the room.

Dr. Kelley, this is Stacey from the national donor registry list.

I sucked in a breath, listening intently. It couldn't be.

Yes? my voice replied.

We're calling to let you know we have matched an organ for one of your patients. It will be ready for transport tomorrow and only take a few hours to arrive at your hospital.

Which patient? The hopeful tone in my voice felt like a branding iron. I still remembered that moment. I still remembered the way I'd looked up at the sky and prayed to God my nephew's name was spoken.

Rocco Kelley.

The recording clicked off, and the man with white hair looked up. "It's amazing what a drama student at the college will do for a quick couple hundred bucks."

The force of my anger propelled me forward. I lunged for him, so fucking pissed off I saw dots before my eyes.

He whipped out the pistol and held it out like it would stop me. I would have laughed if I hadn't been so intent on my prize.

I knocked the gun out of his hand faster than he expected and bulldozed into him as it went clattering across the floor and slid beneath some equipment.

"Backup!" he hollered as we both smacked into the floor.

I reared my fist back and slammed it into his face. Then I did it again. Blood spurted across his face and peppered my knuckles, and the red was like a flag to a bull.

Instead of punching him again, I hauled the chain up and slipped it beneath his head so I could wrap it around his neck.

The cold nose of a gun pressed against my temple.

I paused and looked up. Taxi Man was standing there, his face flushed. "Get up."

I squeezed the chain tight. The man beneath me gasped.

"Go ahead and shoot me," I growled.

He shuffled beside me, clearly not prepared for this. Still, he hesitated in harming me. Was I really that goddamn important? Couldn't they just cut out her organs themselves?

"Ro-c-co," he wheezed.

My grip loosened at the mention of my nephew. "Don't say his name!" I raged, clenching the chain once more.

"If you kill him, your nephew is as good as dead," Taxi Man said.

With a shout, I let go and pushed up off the man. I wanted to kill him, but first, I wanted to know everything.

"How do you know about him?" I yelled. The rise and fall of my chest was rapid. My heart no longer pumped slowly but galloped beneath my ribs like a race horse.

"You think I wouldn't do my homework before a million-dollar job?" the boss rasped, getting up off the floor while holding his neck.

"A million dollars?" Rose gasped.

I was ashamed to say I'd forgotten she was there.

"Job of a lifetime," Taxi Man drawled.

Rose's voice was bewildered. "There's no way one of my organs would get that much."

"No, but all of them would fetch enough to set me up for the rest of my life." His voice was strained from being choked.

Rose gasped again. I glanced at where she stood, not where she'd been, but on the other side of the table. Her face was whiter than a sheet of paper, almost translucent. Her eyes looked unnaturally large in her face, and her red hair was wild around her shoulders.

She finally understood completely. It wasn't just one organ they wanted.

These motherfuckers wanted me to literally carve out her entire body. The only reason they hadn't killed her immediately was because the organs would only be viable for so long. This way, I could cut them all out and they could transport them immediately.

After they killed me of course.

"Do it, and we'll give you a kidney. Your pick of either of hers. You can take it to the hospital right after you're done. Hell, I'll drive you there myself."

They were trying to use Rocco to make me do it.

His life in exchange for hers.

"I don't trust you," I growled. "There's no way in hell you'll let me live."

"No reason not to let you live." He shrugged.

I glanced over at Rose.

As I stared at her, I was taunted.

"Take the kidney. Go save your nephew. He's ten. He's got a whole life in front of him. If you do this, he'll have that life. By the time you get out of surgery, I'll be long gone. It won't matter if you go to the police, because they'll never find me."

"We'll be long gone." Taxi Man corrected.

My eyes shifted away from Rose and then back to her face. I looked away abruptly. "She's not a match. Her kidney won't save him."

"But it will. She's AB negative."

I sucked in a breath.

Rose did, too. "How do you know my blood type?"

"Research."

I glanced back. "You're AB negative?" I couldn't help the gravelly way I said it. Rocco was the rarest blood type there was. Matching him with a kidney was even harder because of it.

"Y-yes," Rose stuttered.

Her kidney might actually save him.

Rocco's cure was right here in front of me.

I felt my insides wavering.

That line I was talking about? The one between desperation and obsession?

I was very, *very* close to that line.

"So is he," I intoned.

Rose took a step back, like she felt the inner tug-of-war going on inside me.

"She's just a girl," Taxi Man said. "She's disposable. You get what you want and so do we. Everyone gets their happy ending."

"I don't!" Rose burst out.

We stared at each other for long moments.

Rocco's face flashed behind my eyes.

I glanced away from her, then back again.

"I'm sorry," I told her. The hollowness in my words made tears fill her eyes.

I took a step forward.

15

Rose

Be careful who you trust.
One lapse in judgement may carry a hefty price tag.

16

Derek

The stainless steel table was cold beneath my clammy hands. Instead of shocking me, it worked as an anchor, grounding me to my decision.

"Get the gun!" I roared. Using all the pissed-off emotion filling my limbs, I manhandled the table around. It was on wheels, which only helped me propel it with even more force.

Rose sprang into action, and the two men standing nearby were completely caught off guard.

The table swung into them, knocking them down like bowling pins after a lucky strike. The sound they made when the steel connected with their bodies was a sound I enjoyed. At first, they skittered along, trying desperately not to go down, but I was unrelenting.

Rushing them with the table between us, I didn't stop shoving until it hit the wall with a great crash and they sprawled across the floor.

When I mowed into Taxi Man, he lost his grip on the rifle, and it clattered to the floor. I picked it up and aimed it at them, glancing over my shoulder to Rose. She was half under the equipment, trying to reach the weapon.

"Hurry!" I called.

The men stirred. Taxi Man rolled out from under the table. A couple of the buttons on his shirt popped and some wiry chest hair and skin was showing.

It was gross.

It was also a shame. Too bad he didn't have half the hair on his chest on his head.

"Don't even think about it," I muttered, totally prepared to shoot.

"You just signed your nephew's death certificate."

Nausea rolled over me. How could it not? They made it out like a choice. I guess in a lot of ways, I did have one.

Was I choosing wrong?

What if Rocco never got that call? What if he would never find a match?

Would I someday stand at his grave and regret the choice I'd made?

Don't think like that.

Rose rushed to my side, the gun in her unsteady hands.

"You okay?" I asked.

She gave me a look that made me feel stupid for asking.

Taxi Man stood. Rose recoiled.

It was definitely the chest hair.

Nasty.

"Don't come any closer," I warned, my gun unwavering. "Throw the keys over here," I demanded.

"I don't have them." He lied.

I shot him in the foot.

He fell back onto the floor, screaming like the little bitch he was.

"The goddamn keys!" I roared.

Sweat dripped between my shoulder blades. What was left of my torn shirt clung to my skin and made me uncomfortable.

A single key on a silver ring landed at my feet.

Rose bent to pick it up while I kept my eyes on the men. The brains of the operation was unconscious. He'd taken the brunt of the hit.

But even passed out, I didn't trust him. He could be faking.

I spared a single glance at Rose. She stared between me and the key. I saw doubt in her eyes again.

"I'm not going to hurt you, fairy." I used the nickname on purpose, trying to remind her how much I really did care.

Do I care about her more than Rocco?

No.

But as I previously pointed out, I didn't have a God complex. I had no right to decide who lived and died. I wouldn't choose between Rocco and Rose. It wasn't up to me.

And I wasn't under any circumstances going to be blackmailed into illegally removing someone's organs.

Rose jammed the gun in the waistband of her skirt.

"Careful." I cautioned. "We don't have time to fix another bullet wound."

Her hands noticeably shook as she fumbled with the key. The gun was still trained on the kidnappers, so she had to stretch around and press close to reach the lock on the cuff at my wrist.

I felt the key slide into the lock, and I heard the mechanism click.

I glanced down as the cuff popped open.

Rose grinned, a spark of hope lighting her green eyes.

I shouldn't have glanced away. Not even for the split second I did.

Taxi Man burst up off the ground, half falling, half leaping at Rose. He was going for the gun.

Without a second thought, I pulled my trigger. The deafening sound of the rifle going off at close range bounced off the metal walls all around us.

The bullet hit its mark, slammed into his chest and knocking him back. Red bloomed out across the white shirt he wore, the fabric soaking it up like a sponge.

He made one sound, a single gurgle, and then fell back onto the concrete, dead.

The second I shot, I wrapped an arm around Rose and pulled her into my chest. She buried her face there, both hands pressing against her ears.

Once the man was down, I pulled her back. "Let's go."

She started to turn, to look at the body.

"Don't look." I ordered and pulled her back.

I would live with the sight of him lying there bleeding out, but she didn't have to.

I half carried her out of the silo. All she could do was hobble at best.

Several yards away, the taxi we were both kidnapped in was parked in the grass. I had no desire to ever get into another damn cab again, but now really wasn't the time to be picky.

"C'mon," I said, guiding her toward it.

"The keys!" she cried and turned back.

"Fuck the keys," I growled. "I'll hotwire it."

We didn't have time to go back. The other man could wake at any moment. He didn't have a gun, but he could still put up a fight.

He wanted his money. He wouldn't just let us go.

As if my thoughts conjured him up, someone shouted behind us. "Hey!"

I let go of Rose, spun on my heel, and squeezed off a shot.

It hit him in the side. I'd been aiming for the chest, but beggars couldn't be choosers.

With a cry, he slumped onto the ground, screaming.

"Get in!" I yelled unnecessarily once the cab was within reach.

I made it into the driver's seat before Rose got in and bent to hotwire the cab. But the keys were hanging in the ignition.

Dumb criminals.

God's gift to victims.

Rose collapsed into the passenger seat as the engine roared to life. I tore across the grass before her door was even closed. In the rearview mirror, I saw the boss struggling to his feet. I pressed on the gas and drove ahead.

"I really, *really* hate cabs," Rose muttered.

I glanced at her and smiled. "You and me both."

17

Rose

When you walk (well, are carried) into an ER where the man doing the carrying is a well-liked surgeon, you don't have to sit in the waiting room. You don't even have to fill out the half ton of forms they give you strapped to the top of a clipboard. Although, I'm sure those would come later.

Derek drove the kidnapper mobile, aka the taxi, right up to the entrance of the ER and left it there. I tried to bring my gun inside with me.

Apparently, that might get me shot.

I'd already had enough of that.

So after Derek pried the deadly weapon (which he said made me look like a terrorist) out of my hands, he swung me up into his arms and tightly against his chest.

It felt too good to argue. I didn't even bother. All I did was lay my cheek against his chest and close my eyes. I tried to block out all my thoughts and focus on the fact we were safe.

Safe.

Something I would never take for granted again.

"Oh my God! Dr. Kelley?" A woman gasped only seconds after the doors whooshed closed behind us.

"We need a private exam room. And the police," he said.

Everything happened fast after that.

I was placed on a hospital bed as nurses bustled around, clucking their tongues and firing questions like they were the police and not the caregivers.

Derek put up with it for about five minutes, then tasked them with different jobs to get them out of the room.

The second they were gone, I slumped into the bed.

He'd been pacing nearby and came over to me. I scooched over, making room, and he sat on the mattress without a word.

"You're safe now," he murmured, brushing the hair from my face.

"Thanks to you." The horrible scene we'd just run from played back in my mind. The split second of mind-numbing fear I'd had when I thought he'd turned against me was in the forefront.

"The nurses will take care of you, fairy. One should be back any second."

"You need to go be with Rocco," I said, not upset he had to go, but maybe a little sad he wouldn't be beside me.

"Hopefully, the surgery started already, but I can at least go be there." His leg bounced with nervous energy. And something else… something I couldn't put my finger on.

"Go," I urged.

Before he did, he swooped in. His lips captured mine in a searing kiss. A kiss from Derek did more for me than medicine or an IV ever would. My lips parted with a sigh, and his tongue stroked in. Deeply he delved into my mouth, and I welcomed him wholeheartedly.

Warmth spread throughout my body as our mouths danced together in a rhythm only they knew.

Before pulling away, he kissed my lips with one last soft kiss, then pressed another to the tip of my nose. "I'll find you later."

I nodded.

On his way out, the nurse came in.

"I'm going up to sit in on Rocco's surgery," he told her, catching the door before it could swing closed.

"Rocco's in surgery?" The nurse seemed puzzled.

"You didn't hear?" Derek asked. He looked exhausted, like he'd been run over with a car. The T-shirt he wore was ripped and stained with blood. His sweatpants were dirty and his hair was a disaster. Frankly, I wondered how he was still standing so tall.

"No," she replied, her brow furrowing.

His eyes slid to me, and the anxious energy I'd felt off him before returned. "Tell the police I'll talk to them as soon as the surgery is over."

"Of course." The nurse agreed, although he was already gone.

Her eyes turned to me, appraising me with a motherly stare. "Let's get you cleaned up and some fluids going. You're being admitted, so we'll move you to a different floor soon."

"Thank you," I said, exhaustion really weighing me down now. My eyes felt as though there was sand in them, and my limbs each felt like they weighed a hundred pounds.

She bustled around and stuck an IV into the back of my hand.

"How long do kidney transplant surgeries normally take?" I asked her.

"Hours," she replied with a frown.

"What is it?"

"No one has said a word about that boy's surgery. The entire staff loves him so much. I should have heard about it before now."

"Well, it did happen very fast." I hedged. My stomach twisted.

She nodded but didn't look convinced. "I'll go hurry along your room and the doctor so you can get some rest."

When she was gone, I remembered what the kidnappers said. I remembered the audio that filled the room and devastated Derek.

The call about the organ match had been a fake. A ploy to force him into cutting me open.

I tended not to believe kidnappers. They did try to kill me after all. Rather, they tried to get Derek to kill me.

They were lying. Derek seemed to think so, too, by the way he rushed out of here.

But... what if they weren't?

18

Derek

I killed a man today.

Maybe even two.

Hell, I hoped the white-haired bastard lay there and bled to death as we drove away.

What did that make me?

Human. It made me human.

It also made me honest.

Honest men didn't like to be lied to, but right now, I was praying I'd been told the mother of all lies.

They had a recording of the phone call I'd had with donor registry. Was it all a setup? A big ruse to get me to do something sinister?

Or were the men preying upon my weaknesses?

I wanted to believe so badly I ignored the truth nagging the back of my mind. I ignored the urge to bite my nails in anticipation, and I tried not to feel like it wasn't just two people I killed today… but three.

If that phone call had been a hoax, *if* I turned down a chance at an AB negative organ, then I *might* have just killed Rocco.

All the ifs and mights were feasting away on my insides. I passed the elevators and rushed up the stairs to the OR. A familiar nurse dressed in scrubs and carrying a clipboard of paperwork was in the hall when I burst in.

"Janet." I heaved. "Where's Rocco?" I glanced toward the brown swinging doors that led back to the operating rooms.

"Dr. Kelley, are you okay?" She frowned.

I waved away her concern. "Where is he?"

Her brow furrowed. "In his room, I imagine."

I stumbled back.

The truth hit me like a train at full speed.

"Dr. Kelley!" Janet rushed toward me, grabbing my arm. "You need to sit down."

"Rocco's not up here?" I whispered, strained.

"No," she replied, worry dripping from the single word.

I pulled away and rushed back into the stairwell. Once there, I lunged down two flights of stairs, then leaned against the wall to catch my breath.

My sister, my God, my sister must be beside herself. I told her he was getting a kidney. I promised her I'd be there and her son would be okay.

I was late. The kidney never came.

She was going to hate me.

Rocco might, too.

Shoving off the wall, I stepped out onto the floor where Rocco was located. I pivoted left and practically sprinted toward his room, which was the last door on the left. Laura stepped out of the doorway, looking straight ahead, like she was lost in thought.

My shoe squeaked against the tile.

Her head whipped around.

"Derek!" she gasped and rushed toward me. "Where have you been?"

I stopped before I got to the doorway, and Laura closed the distance between us.

"Oh my word! What happened?" she exclaimed, three fingers pressed against her lips as if to hold in a screech.

I didn't answer at first, instead taking a moment to appraise her features. Laura was a beautiful woman, with dark hair and eyes like mine—more fine boned, a narrow nose, and thinner lips. She was older than me by several years, but it had never been evident.

At least until the last year. Until right now.

It was like she'd aged five years since I'd seen her last. Her skin was sallow and pasty, her normally warm eyes bloodshot and dilated. For the first time, I noticed fine lines at the corners and just beneath her lower lash line. The thick strands of her hair were pulled back harshly in a low ponytail at the base of her neck, the ends frayed and lackluster. The tip of her nose was red, and her skin was dry. Beneath her bottom lip was a red welt from where she'd clearly been chewing at it.

I'd done this to her.

I made a promise—*a life and death promise*—and didn't keep it.

"How's Rocco?" I asked, keeping my voice low.

"He's sleeping. It's been a long day. He's been upset."

I felt like a sailboat without any wind in my sails, drifting… drifting along like I'd lost my way.

"We need to talk," I murmured, fighting the urge to go into my nephew's room and wake him just so I could hug him.

She nodded, and I pulled her across the hall into an empty room.

"Your face." She fretted, staring at the black eye I sported. Then her eyes trailed to my clothes. "You're hurt."

"I was kidnapped." Yeah, it was a blunt way to say it, but I didn't have time to pretty up the words. Now wasn't the time for gentle bedside manner. She'd been waiting, wondering.

She deserved a straightforward explanation.

Laura sucked in a breath. "What?"

I nodded. "Last night when I got home, I was shot with a tranquilizer and taken out of my driveway."

Her voice was low and shocked. "I tried to call you so many times."

"Well, now you know why I didn't answer."

"Were you hurt?" She began pacing along the length of the wall and wringing her hands.

Just watching her made me exhausted. I sank on the end of the nearby hospital bed. No sleep, the adrenaline rushes… It was all catching up to me.

Maybe that's why it seemed she was repeating herself. I felt like I could sleep for an entire week.

With Rose beside me.

With thoughts of the red-haired coffee fairy at the front of my mind, I said, "Not too bad. They didn't want me hurt. Rose was a different story."

"Rose?" She paused in pacing and swung to stare at me.

"You know the coffee truck girl outside?" I told her.

"The one you totally like?" She didn't say it with a teasing note in her voice like usual. When I—a non-coffee drinker started showing up with coffee cups in hand, it was like open season to pick on her little brother who clearly had a crush.

I told her she was delusional even though she wasn't.

Right now, though, she wasn't amused. Instead, she seemed horrified, and as soon as the words escaped, she slapped her palm over her lips.

I nodded. "She was kidnapped, too."

"*Oh my God*, Derek." Her voice broke. "I'm so sorry."

"It's over now."

"They let you go, then?" she said before I could continue. "Where is it?"

"Where's what?" I frowned.

"I meant to say she. Where is *she*?" Laura amended.

"Rose is downstairs, admitted for the night," I replied slowly.

"Is she all right? What's her condition like? Will she recover?" She started pacing again, the nervous, anxious energy surrounding her beginning to penetrate my exhaustion.

She was acting weird.

I watched her closely. "Why wouldn't she recover?"

"Of course she will," she reasoned almost as if to herself. "You're the best surgeon at this hospital."

"Why would Rose need a surgeon?" I said, steady.

A very, *very* bad feeling came over me. It seemed to suck every bit of oxygen from my lungs.

Laura stopped pacing and glanced up. "Tell me you got it." Her voice was pleading.

I jolted to my feet, my heart galloping against my chest. I could barely force the words out of my mouth. "Oh shit, Laura. What did you do?"

A half cry, half moan escaped her throat.

No.

So quickly, my feelings changed. Comprehension washed over me.

"Tell me you weren't involved in this." Disbelief and shock consumed me. Memories flashed behind my eyes, memories of my sister at various times in our lives.

Never in a million years would I have ever thought she was capable of something like this. Hell, part of me still awaited her denial. All she'd have to do to convince me I was totally off base was say the word no. I'd believe her.

I'd believe her in an instant.

It just wasn't possible my sister, the girl who had literally been in my life since the day I was born, would do something like this.

"He's just a little boy." Her voice was broken.

In that moment, I was, too. The statement shattered me. My knees actually felt weak.

She did this. Laura had me kidnapped. She had me chained up by criminals to try and force me to steal an organ for my nephew.

The kidnappers hadn't lied to me.

My sister did.

I dropped back onto the bed, my eyes not really focused on anything at all because the thoughts and feelings inside me made me blind to everything else.

"Please understand," she begged, rushing close.

Her movement snapped me back to reality. My head whipped up. Whatever she saw in my eyes made her pause. Her stature became tense.

She should be nervous.

I rose. She took a step back.

I found that very telling about the way I must have looked. Black and blue from the hits I took, blood smeared all over my ripped and dirty clothing.

But not my blood.

Rose's.

My sister did this to Rose.

I took another step closer, my hands clenched. At my side, my raw wrist burned. I stopped in front of her, just short of arm's distance. I was genuinely afraid if I went any closer, I'd do something I'd regret.

"You had Rose kidnapped, an innocent woman, a woman you knew I wanted."

She started to protest. I watched it form on her tongue.

I silenced her by cutting my hand through the air between us. She flinched.

If I wasn't so angry, I'd be offended. It was true; I felt deadly, and I was beyond betrayed. Even still, I'd never physically hurt Laura.

Apparently, I couldn't say the same about her.

"You had me kidnapped, dumped into the back of a taxi, and carted off to some abandoned farm where I was chained up and threatened. Those men… the men I assume you paid?"

She nodded, and I made a choked sound.

"It was for Rocco!" she burst out. "He needs a kidney *desperately*, Derek. I can see it in your eyes every time you look at him. I watch him lie in that bed day after day as life slowly drains out of him." Her cheeks became flushed, and the resolve of a mother filled her gaze.

She was no longer worried about me, no longer frightened of what I might do.

She was unrelenting. She was fierce, and she would goddamn do what she had to do to save her son's life.

"My little boy is dying because his body is betraying him. Because two organs won't do their job. People walk around every single day with perfectly good organs. He only needs one. *One.*"

"You can't just take an organ out of someone else's body!" I roared.

"The hell I can't!" she bellowed back. "I made a promise to that child, to myself. I promised him I would protect him and love him. I promised him a good life. I thought you promised him the same!"

I sucked in a breath.

"But you wouldn't do it, would you? You wouldn't just go against your morals for one hour to save the life of a boy you claim to love like a son."

"You think me murdering someone is the way I should prove my love?" I disparaged.

"It's not murder. She would be fine with one kidney." Laura's eyes flashed. "You chose your dick over your own flesh and blood."

I was moving before the words even left my mouth. I shot forward and grabbed my sister, moving until her back hit the wall, and I pinned myself against her. My breath heaved, and I knew she could likely feel it blowing in her suddenly pale face.

I was so fucking pissed I couldn't even see straight. Maybe I would hurt her… Maybe she'd pushed me way, *way* too far.

"How dare you?" I growled. "I've treated him like a son his entire life. I pay his damn hospital bills. I give him the best care I can humanly give. I've been killing myself for years now trying to find that boy a kidney. I've had myself tested three times, each time giving myself false hope I would miraculously be a match. I've even been trying to find his good-for-nothing father."

She gasped. She had no idea I'd been searching for that douchebag.

"Don't you dare say I don't love him. Don't even fucking think it. I want him to be whole again just as badly as you." I felt my eyes flashing down at her.

She swallowed thickly.

I shoved away from her. She made me sick. I felt like she was a complete stranger now.

"You've been trying to find Daniel?" she whispered.

"My private investigator keeps coming up empty," I replied, not looking at her.

The vulnerability in her voice cut me, and that made me angry. I guess even a betrayal this heavy didn't keep me from caring.

"I know what I did was terrible," she whispered.

My back muscles bunched. I wanted to laugh. What she did went way beyond terrible.

"I can't keep letting him deteriorate. One night when I was researching online for something, anything that could save him, I saw some articles on black market organs."

My eyes closed.

"People pay for organs. They just buy them." There was a hint of wonder in her voice, like she'd never heard of it until she accidentally stumbled across the information on the web.

"It's illegal, Laura. That's why it's called *black market*. They steal the organs out of unwilling donors."

"I started looking deeper," she said, ignoring my words. Maybe that was how she did this; she ignored the parts she didn't want to think about. "I made some calls. I paid someone here at the hospital to see if there were any matches for his blood type. I didn't want anyone not in the States. I wanted a viable, healthy organ."

Insanity. How had I completely missed that my sister was bordering on insanity?

"The hope I'd felt when I heard there was a match…" Her voice broke, and she finished her sentence with a sob. "I hadn't felt that kind of hope in a long time."

"Laura," I rasped, still unable to look at her.

"So I made some calls. I found some men who were willing to kidnap the match. I never asked much about her identity. I never even read the personal information I was given. I thought it would be easier—"

"She was just a means to an end for you." I cut in.

"No! Not at all. But I had to do this. I gave them strict orders not to hurt her any more than necessary. Once the kidney was removed, she was to be taken to a hospital a few hours away. The men would disappear with their hefty fee, and you could do the surgery and save my son."

"And me?" I asked.

"I got scared," she whispered. "I worried I was doing all this only to let a criminal cut out the thing that would save Rocco. So I took out a second mortgage on the house. I offered them more money to kidnap you…

I knew you'd cut out the kidney the right way. It was safer. Not just for Rocco, but for the donor."

"They were going to kill her," I snapped.

"What?"

"You hired criminals. Did you think they would do everything you said? They wanted me to cut out *all* her organs. Not just one. They planned to only give me the kidney if I cut out all her other organs to be sold on the black market. Rose would be dead."

"That's not what I wanted!" she insisted and started to cry. "I only wanted to save my son."

A slew of curses filled the room. Roughly, I turned and yanked her into a hug.

I couldn't help but feel like she was a victim too.

"Why couldn't you have just saved him?"

Her tortured cry cut me like a knife. I'd probably bleed from that statement the rest of my life.

Why couldn't I have just done it?

Why did it have to be Rose? Would I have done it if it hadn't been her? Why did life have to be so fucking unfair?

"I'm sorry." The apology ripped from my gut.

Deep, gut-wrenching sobs tore out of her as she clung to my chest. How in God's name did I find myself here? How did she?

"What happened to the men?" she asked after long, long minutes.

"I killed them."

It struck me then how I hadn't even hesitated in killing them, but with Rose, it had been an internal battle. At least not there in the end.

It was because it came down to them or us. Eat or be eaten. They'd been trying to hurt me by using my nephew. I thought they'd been lying. They hadn't lied about him, but they lied about everything else.

Regardless of what my sister thought, I wouldn't have walked out of there with my life. Neither would Rose. No one would have been any better if I'd done what they ordered.

But what about Rocco?

Now they were dead.

I was here.

And I would wonder if the choices my sister made and the choices I made would ultimately cost Rocco.

"Have you spoken to the police?" she asked, pulling away from me and wiping at her face.

"Not yet." My tone was hard and clipped. I looked away from her once more. It hurt too much to look. My resolve weakened when I did. Part of me just couldn't be as livid as I knew I had the right to be.

Part of me understood why she did it.

"I can't look at you right now," I growled and spun to leave.

"Wait," she called.

I stopped but didn't turn.

"What will you tell them?"

I didn't answer. I couldn't. Instead, I walked out, leaving her behind to wallow in what she'd done. I went directly across the hall into the darkened room.

From the foot of the bed, I stared down at my sleeping nephew.

His hair was on the long side like mine. A while back, he told me he wanted to grow his hair, and I promised I'd grow mine, too.

Rocco's hair wasn't quite as dark as mine. It was more of a medium brown, where mine was just dark. It flopped over his forehead and eyes. His cheeks were pale, his complexion sallow. He was small and frail beneath the quilt my mother had made him out of T-shirts from all the places we'd been and places he'd yet to see.

Places I wondered if he would ever get to see.

There was a stuffed dinosaur on his left and a giant stuffed shark on his right, monitors hooked up all around, and several decks of cards nearby.

The physical pain of staring down at him was the worst pain I'd ever known. It was the absolute in grief.

If I could trade my life for this boy's, I would in a heartbeat.

But I couldn't.

And it was that which would haunt me forever.

19

Rose

I didn't expect to see him here.

Yet he was.

My throat felt like the Sahara Desert, dry and sandy but also swollen and tight. It was that feeling that woke me from deep sleep. Well, that and the dream I'd been having.

I had a feeling I'd be dreaming about chains and duct tape for a long time.

Those images and gut-tightening fear didn't last, though, because when I opened my eyes, it was him I saw. Derek wasn't a small man. He wasn't so huge he was intimidating either. He was just the right size.

You know. A size that carried presence. A size that inspired confidence and strength. Even though he wasn't my doctor, I knew he had a really good bedside manner.

Crap, he made me feel better just by being here, even slumped in an uncomfortable-looking chair with his feet propped up on the end of my bed. He wasn't wearing the ripped-up T-shirt anymore or the sweats. Those ruined clothes were switched out for a set of green hospital scrubs.

The messy way his hair looked the last I saw him was also fixed, like he'd combed it or run his hands through it so much it was lying down, tamed.

The bruise on the side of his face seemed darker now, the skin around it puffy. His wrist was bandaged just like mine, and up until this point, I hadn't noticed the cuts and scrapes on his knuckles from the fighting he'd done.

But even with his injuries, he still looked strong.

My heart swelled. Not at his injuries, the sight of his chin resting against his chest, or the way his arms wrapped across his middle while he slept. It was the sight of his bare feet atop my scratchy blankets.

No, I don't have a weird foot fetish.

But there was intimacy in waking up to find him here, to find his naked feet on my bed. I liked it. I liked it so much everything else seemed to be forgotten for long, blissful seconds.

There was a large no-nonsense clock hanging on the wall across from the bed, the kind with a white face, black numbers and hands, and a cheap-looking plastic frame. It was already morning. I'd slept through the night.

The IV was still in the back of my hand. The needle and tape tugged and pulled, but I barely noticed.

"Derek," I whispered, but it came out as more of a croak.

His body jolted, arms flew out, and those bare toes hit the ground. The chair beneath him skidded backward with the force of how quickly he stood. "What's the matter?"

"Everything's fine." I assured him. "I didn't mean to freak you out."

His large exhale filled my ears. "Guess I'm still kinda on red alert," he said, rubbing the back of his neck and glancing up at me from beneath lowered lashes.

His eyes were sheepish, and the dark length of his hair fell, creating a short waterfall over his forehead and part of his brow. He was completely adorable, but not in a cutesy way. In a knight in shining armor way.

"That's understandable."

Both his hands dropped to his sides when he came closer. I couldn't help but notice there was something wary about the way he approached me. Almost as if he were apprehensive. "How you feeling, fairy?"

Derek had never been very apprehensive around me.

Well. *Wait.*

I guess he'd always been a little cautious around me, up until we'd been kidnapped. He always hesitated to ask me out, even though he said wanted to. He always tried to just keep things friendly instead of going a little further.

Was there a difference between hesitation and apprehension?

Sure felt like it.

It seemed like whatever held him back before was a lot different than the guilt I read in his eyes now.

I made a split-second decision right then and there. *I am going to go more with my gut and less with my head.*

If I'd gone with my gut the night at the bar, maybe I wouldn't be sitting here right now.

But then you wouldn't be here with Derek.

I pushed away that little nugget of a thought. Getting kidnapped, shot, and almost dissected was never going to be classified as okay steps to getting a date.

Desperate much?

Following my gut had yet to lead me astray. In fact, I had a successful business because of it.

"What's the matter, doc?" I pressed.

His dark eyes flashed up to mine. The shield he'd held between us crumbled, and amusement lit up his face. "Doc?"

I shrugged and rebutted. "You call me fairy."

One dark brow arched up his forehead. It totally made my stomach flip. "I can stop."

"I hope you won't." Damn my breathless voice. I totally loved that he called me fairy. Made me feel special. I had a feeling there were lots of women that would line up just for a chance to be special to him.

The way his full lips pulled taut into a satisfied, arrogant smile just might be my undoing. His arrogance made me curious. Curious because someone like Derek was only arrogant when he knew he could back up whatever he was feeling smug about.

Clearly, in this moment, that something was me.

"Doc it is," he drawled.

Southern charm. He wore it better than those scrubs.

He was distracting me. Again. I forced my brain back to the matter at hand. "You were sleeping beside my bed."

"Thought it was too soon to climb in with you." He winked.

Don't get distracted.

"Why didn't you go home?" *Why aren't you with your nephew?*

The playfulness in his presence left the building. "Came in to check on you. It was just too hard to walk back out."

Oh, I liked that.

I liked it way more than I should have.

"How's Rocco? The surgery?" I pushed hesitantly.

A bitter, almost livid expression crossed his features. It transformed him into someone I almost didn't recognize. It was as if my question drained him completely, as if energy bled right out of his pores.

"They weren't lying," I surmised.

It was what I'd been afraid of, and really, Derek had been afraid of it, too. I recalled the way he looked when he drove the taxi to the hospital. God, had that only been last night? Felt like years ago. Time dragged so slowly since I was first taken. I felt like I'd lived a couple lives in the span of a couple days.

Derek had been solemn and intense as he swerved through the streets, bringing us to the ER. We weren't euphoric from escaping with our lives. We weren't kissing and laughing because the excitement of freedom overshadowed everything else.

"They could have been lying," I'd whispered. Those were the only words I'd said in the cab.

His hands clenched the steering wheel. He didn't glance at me at all. *"They have to be."* The words were an ominous prayer.

But…

It hadn't stopped him from hoping.

And now his hope was crushed.

A feeling of someone snapping a giant rubber band inside me seemed to give me a jolt. Beneath my skin, my insides stung.

Derek was here.

In this room.

What if he regretted what happened? What if now that he knew his nephew didn't get the kidney he desperately needed, Derek was sorely sorry he hadn't done what the men wanted and cut me up?

"Derek," I whispered, his name so heavy it lay in the room like a gigantic rock.

He shifted from one bare foot to the other. "Rose. We need to talk. There's something I need to tell you."

Oh.

So that's why it was so hard to walk out when he first arrived. It wasn't me he felt connected to. Not me who made him want to say.

Just a piece of me.

My kidney.

20

Derek

Her face was beautiful.

Even in exhaustion, Rose had a luminosity about her I rarely saw in patients lying in hospital beds. She was one of those truly beautiful people, her outside made stunning by the heart held captive in her chest.

The long, light-red strands of her hair waved down her back. One lone strand looped over her shoulder to fall incongruously across her chest. Freckles spattered lightly over her cheeks and nose. Despite the dark circles beneath her eyes, she appeared alert. The injuries inflicted upon her turned my stomach and made me even angrier with my sister.

The whole one side of her face was black and blue from being hit, and there was a swollen cut at her hairline with a butterfly bandage pulling it together. I was pretty sure it was from being hit with the butt of the gun. Around her wrist was a thick bandage. The way it rested against her lap told me it was painful. The makeshift bandages I'd used on her hands were gone. All the red cuts, torn skin, and scrapes were exposed. The sheen across them indicated they were cleaned, medicated, and probably had some sort of liquid bandage coating them. That was good; it would protect them for a while.

I couldn't see the leg where she took the bullet, but I knew it was likely well covered and taken care of. She seemed fragile to me, not really in spirit, but in the flesh. How vulnerable she'd been to those men—to my sister—it made me sick.

But even with all her injuries, the stark reminders of her own mortality, she was still beautiful. Her face was flawless to me.

Natural. Not pretend.

Real.

God, as much as I craved her from the minute I heard her laugh and tasted her magical brew, I craved her even more now.

Nothing felt real anymore.

Except for the way she looked at me.

How would I do it?

How would I tell her she was kidnapped because of me? How could I explain the twisted place we found ourselves in?

"You don't have to explain." Her voice was hollow and far away. The stoic way she watched me stirred a gust of wind through my middle. In its wake, a feeling forlornness hunkered down like a storm that planned to stay a while. "I understand."

"You can't possibly," I rasped.

Her eyes turned to stare down at the blanket covering her lower half. God, how small she looked lying in that bed. Barely a lump beneath the covers.

I'd come in here to confess what I learned. The resolve I'd known dissolved like sugar in a glass of warm water, instantly, as if it hadn't even been there at all.

How could such a small woman with a mop of red hair and pale cheeks offer me such solace? How did I not know it was solace I was seeking, rather than to spill my guts?

I was used to cutting up people for a living. I was trained in how to sew them back together. I always left them in better condition than when I found them.

I couldn't do that this time.

I didn't know how to fix this. If I spilled my guts to her, here, now… I was very afraid I wouldn't be able to sew myself up again. Or her.

"You regret it."

My eyes snapped up. "What?"

She still stared down, fiddling with an invisible thread on the damn blanket. I wanted her to look at me. I wanted her green eyes on mine.

"If you'd done what they wanted, your nephew would be whole again." She elaborated.

Rose thought I regretted saving her life. The realization was almost as hard as knowing my nephew didn't have a kidney.

I rushed forward. She still refused to look at me. My hand covered both of hers where she worried with the string. Guess it wasn't invisible after all, but apparently, some other things were.

Her entire body stilled beneath my touch, and she stared at our connection. Without an invite or a word, I sat on the mattress and rotated so I was facing her and my feet were flat on the floor.

The side of my hip brushed against her leg when I moved. She didn't pull away.

That was something.

"When you called my name just a minute ago, did you see my reaction?" I asked, keeping my voice low and even.

I felt her look up, but she didn't lift her head.

I had her attention.

Her head bobbed once.

"I thought there was a threat, and I literally jumped up out of sleep. Granted, it wasn't the best sleep. Those chairs belong in hell," I muttered.

She giggled.

It was almost silent, but her shoulders shook.

My heart dented a little. Tenderness consumed me.

How she thought I could ever regret not hurting her was the biggest mystery I'd ever know. Seriously. I'd figure out how the pyramids were built before I unraveled a woman's brain.

"It wasn't a threat to *me* that had me up and moving, sweetheart." I went on. "It was danger to you."

That got me the green eyes.

Just feeling the brush of her stare loosened some of the tightness in my body.

"I'd been kidnapped by a fucking taxi driver," I muttered offensively. "Hit with a tranquilizer and dumped in a silo. The second my eyes found you, thoughts of my well-being ceased. You were there. You know. I went into full-on protection mode."

Frankly, it kind of shocked the shit out of me. I was still processing it.

"You're a doctor," she said like that was the answer to it all.

I laughed. "Even doctors have a sense of self-preservation, fairy."

Her wide eyes regarded me, prompting me to go on.

"I went upstairs. I saw my nephew. I found out some things… bad things. Facts that shake me more than what happened in those silos ever could. Know the first place I came? Here. To you. Just sitting in that lumpy, godforsaken chair and propping my feet on your bed made me feel a little better."

"What happened?" Concern darkened her face, her frown pronounced.

She did it, too. She forgot to be upset even though she suspected I was sorry she was still alive. She forgot about herself the instant I said I was shaken.

I was going to fall in love with her.

Hard.

Fast.

Deep.

I cupped her face, letting my thumbs brush across her cheeks. "I don't regret not hurting you, Rose. There are a ton of reasons I would never have done what those criminals wanted. One, because it was morally depraved and sick. But that's not the main reason."

"No?" Her bandaged hands came up to grip my wrists. The pressure of her fingers on my skin was delicious. A bite of desire pierced me. Sexual arousal swirled upward.

Now was not the time, but really, I wasn't surprised.

It didn't seem to matter with Rose. With her, I was always capable of want.

I shook my head. "Can you feel it between us?" I whispered. "I tried to avoid it. My hours as a surgeon aren't very conducive to a relationship. But you, Rose, you bring out something in me. I want you. I want you in so many ways. Most of all, I want you safe."

"Derek…" Her body swayed toward mine.

The distance between us evaporated. My mouth fused to hers like a flame to a wick. I was fierce and hungry. Where I once held back, I couldn't anymore. Suddenly, the urge to make up for lost time with her hammered through my veins so hard it replaced my heartbeat. Our lips met again and again. The sound of my ragged breathing as I sucked in air only when absolutely necessary filled the quiet room.

When I started to draw back, her fingers slid into my hair and pulled me close again. With a groan, I surrendered and glided my tongue across the fullness of her lower lip. She opened. Our tongues tangled even as our lips remained in motion. Her body fidgeted, trying to get closer, like she too was suddenly impatient with need. My hands shot out so I could lift her into my lap, but instantly, I was distracted.

One hand brushed over the thin fabric of the hospital gown, the hardened pebble of her nipple was unmistakable. The accidental touch caused a shiver to work its way up her spine, so I did it again.

With both hands.

The pad of my thumbs slid over her nipples at the same time. Her mouth ripped free of mine with a gasp, and her forehead hit my shoulder. Her nipples tightened even more, so much I knew it probably hurt, so I gave them both a gentle pinch.

An incoherent sound ripped from deep in her throat. I clutched her body, fiercely yanking her against my chest.

Her nails clutched at my back, and the length of the IV tube in her hand brushed against the back of my arm.

"I won't ever hurt you," I vowed against her hair.

The promise cut me like a knife. The moment was broken, like a dog with its tail between his legs, running into a corner.

I shot up off the bed instantly. So fast she fell forward without my body to lean on. I reached down to steady her before pulling away again.

"Fuck," I growled.

"Tell me what's wrong."

I swung on her, anger propelling me. "What's wrong is I can only partially keep that promise. I hate it. I hate this. I won't hurt you physically. I swear to God."

"Just say it." Her voice was anxious yet also frustrated. She wanted out of her misery.

Jesus, so did I.

"My sister is the one who had you kidnapped. She's the reason you almost died."

21

Rose

I would not be playing the lottery anytime soon.

Know why?

The odds were not in my favor.

In fact, I was beginning to suspect the universe had it in for me.

How much more out there could this situation get?

Maybe I should put in a call to CSI and offer them the storyline.

No. I would never want to relive this twice, even if it were on some TV show I watched from my living room.

Derek was clearly distraught, the way he paced back and forth. Back and forth. The conflict in his eyes flashed every time he glanced my way. He felt guilty, embarrassed, hurt…

Torn.

How I honestly could have ever thought he regretted not stealing my organs I just might never know.

I could call it a lapse in judgement. Temporary insanity. A brain fart.

Whatever it was, it was long gone.

His kiss annihilated those thoughts. But his actions… his actions right now—that's what convinced me wholeheartedly.

Even now, he was concerned what this news would do to me, how hurt I would feel.

Maybe I was messed up in the head, but honestly, it didn't matter to me the details of why and how I was kidnapped.

Not anymore.

I was safe.

And frankly, the result was still the same.

This information affected Derek far more than it could ever affect me. He was kidnapped and betrayed at the hands of his own family. *His sister.*

I shook my head, trying to wrap my thoughts around it all.

"Wait," I finally said. "But you were kidnapped, too." His sister couldn't possibly have arranged his kidnapping as well.

"That's why they weren't supposed to hurt me," he half growled.

I felt my mouth drop open. "You mean your sister had *you* kidnapped?"

It was absurd.

His expression was grim. "Yeah." A stricken look crossed his features. "You wanna know the worst part?"

"What?"

"I can't even blame her."

The audible sound of me sucking in breath was all that could be heard for a long second.

Derek's shoulders slumped, and he moved even farther away from the bed. "I've spent a lot of time around patients who need an organ transplant. I've watched families sit at bedsides and gather when a patient draws their last breaths. The truth of a failing organ or any kind of life-claiming disease changes people. People who are ordinarily good, who inherently know right from wrong. Individuals who don't even have so much as a speeding ticket or a mark on their record… Death alters them. It makes them desperate. I understand that feeling so well. Not because I've seen it, but because it lives inside me."

Derek lifted a hand and pressed it against his chest, absentmindedly rubbing. I thought about the look in his eye—the haunted, tormented look—when the kidnappers were taunting him with the fact that my organ would save his nephew.

He debated.

I'd seen it right there at the forefront of his stare. He asked himself if he could sacrifice my life for that of someone he loved.

I'd been alarmed and afraid… but at the same time, I also understood his debate.

Rocco was just a little boy.

"No parent should ever watch a child suffer. No mother should have to see her son stare death in the face." He spoke with the kind of passion that could only come from experience.

"You're more like his father than his uncle, aren't you?" I asked quietly. I felt the waves of pain coming off him. The very tinge of the desperation he spoke of clung to the air.

"His father left him when he was just a baby." He shook his head. "How anyone could leave that boy I will never, ever understand."

I couldn't sit here and say I understood how Derek felt. What he was describing was something I'd never experienced.

But I could imagine.

And I could see.

I could see so clearly what Rocco's failing body was doing to Derek.

"Laura knew what I never said out loud. She knows his body won't hold out forever. Day by day, she grew more desperate. Hour by hour she sat by his hospital bed, and she went a little madder. For that, I blame myself. I should have known. I should have recognized how hard she was taking it." Derek's bleak stare penetrated my heart. "I might not be the one who set this plan in motion, but it's my fault you were kidnapped."

"This is *not* your fault," I immediately replied.

"If I had seen her spiraling into darkness, this might not have happened." He sounded so tortured, so willing to take the blame for someone else's mistakes.

"You can't save everyone, Derek. I know you know that. The lines are getting blurred because this is family. None of this is your fault. You're a victim, too."

"I was never really part of it. Apparently, the plan was for one of them to cut out the kidney. But once they had you, she got scared," he explained, not agreeing nor disagreeing with my statement.

"She was worried they would ruin the organ and it wouldn't be viable." I surmised.

He nodded once. "So she had me kidnapped, too. She thought I would just do it." The bewilderment in his tone as he spoke was not lost on me. "She thought I would buckle to the pressure, toss all my training, all my morals aside, and just cut out your kidney. After that, I was to be let go. They were supposed to deliver it to the hospital without me knowing, and when I arrived, I would never have known I was putting the very same kidney I'd just stolen out of your body into my nephew."

"What about me?" I whispered, hoarse. "She was going to sell the rest of me to the highest bidder?"

He made a choked sound. "She swears she ordered you be kept alive as well. They were supposed to drop you off at an entrance to some emergency room a couple hours from here."

"But we both saw the kidnappers' faces." I objected. It puzzled me she wanted me left alive. That wasn't what those men had said.

"They were supposed to be out of the country by the time you were coherent enough to talk and I was out of surgery and preoccupied with Rocco's recovery. So even if we gave their descriptions, those assholes would have been out of reach." He paused.

"But they were going to kill me." I argued.

"Of course they were," he muttered. "What the fuck did she think would happen, dealing with black market thugs? She thought they would listen and do what they were told. Men like that have their own agenda. They saw you as giant payday, and they saw me as an easy way to get clean, viable organs so they could charge even more."

"What if they killed you?" Anger began to work its way up the back of my neck. I felt it flushing my skin; soon it would be in my cheeks.

How could Derek's sister take a chance with her brother's life—the man who stepped in to help raise her son?

"She was going to pay them very handsomely to leave me alive. She convinced them if I ever found out, I wouldn't say shit because he's my nephew."

"That's why they tried to use him when you balked," I added.

"Yeah," he muttered.

He rubbed a hand over his head. His floppy hair went every which way. "But she made one fatal mistake. There was a giant, gaping hole in her not-so-well-plotted plan."

I tilted my head to the side, feeling the ends of my hair tickle my arm. "What's that?"

"She picked the one person on this entire planet no one could ever convince me to hurt."

So many emotions. This conversation—okay, no. That last sentence Derek just spoke singlehandedly caused an uproar inside my chest.

On one *very* large hand, I was charmed and amazed it was me he wouldn't hurt. It made me want him more. On the other hand (maybe not so large as the first one…) was a little bit of concern for the man I wanted.

"Are you saying you would have done it if it had been anyone other than me?" I asked, my voice small.

"No." He glanced away. "I don't know!" In a burst of frustration, he shoved the hard, lumpy chair away (his words, not mine), and it skidded across the room to clatter against the wall.

I winced but otherwise didn't cower. I wasn't afraid of Derek. I doubted I ever would be.

But I was afraid *for* him.

Of what he might do to correct his sister's wrongs.

It took me a minute to shove the tightly tucked blankets down the mattress. Once I had enough space, I ignored the protests in my body and the stinging in my wrist to crawl over the bed to the opposite side where the IV pole stood. The hand with the needle in the back gripped the cold metal gently as I rolled it around the bed toward where Derek stood. I used it as a crutch to help me walk because the leg with the bullet wound was more sore now than ever.

He faced away from me, staring at the wall. His back and shoulders heaved, like he couldn't catch his breath.

What his sister had done was beyond cruel.

I might have been the one sacrificing body parts (maybe my life), but the biggest victim in all of this was him.

Betrayal by those you love and are supposed to be able to trust more than anyone cuts deep. It leaves permanent scars in places no one ever sees but the afflicted feels forever. She took advantage of him, of his position as a surgeon. She lied, plotted, and played with his life.

Not only that, but she put him in a position where he had to basically chose between his nephew, the boy who was most important to him, and his morals.

Clearly, he had a well-developed sense of right and wrong.

Laura pitted himself against himself. She pitted his love for family against the core of who he was.

I, too, understood she must have been terribly desperate. But that was no excuse.

She'd gotten caught. Her son might lose his mother after already losing his father.

He would be left with Derek.

They would be two victims of desperation.

And what if Rocco died?

Derek would be left all alone. Silently suffering and silently blaming himself for the death of a boy he might have prevented if only he'd sacrificed himself and killed someone else.

A very real ache was developing behind my eyes.

A very real ache was developing in my chest.

Without hesitation, I reached out to him. My hand glided over the small of his back. The green scrub shirt felt soft and worn beneath my skin.

Derek stiffened and whipped his head around, shock in his face, like he hadn't even heard me move.

"Hey," I murmured.

His body rotated around. He was so tired, his eyes appeared bruised. I lifted a hand to swipe gently at the dark marks ringing them. I wanted to tell him it would be okay, but I didn't want to lie.

Seemed he'd been lied to enough, even for just a statement made to comfort.

Instead of speaking, I wrapped both my arms around his middle and pressed in close. My cheek pillowed on his chest, and a rumbly sound vibrated my ear. Both arms came around me until I was consumed by his body.

My eyes slid closed as I stroked a hand up and down the lower portion of his spine. Hair from the top of my head tangled in the scruff of his beard, but instead of pulling back, Derek settled in closer.

"I wish I knew what to say," I whispered. "But I don't. I'm sorry this is happening."

"I should be apologizing to you." He corrected.

I squeezed a little tighter. "This isn't your fault, Derek. Nothing leading up to this and nothing that might happen from here on out. I know you don't believe that, but I do."

"How can you not blame me?"

"No offense, but that's a stupid question." I leaned back enough to look up.

He made a sound. "No more stupid that you thinking I regretted not killing you."

"Touché," I murmured and laid my head back on his chest.

"I thought about it," he rasped. I heard the self-loathing in his tone. "It makes me ashamed."

"Don't be ashamed of loving someone so much you would consider doing anything possible to save them." My words were gentle, truthful.

His arms tightened around me. "I can't hurt you. Not even for him."

I didn't say anything because I just wanted to feel those words. I wanted to let them linger in the air a little while.

We didn't speak. I continued to stroke his back while we took comfort from each other.

"Derek?" I asked after a short while.

"Fairy?"

I smiled. "Why me? Why did your sister pick me to kidnap?"

Against me, his body went taut. The steely way his muscles froze almost made me shudder. He was powerful; there was a lot of physical strength in this man.

"She paid someone on staff here at the hospital to do a record search for someone with Rocco's same rare blood type."

Of course. "And I was in the records because I donate blood here but also because they have a sort of employee file on me because of Curbside Coffee." I finished.

"Not only that, but you're young, healthy, and small." He spoke in his professional tone I'd come to recognize.

"Wouldn't she have wanted someone bigger?" I puzzled.

"Rocco's only ten. A smaller organ would fit him better. Less chance of rejection."

"Basically, I'm a perfect match."

His body went tight again. "On paper."

I glanced up. "What do you mean?"

"There are other tests that need to be run to help verify if you would actually be a good match. My sister was desperate and willing to take a chance."

I gasped. "What if his body rejected it?"

"There's always a possibility of rejection. Even with a perfect match. It all depends on how the body responds to the new tissue of a foreign organ," he explained, slipping a little more into doctor mode. "But the chances are reduced with, say, a candidate like you. He would have received the transplant and started anti-rejection meds immediately. If anything, the new kidney potentially would have bought him some extra time."

The weight of that little boy's life suddenly settled on my shoulders. It was probably one quarter of the weight Derek carried, and I was already overwhelmed.

I almost felt guilty, too.

Here I was walking around with two healthy kidneys, and there were some people that desperately needed one. One was a little boy Derek loved unconditionally.

I knew I wasn't selfish. But I kind of felt like it in that moment.

Why me? Why did I have health while others didn't?

"But the kidney could be a match? It could give him a whole new life?" I asked.

"That's what my sister was banking on."

"What do you think?" I pulled away and faced him.

"I think life's unfair. And I think the only being that gets to decide who lives and dies is God. Not me. Not black market criminals… and not desperate parents willing to do anything to save a child."

"You wouldn't have done it," I said.

His eyes bounced between mine. "What?"

"A few minutes ago, you said you weren't sure if you'd have done it if it had been anyone but me."

He made a face like he was disgusted with himself.

I smiled. "You wouldn't have done it no matter who it was."

"What makes you so sure about that?" He pressed.

"Because you respect life. That's why you became a doctor, isn't it? Not only to help people, but because you have a deep respect and understanding of the cycle of life."

"Maybe I just like the salary attached to my job title," he quipped.

I gave his shoulder a light shove. "You always use humor and sarcasm when you want to distract someone from the truth."

His coffee-colored gaze settled on me once more. "I feel like I've known you a really long time. And not just what your job is, how cute you look peeking over the counter of your coffee truck, or how much I like to kiss you. I feel like I *really* know you."

"I feel the same way." I admitted.

He tilted his head to the side. "Product of the life-and-death situation perhaps?"

"Maybe," I allowed. Though, deep down, I felt there was more. We'd been circling around each other for a while before any of this happened. "Where is your sister now?" I asked.

His mouth flattened into a thin line. "Upstairs with Rocco."

I was surprised by this. I just assumed she'd be in jail.

"Have the police been by yet?" I asked. "Did I miss them?"

"They were here." He hedged. "I told them to come back this morning. You were sleeping, and I didn't want anyone to bother you."

"Or maybe you were putting off giving a statement," I suggested.

He lifted the ends of my hair and rubbed them between two fingers, saying nothing at all. Suddenly, I felt self-conscious about how I looked and smelled.

"I need a hot shower and some clothes." The yearning in my voice earned me a little smile.

"I could probably get you sprung this morning."

"Yes, please," I groaned.

"I'll see what I can do." He started to move away.

I caught his hand. The way he automatically entangled our fingers caused my heart to skip a beat.

"Did you talk to the police yet?" I asked.

His fingers jerked against mine, but he didn't pull away. "Yeah. I told them what happened, where to find the bodies…"

"Do you think they both died?" I whispered, feeling myself go cold. Even though I hated those men, thinking about their dead bodies lying at that farm was not a pleasant thought.

Honestly, though? Knowing they couldn't hurt me anymore was comforting.

"The taxi driver? Absolutely," Derek replied. Then he turned thoughtful. "The other man? More than likely. It was a gut shot. He probably slowly bled out."

I squeezed my eyes closed.

"Shit," Derek swore and tugged me into his chest. We still held hands, neither of us willing to let go, so he wrapped only one arm around me. "I'm sorry, sweetheart. I shouldn't have been so graphic."

"After what happened, it really wasn't graphic," I muttered.

"You don't need any reminders, though."

"Did you tell them about your sister?" I asked, finally putting voice to the question I really wanted to ask.

Against me, his chest puffed out and he exhaled. "No."

I heard what he didn't say.

"If both kidnappers really are dead, then there's no one left to point the finger at her but us," I said.

Derek released me all the way, pulling his body and his hand from mine.

It made me feel cold.

"I'm not saying she should get away with this. I'm not excusing it or even forgiving it. I'm so fucking pissed. I'm so torn up inside I can barely think about her without seeing black." He paused and took a breath. "But I couldn't do it. The words were right there on the tip of my tongue when the police were standing in front of me. But I couldn't tell them. How could I take away his mother?"

Again, the position his sister put him in qualified her as the worst relative in the history of relatives.

"I'm gonna go see about your release," he said. "I'll be back."

"Derek?" I asked when he was at the door.

He glanced back.

"I'm not asking you to not tell them," he told me. "I won't be mad if you do. She deserves to be punished... I just..."

I held up a hand. "I understand."

And I did.

He left the room, and I climbed back into bed.

All of the sudden, I was the one with a choice to make.

22

Derek

The police were coming out of her room when I returned. It was the same two men from just hours ago. They didn't appear tired, though. In fact, they looked fresh and well rested.

I was starting to wonder if I would ever be well rested again.

One man looked up and saw me coming. My steps slowed the closer I got.

"Officers." I spoke formally. In the back of my mind, I couldn't help but wonder if they would ask me about Laura. If they were on their way to arrest her right then.

She deserved it.

Right?

Did a grief-stricken mother deserve to be punished for doing everything humanly possible (no matter how despicable) to save her child?

I was starting to think she didn't.

But like Rose said, the lines were beginning to blur for me. I was entirely too close to this situation.

After I got Rose's release in motion, I went back upstairs. I didn't want to see my sister, but Rocco was a different story. I needed to see him. To talk to him. To apologize for his kidney not being here like he thought.

The whole way up the stairs, I dreaded the look in his eyes. The innocent, forgiving look of a child. I dreaded telling him the kidney wasn't coming.

Laura was beside his bed, just like always.

Rocco was laughing when I stepped in, a sound that socked me right in the gut. His mom was holding an album of photographs, and the pair were bent over it laughing.

"Uncle Derek!" he called out. "Come see these baby pictures Mom has. There's one of you in here… We look just alike!"

I avoided my sister's searching eyes and directed all my attention to my nephew. He was like a son to me. In fact, I couldn't imagine loving my own child any more than I loved him.

After we laughed over the pictures and I teased him about his hair (when he was a baby, it stuck up constantly, no matter what any of us did to tame it), he turned serious, and I braced myself.

Rocco had blue eyes. The one trait he'd gotten from his dirt-bag father. They were a true blue, and when they focused on me, I felt the weight of a thousand men.

"Mom told me about the kidney."

I glanced at Laura. She glanced back with a lost look.

"I'm real sorry it didn't get here," I told him, not sure what to say. Laura couldn't possibly have told him *why* the kidney didn't come.

"It's okay. Someone else needed it more than me."

I cleared my throat. Was it possible for a person's chest to collapse without any kind of blow? My eyes slid back to my sister.

She spoke up. "An emergency came in at the hospital where it was being harvested, and the patient there needed it right away."

So she made her son a victim, too. A victim of her lies.

I hated her in that moment. So much it hurt to not rat her out.

But spilling my guts to a ten-year-old boy who loved his mother was not revenge. It was cruel.

I sat on the side of the mattress, totally turning my back on her. "That's really big of you, dude. To not be upset."

Rocco shrugged. "Mom always taught me to share. If they'd sent it here, that other person would have died."

Laura bolted up out of her chair. Both of us turned to look. "I'm just gonna go grab some coffee. Do you mind?" she asked me.

I shook my head.

"Rocco, I'll see if I can find you something good in the cafeteria."

"Thanks, Mom."

When she was gone, the tightness in my chest didn't lessen. I ruffled the top of Rocco's hair. "You know I love you, right?"

He nodded. "Love you more." Then he nabbed the cards nearby. "Wanna play some poker?"

We played a couple hands. He won them all. And then I noticed my sister hovering in the doorway.

"I had a long shift last night," I told him. "I'm gonna go home and grab a shower and some rest. I'll come back later, and we can play some more."

He nodded and shuffled the cards around for a game of solitaire. A ten-year-old shouldn't have to play solitaire. He should be outside with his friends.

Out in the hallway, Laura stared at me, her eyes begging the question she didn't ask.

"I didn't tell them," I said low.

She made a whimpering sound. "Your team showed up last night, ready for the transplant. After a while, I told them you called, said the surgery fell through and you'd brief them soon." She looked up, her eyes begging me to understand.

I couldn't. At least not right now.

"They all went home, assumed you were too upset to come in." She went on.

I made a motion with my hand. I didn't want to hear any more about all the lies she told.

"I won't hurt him like that," I intoned, motioning toward Rocco's door. "But I didn't ask Rose not to say anything. She has every right to seek justice for the shit you put her through."

Laura's face went stark white.

I stared at her long and hard.

And then I walked away without another word.

And now I stood before the detectives, awaiting the verdict.

"Officers," I said by way of greeting, pushing aside what happened just moments ago.

"Dr. Kelley," the one who saw me first replied. "We've just come from speaking with Rose."

I nodded, waiting to see what else they would say.

"Her story seems to corroborate everything you told us."

I nodded. "And the men?" I asked, hoping asking about the kidnappers might make the nerves in my voice understandable.

"Both the bodies were recovered this morning."

"*Both* of them?"

He nodded. "It appears he did bleed out as you surmised. We found him a short distance away from the silos. Clearly, he was attempting to escape when he collapsed and died."

I didn't feel bad.

It was the first time in my entire life the loss of a life didn't affect me at all.

"We're going to need you both to come down to the station soon to identify them as your kidnappers."

"That's really necessary?" I asked, thinking of Rose.

"It's a formality, yes. We'll also need your signatures on the formal statements we're having drawn up."

I nodded, grim. "Of course." I cleared my throat. "So will I be arrested for murder?"

The officer shook his head. "No. It was clearly self-defense. Everything at the scene proved both of your testimonies."

I nodded, not really relieved. Honestly, being arrested had barely even occurred to me. There were other things to worry about.

"You still have my card?" the officer asked. His partner just stood nearby and listened to our exchange.

"Yes," I replied.

"Good. Would later this evening work for you to come in?"

"That should be fine," I said, even though there would never be a fine time for this.

The two officers took their leave, and I held my breath until they were gone. When they stepped into the elevator and it closed, I rushed after them to see which direction the elevator was going.

Down. Not up.

They weren't going for my sister.

Rose hadn't told them.

I let myself into her room without knocking or saying a word.

Her room was private. I'd made sure of it before I'd gone in search of my sister when I'd first left her in the care of the ER nurses and staff. She'd been through too much. She needed some space and time, not some strange roommate breathing down her neck.

Plus, it was selfish. I'd wanted to be alone when I saw her. At the time, I hadn't realized the curveball coming at me. At the time, I just wanted to spend time with her away from prying eyes.

She wasn't in bed, but standing across the room at the window. The sun was bright even though it was still early. The yellow-gold rays shone through the glass and created a sort of halo around her body. What didn't touch her moved past to stretch out across the white floor in vibrant streaks.

Her wavy hair appeared on fire, glowing in the brightness. Some strands were deep red, while others sparked with hints of gold.

The IV had been removed from her hand, so she stood with both arms folded in front of her, the position stretching the gown at her back. It was haphazardly tied, so there was a long, wide opening that revealed her creamy skin.

What was exposed looked soft, like the skin on a peach. I ached to run my fingers across it, back and forth, to let the velvet texture delight my senses. My eyes refused to leave the small of her back, the way it dipped in and the gown fell straight down without touching her curves. It looked like the palm of my hand would fit there, the perfect place to rest and pull her up against my body.

All she wore beneath the gown was a pair of panties. They were white lace. See-through.

Sexy.

Yeah, it might be wrong to think about how much I wanted her when we stood in a hospital room in the center of a chaotic event, but I didn't care.

I wanted her.

Seeing hints of her body like this only made me want her more. It didn't matter where or when. As long as I made her mine.

She hadn't heard me come in. I could tell she was lost in her own private thoughts. Even though when I opened the door, I'd been in a hurry to talk to her, I wasn't anymore.

The length of her hair fell farther down her back when she lifted her face to let the bright light of the sun caress it.

With the slight shift of her body, my eyes dropped down again. White lace stretched out over her well-shaped ass, and my dick jumped in my boxers. Her ass was also like a peach. Juicy and ripe, begging for my touch.

I had the sudden instinct to push down my bottoms and go up behind her, shove aside that lace, and claim her right there in the glow of the sun.

Now I understood all those stories I heard about people getting it on in closets around the hospital. When it came to Rose, I had close to no self-control.

"Only about two days without the sun and it felt like an entire lifetime," she said, her voice low, almost thick.

So she had heard me come in.

She knew I'd been staring.

She let me.

"I saw the cops on my way in," I said, my eyes still feasting on her form.

She made a sound but said nothing more.

I prowled across the floor to stand so close behind her my chest touched her back. She swayed ever so slightly toward me, and I took it as an invitation. My arms wrapped around her from behind, the heat from her sun-kissed body seeping into my pores.

Hunching around her, I let my lips play against her ear. "You didn't tell them."

One of her hands glided along my forearm and tucked around the bend of my elbow. "No."

"Why?"

"Because I don't think it will change anything."

I nuzzled the side of her neck and she tilted back, giving me better access.

"I'll take you home," I murmured.

"Will you stay?" Her body arched into me a little bit farther.

I groaned. "If you want me to."

She turned to face me, the sun now glistening at her back.

"You should get off that leg," I told her, palmed her waist, and lifted, perching her on the windowsill.

Without hesitation, the distance between our mouths closed. I brushed my lips over hers, once, twice, and then on the third time, I didn't lift my head. I'd never wanted to kiss someone so thoroughly before.

I couldn't get close enough; my lips couldn't press deep enough. I licked into her mouth like she was a melting, sinful desert and I wanted every last taste. Her lips closed around my tongue and sucked it deep, and I damn near exploded in my jeans.

My fingers dug into her cheeks, and she pulled deeper, making a small mewling noise as if she'd been craving me all along.

When at last she relented, I ripped my mouth away and stared down at her. Her lips glistened from our kissing. They looked slick and plump. I wanted to lower my head again but knew if I did, I might not be able to stop.

"C'mon, fairy, let's go."

"I don't have any clothes." She grimaced.

"Well, you aren't wearing that," I drawled.

"And why not?" she demanded, a hint of that stubborn streak I'd seen before reasserting itself.

Oh yes, I was going to love her.

"Because your entire luscious ass is on display back there."

She lifted a brow. "You didn't seem to mind."

"I didn't. But I sure as hell will mind if everyone else gets an eyeful."

"Maybe I'll catch the eye of a handsome doctor."

She was teasing me. I liked it.

"Maybe you already have."

She started to laugh, but it turned into a yawn.

I frowned. "Be right back."

I found her a pair of scrubs in the doctor's lounge and a pair of itchy-looking socks. While I was there, I realized neither of us had a car.

I wasn't calling a cab; that was for sure.

With the scrubs in hand, I ran upstairs and got the keys to my sister's SUV. She handed them over without blinking.

The least she could do after everything was let me borrow her car.

"Derek?" she said, coming out of Rocco's room behind me.

"What?"

She winced at the bite in my voice, but I didn't feel bad.

"Are they coming for me?" she asked, her voice small.

She was waiting for the police. I supposed it was good punishment. To sit and wait. To wonder. She could go to jail for a very, very long time for this.

"As of right now?" I began. "No."

Her shoulders slumped and tears filled her eyes.

I looked away.

"But that doesn't mean they won't," I said, perhaps a little colder than necessary.

"Rocco," she said.

My eyes snapped back to hers. I felt the anger burning in their depths. "You should have thought about him *before* you did this. But don't worry, Laura. I'll take care of him if and when you aren't able."

She pressed the back of her hand to her mouth, tears streaking down her cheeks.

"I don't want to miss what time he's got left," she whispered.

A piece of my heart turned to stone. The thought of my nephew no longer being here was my worst nightmare. And what's more, if it ever did come to that, he shouldn't have to leave this earth without his mother by his side.

I couldn't.

I couldn't do it right then.

I was so tired and so pissed off and so twisted up inside I was on some kind of emotional rollercoaster, speeding downhill.

I needed a break.

I needed Rose.

23

Rose

Everyone handles grief, even chaos, in different ways.

I don't think a person ever really knows how they'll handle an extreme situation until they're thrust in and have no other choice but to react.

After I signed the final paperwork presented to me by a few nurses, who obviously had huge crushes on Derek, I pondered this.

I also pondered the fact I wasn't too thrilled the nurses had crushes. I consoled myself with the memory of how his fingers felt teasing along the gap of skin exposed at my back due to the ill-fitting hospital gown. Most people hated the things. I could be put on that list as well. However, I can't say I didn't have a newfound appreciation for the flimsy, pathetic excuse for a cover-up. After all, it had enticed Derek to touch me.

And those were the kinds of thoughts that led back around to pondering my reaction to being kidnapped by a psycho taxi driver and chained up for my organs.

Well, he probably wasn't *actually* a taxi driver.

I'd been on the verge of falling apart several times in those silos. I'd been terrified to the point I honestly thought I was going to die.

Yet here I stood, thinking about Derek's hands and the way my skin raced with chills (the good kind) whenever he touched me. I thought about more kisses, because the ones we'd already shared weren't nearly enough.

Did this mean I was some cold, unaffected woman?

No.

I was profoundly affected.

But on the inside, not the outside.

The alterations I felt weren't the kind that came with tears and panic attacks.

I certainly wasn't chipper or in a bright and happy mood. But I was grateful.

Grateful to be alive. Thankful for the air in my lungs and the bandage around my wrist. Because although my injuries hurt, I knew I would heal. I knew I would see tomorrow.

In a way, I felt stronger than before.

Why? Because I survived. Because I faced all those awful things, and I made it through.

I felt a fresh sense of myself.

No, I would likely never ride in a cab again. I'd probably look at strangers on the street and wonder who they really were for the rest of my life, and bondage (like with chains) during sex…

That would be a hell to the no.

But I wasn't going to let what happened cripple me. I wanted to live the life I'd managed to keep. I wanted to be happy.

If I learned anything at all (besides never get into a cab or walk alone in the dark) from all of this, it was not everyone gets a full life. Some people are robbed of days, even years. Not just from criminals, but by failing bodies.

Even when I felt the effects of what was done to me, I was going to push on. I was going to live.

When I came out of the bathroom, I felt a little silly dressed in a pair of all-pink nurse's scrubs, the hems of which dragged the floor.

Derek was leaning against the wall with his arms crossed in front of him. The look on his face was intensely dark. Until he looked up and saw me.

That darkness was replaced by amusement.

"What?" I asked, looking down.

"You look adorable."

"Adorable?" I echoed and rolled my eyes.

"You ready?"

I nodded enthusiastically. I turned to grab my things and realized I didn't have any. I had no idea what happened to my purse, my IDs, my evil shoes… My phone.

By now, surely someone had missed me. I talked to my mother on the phone almost every morning. She was probably worried sick I didn't answer. How many times had she tried to call me? Five? Ten?

As soon as I got home, I made a mental note to call her from a landline.

Just the idea of having to tell my parents what was done to me made me want to weep. They were going to be beside themselves, and honestly… I just didn't have the energy for it.

"C'mon, then," he said and bent low in front of me. Thoughts of telling my family about my recent ordeal went away as I stared at him.

He glanced over his shoulder. "You got something against piggyback rides?"

"I can walk."

He lifted an eyebrow. "With a bullet hole in your leg?"

"I'm getting around okay." I protested.

"You look like the damn Easter Bunny hopping around. You haven't even touched your crutches."

I made a face.

"Fine, I'll call for a wheelchair."

I made a defeated sound. He laughed. I liked the way his teeth looked extra white against the darkness of his stubble. "A man always gets an ego boost when he's preferred over a chair with wheels."

I started to grin, but he swept me up into his arms, against his body.

His chest was wide and solid, his heat radiant and delicious. I melted into him like chocolate too close to a flame, and my cheek fell against his shoulder.

"I thought it was going to be a piggyback ride?" I murmured, my eyes slipping closed.

I was such a sucker.

He bent, his lips brushing the top of my head as he spoke. "I think I like you right here."

On the way out of the hospital, I heard some nurses whispering. I smiled a little to myself and didn't lift my head.

We managed to snag an elevator alone. Once inside, Derek hit the button and then leaned against the side. I looked up; he looked down. Our lips met softly.

When the elevator slid to a stop, he pulled back, and I sighed.

"Derek!" someone called when he stepped out. His muscles tensed, and he turned with me in his hold.

I glanced up, knowing this wasn't just some busybody nurse. It was a woman with long blond hair and a tall, willowy frame.

"Hey, Reggie," he said. The way they used each other's first names spoke of familiarity.

"I heard you were kidnapped. My word!" She rushed to close the distance, her eyes flicking to me, then back up. "Let me get you a wheelchair for her."

She started to lift her hand to signal someone.

"Not necessary," Derek replied and pulled me a little closer against him.

Her eyes came back to me, more interested this time.

"We were just on our way out. It's been a very long night."

"I can imagine," she murmured, still looking at me.

"Do you know Rose, from the coffee truck outside?" he asked, glancing down at me.

I smiled at her, but didn't bother straightening. I was too comfortable.

"I don't drink coffee," she replied smoothly. "I prefer tea."

Remember what I said about how I didn't judge people who didn't like coffee?

Well, I was judging her.

She was getting a low score.

"I'm sorry," I said, forlorn. It was a joke. I made it all the time. But it was also a little dig. She knew it. Women understood women and their bitchiness.

As usual, Derek had no clue about the undercurrents between me and this doctor (she was wearing a white lab coat), and he chuckled at the joke. I felt it rumble right against my side. It tickled.

Her eyes flashed a little at that. She was jealous. If she wasn't involved with him, she sure wanted to be.

I laid my cheek back against his chest and sighed.

Finders keepers… I don't know why the words sang through my brain. I had no idea which one of us "found" Derek first. I mean, really. This wasn't grade school.

But I wanted to keep him anyway.

"Well, we should go. I'll see you in a day or two when I'm back on rounds," he said.

"Of course," she purred. "If there's anything I can do to help you out around the hospital, don't hesitate to ask. I know I don't see post-surgical patients, but I can make an exception for you."

"You're the best," he called and headed for the exit.

"She wants to date you," I said the second he stepped onto the sidewalk outside.

"How'd you know that?" he mused.

I rolled my eyes. "She practically whipped out a bridal magazine right there."

"Someone's jealous," he sang.

"No, I'm just tired from being kidnapped and shot," I barked.

"Jealous," he whispered loudly.

I ignored him.

When he realized I wasn't going to engage in this ridiculous conversation (I wasn't about to tell him I *was* jealous of the blond, Amazonian, smart doctor), he spoke up. "I'm not interested in her, fairy. I'm interested in you."

I snuggled against him a little farther.

"Is this your car?" I asked when I was placed gently in the passenger seat of some kind of Jeep SUV.

He blanched. "It's my sisters. My car is at my place. I didn't want to call a cab."

"How nice of our kidnapper to offer us a vehicle to get home in." I deduced.

Hey, I said I was grateful to be alive; I didn't say I forgave that woman.

"You can still turn her in, you know," he murmured, caressing the side of my cheek.

I turned my face to look at him. "You could, too," I said soft.

"Yeah," he replied, short, and shut my door silently to go around to the driver's seat.

It was wrong to say that. He had to be so conflicted inside. On one hand, he probably wanted her to rot in prison. On the other, she was his sister and the mother of his nephew.

To put him in the middle like I just did was wrong.

"Derek…" I admonished and put a hand over his when he placed them on the steering wheel.

He paused and looked out the windshield.

"I shouldn't have said that," I told him.

"You have every right," he replied.

After that, we said nothing at all. The ride to my place was filled with awkward silence, except when I told him where to turn.

When my apartment came into sight, I started to cry. Not like heaving sobs, but there were some tears. The relief I felt to be at home was undeniable.

"Want me to walk you in?" he asked gently, pretending not to notice the wetness on my cheeks.

"Please," I whispered.

"Stay there," he said and jogged around to get me.

The awkwardness from the car wasn't there the second he pulled me into his arms. It just didn't matter with Derek. His touch eclipsed all.

I told him the number, and when we were outside the door, he glanced down. "Key?"

"There's one under the mat," I said, not bothering to whisper. After this, I'd never hide a key outside my place ever again.

I knew the kinds of things that could happen now.

He placed me down, and I favored the leg without the stitches. It didn't hurt terribly, but I knew once the good pain meds they'd given me before I left wore off, it would be worse.

Derek opened the door and gestured for me to go ahead.

The familiarity of the place hit me instantaneously. More tears pricked the backs of my eyes when I took in the cream-colored walls, colorful artwork mostly dedicated to coffee, and brown leather couch with too many pillows.

The lamp beside the sofa was still on from before I left the last time. I always left a light on for myself when I knew I'd be coming in late. I just hadn't even slightest idea I'd be *this* late.

I went and clicked it off. Then I looked behind me toward the kitchen where there were still a few dishes in the sink and my coffee mug collection was neatly displayed on open shelving above the black granite counter.

"Nice place," Derek said, standing near the door.

It was nice. Simple, but I liked simple.

"Bedrooms and bathroom are down the hall." I gestured, pointing in the other direction. The floors were laminate made to look like hardwood, but I had a large patterned area rug in muted tones covering a lot of the living room.

I should have given him a tour, not that there was much to see. It was just a two-bedroom apartment. But it would be polite, wouldn't it?

Problem was I was suddenly exhausted, and the quiet of my home seemed to make my thoughts even louder.

"You okay?" Derek asked, concern evident in his words.

"Yeah." I paused. "I just… I thought I'd never see this place again." I sniffled.

Dammit.

If Derek hesitated near the door before, my words broke that reluctance. He crushed the distance between us with just a few strides. I found myself swept against him, in the protective circle of his arms.

I was safe with him.

Yeah, the fact that he'd saved my life (technically, more than once) contributed to that feeling. But it wasn't just that. Beneath the strong exterior, deep intense stare, and willingness to kill was a gentleness I didn't often see in people.

Or perhaps it was his compassion I felt. Whatever it was resounded with me in ways I'd never felt before.

"Everything's okay now," he whispered. "You're safe."

Everything was okay because I was in his arms.

I pulled back and gazed into his dark eyes. "Will you stay?"

"Of course I will, fairy." His voice was soothing, and his fingers moved to brush all the hair off my cheeks. As he stroked, his thumb brushed away what was left of my tears.

"No more crying," he murmured, bending to gently kiss my cheeks. "I don't like to see you cry."

Just knowing he wouldn't be walking out the door in the next few moments made me feel better. I exhaled deeply and said, "I need a shower. A hot one."

"Go on." He released me. "I'll be right here."

I took two steps and turned before retreating down the hall. "I have an extra towel if you wanna shower, too."

Desire flashed in his gaze. The air practically sizzled with his reaction. "You need some time," he murmured, shaking his head and stepping toward the sofa.

"I have time," I said. "I want to spend it with you."

He straightened. "I don't want you to do something you'll regret when you aren't feeling so vulnerable."

I wanted to argue I wasn't vulnerable. But that would be immature. I was vulnerable, even if I did feel strong. But it wasn't because of him. I wasn't going to regret this.

We were all vulnerable in one way or another.

Mostly, we were vulnerable to time.

Just like inside a cab, our meters were running...

They could stop at any second, and the fee wasn't paid in dollar bills.

It was paid with life.

"I know what I want," I told him boldly. "I wanted this before we were ever kidnapped."

"I've wanted you from the second I heard you laugh. Even before I caught sight of you."

"Take me, then." I challenged.

His eyes flared.

I turned and disappeared down the hall. Beside the bathroom was the linen closet, I reached in and pulled out two oversized white, fluffy towels. The scent of laundry detergent and dryer sheets teased my senses, and I breathed deep.

Derek appeared behind me, his hand curling around my hip. He drew me against his body, thrusting his hips against my ass.

He was hard. Unbendingly stiff.

I arched against his cock and purred like a cat.

The bite of his fingers against my hip was delicious, and I looked up, need already hammering in my veins.

Derek swooped over my shoulder and claimed my mouth. I felt like he slapped a giant *I am here* sign across my lips the way he took them.

He was undeniable. Insatiable. Utterly lickable.

With a groan, I dumped the towels at my feet and spun. He pinned me against the doorjamb of the closet, and I dragged my hands up his chest to grab handfuls of his shirt.

My knees went weak, but it didn't matter. He pinned me so tightly with his body there was no way I would fall. I surrendered to his heat and gave him the best I had.

When he rocked his dick against me, I bit down on his lower lip and he moaned.

After another deep, long kiss, I pushed him back. His eyes were unfocused, and my chest was heaving.

"Shower first," I said, breathless.

He moved back so I could go ahead of him in the bathroom. As I went I let, my fingers trail across his jutting cock and enjoyed the way he sucked in a breath.

In the bathroom, I flipped on the overhead light but left off the ones above the mirror. I liked it a little dim in here. Once the spray was on and warming, I turned back and locked eyes with him.

He was in the doorway, looking a little like danger, but not the kind of danger you ran from. The kind you asked for.

Holding his stare, I grasped the hem of my shirt and stripped it off over my head. I wasn't wearing a bra. The cool air brushed over my newly exposed skin, and I felt my nipples pinch into hard buds.

Derek's eyes glittered like black diamonds, and wetness coated my panties.

"Take it off," Derek ordered, his voice rough.

I slid off the scrub bottoms, letting the lace panties go with them.

I wasn't embarrassed with him; I didn't feel awkward or insecure. There was no way I could feel anything less than confident when he stared at me the way he did.

And also because he was so hard his dick stuck out from his body, pointing at me with absolute certainty.

Derek ignited a primal urge in me. Something I didn't even know I was capable of. I had always been a passionate person, so passionate I built a business out of an old beat up Vanagon.

But this was a different kind of passion. It felt basic, like a fundamental instinct that had only just awakened.

By him and him alone.

The rush was incredible. It tingled through me, making my fingertips itch with the urge to explore his body.

I stood before him, completely naked, letting him boldly stare at my curves. At his sides his fingers flexed, my skin yearned for his touch.

"Your turn," I said, and motioned for his clothes.

Just the mere act of watching him peel away layer by layer of fabric to reveal sharply cut skin, sinewy muscle, and lean, long legs made my mouth run dry.

Between my legs my pulse literally hammered. I was soaked, so saturated with want silky desire coated my inner thighs.

I shivered lightly the second I allowed my eyes to take in his manhood. The skin was so taut across the muscle, I almost moaned because I knew the way it would feel when he finally entered my body. His hardness would stretch me, penetrate me, and I would likely pant.

But first I wanted to taste him. I wanted to lick my tongue across that silky skin and swirl it around his head.

"You keep looking at me like that, I'm gonna come right here." He warned.

I smiled, stepped around the curtain, and disappeared.

The water felt so good cascading over my skin I moaned. The curtain was ripped back, and I glanced over. Dark eyes glittered as he took in the way the droplets dripped over my body and slicked my limbs.

He crowded me as he stepped in. I used it as an excuse to rub my breasts against his chest. My nipples were sensitive, almost aching. I never realized how large his hands were until he wrapped them both over my flesh.

Even as I pushed closer against his palms, his hands moved, grabbed my hips, and lifted me off the shower floor.

"You're a water hog," he told me, moving so his back was against the spray and I was completely out of it.

Ignoring the way my beat-up hands burned and stung beneath the water, I poured too much body wash on a loofah and worked it until it was covered in suds. "I'll wash you if you wash me."

"You got yourself a deal, sweetheart." He agreed, his voice lazy.

When he reached for the loofah, I pulled it back. "You first," I whispered, and then I put my hands on him.

I loved the way suds slid over skin, the way his body looked beneath my touch. There was a lot of restrained power there. I felt it hum beneath my fingertips.

I washed his chest, his shoulders, and down his arms. When I dragged across his abs, his nipples tightened, and I went just a little lower into the short, neat curls just above his cock.

I played in them, stroking my fingers through the damp strands. His hips thrust out, and I was tempted, so very tempted, to wrap my hand around his dick and pump.

But I held off. I wanted to make him crazy the way I was beginning to feel. When I was almost unable to hold back, I guided him around so I could wash his back.

He turned, pressed both palms flat against the wall, and offered me his body.

My breath caught.

"You have a tattoo?"

His back muscles flexed, giving the design life.

It was a simple black ink design. A mark of a doctor, but a mark of more.

I abandoned the soap and lifted on finger to trace over the line.

It was an EKG. You know the line on a machine that measures the beat of one's heart? It rose and fell with perfect symphony, stretching across his back from shoulder blade to shoulder blade. On the left side at the end the line curved into the outline of a heart. On the right, the EKG measurements flowed right into a word written in script, making it look like it was part of the line.

I knew what it was.

A visual, physical reminder to have faith in life. In the beat of a heart.

After all, life was measured in heartbeats. We just never realized it until we thought ours might stop.

It was also a tribute to his nephew, the one he loved above all others. For within the outline of the heart was another name in script.

"Derek," I whispered, still tracing the beautiful lines.

"You like?" he said, his voice slightly muffled because of the rushing spray.

"Love," I replied. It was stunning and beautiful… It was everything he made me feel and more.

Both my palms smoothed out over his back, I stretched up onto my tiptoes and pressed my lips to the design. Water rushed across my lips, and I lapped at it, getting my first taste of his skin.

He was my new favorite flavor.

Not coffee. *Him.*

There was no way in hell I was going back to just washing him. My lips were not done. I kissed down his back and across the side of his hip. I loved the sound of his ragged breathing, and it spurred me on, making me a little bolder. I crouched lower and literally brushed my lips across his taut and nicely shaped ass.

As I kissed on, my hand snaked around and finally, blissfully, wrapped around the base of his cock.

His body tensed, and a low moan filled the shower stall.

I pushed against the side of his hip so he would turn, and he obliged. I knelt before him, water raining over me while his penetrating, molten stare pierced me.

Without a word, I jerked his rod out and away, held his eyes, and licked up.

My tongue dragged upward and, just like I wanted, twirled around the head.

He moaned my name.

My attention melted down. I was consumed only with this one part of him. I sucked deep, taking him as far as I could and holding him there while he pulsed with desire, rubbing against the back of my throat.

When I pulled back, I let my teeth glide over him before sucking deep again.

His back hit the wall, and his thighs parted, giving me greater access. After only a few minutes of working him with my mouth, I bent to gently suck his balls into my mouth. I laved the sensitive flesh with my tongue, taking care to lick and stroke him until I felt his muscles quiver.

I still wasn't satisfied. I wanted more.

While my mouth still caressed his sack, I used my hand to pump him. I went slow and fast, alternating speeds before pulling back to plunge down over his entire length and suck hard.

"Holy fuck, Rose." He grabbed at me, trying to pull me back.

My lips dragged over him, releasing with an audible sound.

"I wasn't done," I protested when he lifted me to my feet.

"If you don't stop, I'm gonna shoot all over the shower." He growled and pinned me against the tile. It was cold against my back, but I barely noticed.

After he snagged the loofah off the floor and added more body wash, he pushed it against my already enflamed skin.

I melded against the tiles, boneless, as he washed and caressed every last inch of me. When his hands delved between my legs and found how ready I really was, he grinned.

His fingers were still between my thighs, and I moved absentmindedly, my body demanding more.

One finger flicked over my swollen clit. I sucked in a breath, and he did it again.

I spread my legs, going as far as to prop one foot on the small bench inside the shower (the injured leg).

"That's it, sweetheart," he crooned and dropped to his knees in front of me.

The sight of his wide, strong body kneeling between my pale, spread thighs was so erotic my vision momentarily dimmed.

"What's your flavor, fairy?" he murmured, parting my folds with his fingers before placing his hot, wet mouth at my center.

I gasped and nearly buckled to the floor.

He chuckled, which made me gasp again because the action vibrated my clit and pleasure shot through me.

One steady hand came up and held me flat against the wall while his tongue and lips devoured my center.

His tongue was wide, slightly rough, and knew all the right places to go. His lips were skilled and gentle when they pulled my swollen bud between them and sucked until I started begging for him to make me come.

"But, fairy," he said, drawing back, "the fun is just beginning."

"Please, Derek," I whimpered.

He stroked my center again, and my eyes closed.

Again, my folds parted. I caught my breath. His tongue plunged deep, actually entering my body.

I cried out as an orgasm ripped through my body. I trembled and shook like an earthquake, but he was unrelenting. He fucked me with his tongue and fingers until I was literally sliding down the wall toward the floor.

"I'm not done with you yet," he vowed, lifting me and sweetly helping me finish my shower.

That meant he washed the rest of me, including my hair, while I tried to compose myself.

When we were both clean, I was slightly tipsy from the orgasm but still hungry for more.

After we haphazardly dried with the towels I'd left lying in the hall, he forced me to sit long enough so he could strip off the large plastic-like bandage over my stiches.

It hurt and cleared up some of the overwhelming lust in my head.

He was gentle and easy, making sure it was dry, and then applied a new one.

"You doing okay, sweetheart?" he asked, worry pulling at his lips when he straightened. I saw him glance at my raw-looking fingers and hands. Before he could demand I allow him to bandage those up as well, I said, "Oh yes," and filled my hands with his throbbing cock.

He moaned.

"Someone needs to be put out of their misery," I murmured, jacking him lightly.

His hands slid beneath my arms, and my butt left my seat. Automatically, my legs wound around his waist. I only winced a little when my wound bumped against him.

"Easy now," he murmured, taking my lips with his.

We kissed soft and slow as he walked toward the bedroom with me in his arms. My center was still saturated, even more so now that I'd reached a climax.

Boldly, I rubbed against him, letting some of my passion skim over his skin.

His nostrils flared when he felt the moisture. His hips worked, and his swollen head met with that part of me.

I ripped my mouth away, pressed my face into his neck, and rocked against his head. The way it slid along my slit and teased my clit made me pant.

The urge to climax came over me once more, and I sucked the flesh of his neck into my mouth. Derek's palm settled over the back of my neck and squeezed lightly.

"Rose," he rasped. I loved the guttural way he called my name.

"Do it, Derek," I urged, rocking more firmly against him.

He hesitated; I felt it in his body. He was trying to wait until we were on the bed. He wanted to take his time with me.

I was beyond that.

I knew wild need.

I took matters into my own hands, or rather, my own entrance.

It only took a simple shift to sheath myself around him. Both of us called out. His steps faltered.

Somehow he'd made it into my room, but his feet stopped working.

Both of us pulled back to stare into each other's eyes. Inside me, his cock jerked, caressing my inner wall.

I rocked my hips. Breath hissed between his lips while fingertips bit into my hips.

"You're so hot and tight." His voice cracked as he shoved deeper.

"Fill me up," I urged and bore down.

His half shout, half groan filled the space. My back hit the bedroom wall, and his chest pinned me there.

I let my head fall back. His lips fastened to my throat as he thrust into me over and over again.

I slid up and down the wall with every plunge. He was powerful and unafraid to show me that power… because he knew I trusted him.

Derek pulled out and rushed back in. He went so incredibly deep I cried out and rocked against him. My fingers clutched at his back as I moved against him, engulfed in the way he felt rubbing against my insides.

"Move, baby," he urged as I rode him.

The next thing I knew, familiar blankets were against my back and all my weight was supported by my bed.

Derek rose over me, pulling himself out and making me reach to pull him back.

He smiled down, tenderness overtaking the fierce possession in his expression.

"You are so beautiful, fairy. This is just the beginning for us. Only the beginning."

I nodded because words failed me.

My eyes dropped to his dick, glistening from my juices and white liquid weeping from its tip.

He saw me looking and grinned. Both his palms flattened on my thighs and pushed wide.

His body filled my line of sight. All I could see was him over me, coming into me… his lips claiming mine.

Inch by inch, he gave back his cock. My body clenched around him tightly, and he moaned.

"I can't hold it anymore, baby." His voice was strained.

I locked my leg (the one without the stitches) around his ass and pulled him deep.

A strangled sound erupted from his throat, and I felt him jerk. Instead of holding still while he emptied inside my body, he began to move, banging into me in a way that made my eyes roll back in my head.

I felt his seed fill me. His swollen cock brushed against my clit.

I splintered apart, falling over the edge and into bliss.

When I finally came back to reality, he was still on top of me, his back slick with water from the shower and maybe even sweat. I clutched at him, pressing our bodies so tightly together it was a wonder I could breathe.

My face was buried against his neck, and one of his arms was thrown back and wrapped around my ass and top of my thigh.

Derek pulled back and looked down at me. My hands fell down at my sides.

"It's true what they say," he quipped.

"What?" I was still trying to comprehend the explosion that just went off between us.

He chuckled. It made the muscles in my stomach tighten.

He was gorgeous. I rubbed my hand along his scruff, enjoying the way it felt against my fingertips.

"Red on the head, wild in bed."

I felt myself blush. Now that reality was coming back, I was a little shocked at my own behavior. I'd never gone at someone the way I'd gone at him.

The way I wanted to again.

He probably thought I was a ho.

I tried to duck back into his shoulder, but he wouldn't allow it.

"Aww," he crooned, rolling away and pulling me onto his chest. "Don't go shy on me now."

I pressed my face into his chest.

He laughed.

"I'm not normally so…" I peeked up at him, and he lifted a brow. "Forward." I finished.

His head fell back with laughter. "Is that your way of warning me next time won't be as earth shattering? 'Cause I call bullshit."

"Next time?" I questioned.

"Mm-hmm." He pulled me against him again to caress my bare back with the tips of his fingers. "I'm not letting you go now."

"You may feel different tomorrow," I told him. "Or once the shock of everything that's happened fades."

He made a rude sound. "I could say the same to you."

"What about your sister, Derek?" The words intruded on our moment before I could take them back. Even though he was my ultimate distraction, even if this wasn't just some kind of release of pent-up tension from almost dying… there were some things that threatened to pull us apart.

With a heavy sigh, he started to move.

He was gentle with me, though, holding me up as he sat up and leaned against my padded headboard.

(PS: I'd made that headboard. I was quite the DIY-er.)

Once he was settled, his legs parted, and he helped me between them. I longed to sit cross-legged and tuck my legs beneath me, but bullet wounds weren't conducive to sitting that way. In fact, my leg was already screaming at me from all the movement and the sex.

It was totally worth it, though.

As if he knew, Derek grabbed two of the many pillows nearby and stacked them up before carefully propping up my wounded leg.

"I'll get you some pain reliever after we talk." He promised.

"How are you?" I asked, thinking he was so concerned for me, but who was concerned for him? He might not have a bullet wound, but he was still a little worse for wear.

I lifted his hand, the one with the bandaged wrist, and brought it to my lips. He watched me with tender eyes as I pressed light kisses to his knuckles and at the base of his wrist.

"You're worried if you press charges against Laura, I'll hate you." He spoke quietly.

Slowly, I lowered his hand, but before pulling away, he tangled our fingers together. I stared down at where we were connected and took a moment to feel the thoroughly satisfied hum in my limbs.

"Won't you?"

He didn't answer right away; he didn't give me an automatic denial. It made his answer more honest, because this wasn't cut and try.

In fact, this entire situation existed in the gray.

"I couldn't never hate you." He paused, searching for the words he wanted. "I would understand if you tell the police tonight. I won't blame you for it. Hell, I may be tempted to turn her in myself."

"But she's your sister." I finished.

He nodded miserably. "Not only that, but she's Rocco's mom. That kid has been through one loss after another. His entire life has seemed like an uphill battle. His father left him, my sister almost fell apart, but she didn't. She held it together for him. She's raised him on her own for ten years. He's an amazing kid. She's a good mom."

His voice implored me to believe. I nodded wholeheartedly. "I believe you."

"My father died a couple years ago. Rocco lost someone else close to him. We all did," he said quietly.

I sucked in a breath. "I'm sorry, Derek."

"Me, too. My dad was an amazing man."

I had no doubt it wasn't true. Derek was probably just like his father.

"Anyway…" He went on. "Between the losses, the challenges, and his failing kidneys… now this. What the fuck was she thinking?" He said the last part to himself, trying to reason it out.

"She was thinking she wanted to protect her son," I said.

"At the cost of your life." His voice grew hard. "I don't know if I can forgive her for that."

I brushed a hand over his jaw. "You don't have to work through it all right now."

"Aren't you angry?" he wondered, caressing my inner thigh with the back of his free hand. "Aren't you so pissed she did this to you?"

"Yes," I said. "But honestly, I'm just so relieved I'm alive that's kind of eclipsing everything else."

"Eventually, that feeling is going to fade." His voice was flat.

"I can understand you not wanting to turn her in. I don't think less of you for it. You're protecting your nephew. Your family."

"What kind of man would let someone get away with something like that?" He swore and grabbed up my face. "What kind of man would I be if I let her hurt you that way and not do anything to pay her back?"

His eyes were desperate. They implored me, begged me for an answer.

"A man who knows great compassion," I whispered.

He kissed me deeply until there was no beginning to him and no end to me. We kissed so fully it was as if for one long moment, we were one.

When at last we parted, I yawned.

A small smile pulled at his lips. "Sleep. You need some."

"Stay?" I asked.

"Always."

After I told him where the pain reliever was, I worked to pull back the blankets and adjust the pillows. Even though I'd slept last night, I was still exhausted. I thought about pulling on a T-shirt, but in the end, I slipped between the covers completely naked.

I wanted to feel my skin against Derek's.

When he came back, I swallowed down the pills and settled against his side. His chest made the perfect pillow, the sound of his heart a lullaby.

As I drifted off to sleep, my mind wandered. To Derek's sister. To what she'd done. Was the reason I hadn't told the police because I was afraid he would hate me? Or was it really because I felt like putting her in jail wouldn't change a thing?

But it would.

Putting Laura in jail might not give me any sense of justice, but it would alter everyone's life.

Especially an innocent little boy's.

24

Derek

I slept like the dead.

Between everything and the mind-blowing, body-draining orgasm Rose literally milked out of my body, it was a wonder I didn't sleep for a week.

Some things were just too enticing to not be awake for.

One of them was Rose.

The other?

Pizza.

When the scent of buttery, deep dish pizza loaded with cheese, sauce, and pepperoni hit my nose, sleep no longer became important. The bed bounced under some movement, and I cracked open my eyes.

Rose was there, trying to climb onto the bed without hurting her leg and carrying a pizza box that was literally half her size.

I took the box and held it up while she slipped back under the covers right beside me.

"Woman, why are you wearing clothes?" I asked, taking in the T-shirt covering her fine-ass body.

"Should I have answered the door naked?"

I grunted and flipped up the lid on the pie and groaned when the steamy, cheesy goodness made me salivate. "I forgive you," I said as I shoved a slice into my face.

"Have you eaten at all?" she asked, watching me.

"Uh, yeah, I grabbed something out of the vending machines at work earlier." I glanced around. "What time is it?"

"After five," she replied, selecting a slice and taking a more reasonable-sized bite.

"Shit!" I swore. "We gotta go to the station."

She shook her head. "I called them, told them I was too tired to come in and I'd see them tomorrow morning, first thing."

I nodded. "I need to call. They're probably wondering where I am."

Her cheeks turned pink. "I told them you were with me."

A slow smile spread across my face. Her words were as good as the pizza.

"You were tired!" She protested. Then her nose wrinkled. "You snore."

"I do not." I shoved more food in my mouth.

"Do, too!" She argued.

"You fart in your sleep." I lied.

What? I needed some kind of comeback because I did snore. Loud.

She gasped like she'd just witnessed some emergency. "I do not!" Her voice was indignant. "How dare you?"

"As a doctor, I can assure you it's a perfectly natural thing for the human body to—" A pillow flew at my face. "Ah!" I yelled and ducked, trying to protect the pizza.

"Don't you use that doctor mumbo jumbo on me, mister!" she yelled and reached for another pillow.

I laughed and made a mental note to piss her off more often. She was fucking hot when she threw things at my head.

"I'm trying to eat!" I yelled, totally amused.

"I'm gonna shove that pizza where the sun don't—" I grabbed her around the waist and pushed her back, coming over her.

And I did it all while still holding on to my eats.

"Now, fairy, I was just teasing." I admonished while taking another bite.

She glared daggers at my face. I kinda liked that, too.

"I do not fart in my sleep." She insisted.

"No, you don't." I agreed.

Her eyes narrowed.

I smiled. "Take a bite." I offered her my slice.

She glared at it dubiously.

"I hear your stomach growling," I told her.

"I want a pepperoni." Her chin jutted out.

I chuckled and plucked a red slice off the top and dangled it against her lips. She snatched it and started chewing.

I let her up, and we went back to eating. "So you told the cops I was your boyfriend, huh?"

"No," she gasped.

I laughed. "I'll tell them, then."

She looked at me like I had ten heads.

"Problem?" I asked.

"You aren't my boyfriend."

"What if I want to be?"

The pizza in her hand lowered from her lips. Her hair was slept on, her eyes bright and finally more rested looking. The shirt she wore slid down to expose one shoulder, and her lips were slightly shiny from the grease on the pizza.

She was like my wet dream in the flesh.

And damn could she make a mean cup of coffee.

"I think it's too soon for you to know that," she replied slowly.

I shrugged. "I know what I want, but I'll wait 'til you do." I wasn't worried about it. I'd make her mine; of that I was completely sure.

"I do want something," she said, cautious.

"Name it." I went after more pizza.

"I want to meet Rocco. And your sister."

Aannd I forgot about the pizza. It hit the bottom of the cardboard box with a slap. "No." The word was flat. Final.

Her eyes narrowed.

No, I didn't think it was cute this time. This was serious.

"Did I or didn't I just sit here and listen to you say you wanted to be my boyfriend?"

I pinched the bridge of my nose with two fingers and sighed. "Rose."

"So you were either lying or you actually planned to date me without introducing me to the most important person in your life." The disgust in her voice was evident.

I backpedaled. "That's not what I meant. You wanna meet Rocco? I'm all for it. It will be amusing to watch him clobber you at poker."

Shit. Maybe I had been too fast to mention the boyfriend card. At first, I'd been teasing her. But then I wasn't. I *did* want to date Rose. I wanted to bury my dick in her body as often as she'd let me, too. But beyond that, I was willing to give making a relationship with her my best shot.

How could it work? I mean, really…

My sister literally tried to have her killed.

What happened if Laura went to jail? I'd probably get custody of Rocco. I'd sure as hell fight for it. Yeah, my mom would be a huge part of his life, like she already was, but I would raise him. I would see to it.

That's a lot to ask of a woman, especially one as young as Rose. She wasn't more than twenty-four. I knew because I'd asked her one day when we'd been flirting.

So already, at the beginning of what I hoped was a relationship, I was asking her to put up with my work schedule and dedication, the fact my sister tried to chop her up like she was an old car being sold for parts… but also potentially raising the son of said chopper?

Goddamn. *I* wanted to run.

How could she not?

But if for some miracle she stuck around, would she hold the sins of his mother against Rocco? Rose didn't seem like the type, but could I risk it with him—a boy who'd already been through too much?

"You're protecting her," Rose said, stunned.

"*No,*" I growled. "I'm not protecting her. I'm protecting you and him."

"I have a right to look her in the eye, Derek, after what she tried to do to me."

I frowned.

"I only know what you've told me. I believe you. But I need to look her in the eye and see for myself what kind of person she is. This is something I have to do."

"Rose." Her name ripped out of me. I felt trapped, caught in the middle.

She was right. Absolutely. She did have a right to this. Even more so she wasn't even asking for that much. A conversation. A chance to understand.

"This is the real reason you cancelled with the cops tonight, isn't it?" I asked. "You want to speak with her first."

Her head bobbed. "Honestly? Yes." Then she added, "But also, you really were sound asleep. And I had to call my mother." She grimaced. "She'd been worried sick. It took me almost thirty minutes to convince her not to rush over here."

Damn, I really had been sound asleep.

"You close to your parents?" I asked, avoiding the topic a few more minutes.

She smiled and nodded. "Yes, and I have two sisters I'm close to as well."

I liked that she had a family, sisters… Maybe that meant it was easier for her to understand this fucked-up situation even better.

I blew out a breath. "Yeah, okay. We'll go see her."

"Tonight." She pressed.

I nodded. "Yeah, but I gotta swing by my place first. I need clothes."

"I'll make us some coffee." She started to slide off the bed, but her muscles tensed and her breath hissed.

"Soreness set in," I murmured, hooked an arm around her waist from behind, and towed her back against me.

"Yeah," she replied pitifully.

I kissed the side of her head. She snuggled close, and my heart turned over. I tossed aside the pizza box and wrapped myself around her. "While we're at the hospital, we can pick up your pain meds."

"All I need is some coffee and you." The softness in her tone awoke the barely contained desire she always stirred in me.

"Coffee is your answer to everything, isn't it?" I mused.

"Of course." Her hand floated low, down to my package. "But I'm thinking you might be, too."

I covered her hand with mine, pressing it a little more firmly against my cock. The action was in direct conflict with my words. "You're too sore."

"Aren't you?"

"I didn't get shot," I rebutted. Even if I was sore, I wouldn't admit it. Besides, I'd never be too sore for sex.

"What if you go really slow?" Her thumb stroked over the most sensitive spot at my head.

My already awakening dick came to full attention. "You've gone and done it now," I told her as it moved against her hand.

"See? You want me, too."

"Oh, sweetheart," I drawled, "that's not even in question."

Green eyes turned up to mine. Her pink tongue jutted out to wet the peach of her lips. I groaned and cupped her ass. I was pleased to see she wasn't wearing any panties beneath the shorts.

My fingers delved between her folds, sliding against the gathering moisture.

She wanted me.

"This time I'm gonna kiss you in places I didn't get a chance to last time," I whispered, pushing on her shoulders until she was lying completely against the blankets.

I lifted up her shirt, baring her breast for my lips, and latched on.

Her breath whooshed out. Fingers dove into my hair as I sucked and licked her flesh the way I'd always wanted to. She tasted sweet, and the sensation of her against my tongue was unmistakable.

She was shaking by the time I entered her, slow and careful, just like I'd been since I first lifted her shirt.

I discovered something while I was making love to her this way. It didn't matter how hard or intensely we went at each other. As long as it was her beneath me, everything else was just details.

25

Rose

What did you say when you faced someone who hurt you?

I'm not talking about eating your last bag of chips or taking the perfect parking spot even though you'd been sitting near it with your blinker on.

The closer we got to the hospital, the tighter I clutched at the mug in my palm. The warmth there soothed me. I'd missed my coffee, not just the taste, but the action of making it, breathing the heady aroma, and how the heat radiated into my palms.

Tonight, I was drinking a vanilla and caramel-swirled latte with a double shot of espresso. I added an extra drizzle of caramel to the top to fortify me.

Well, that and because… caramel.

Derek was drinking his usual, the same cappuccino I always made for him. He'd watched me make it in my kitchen before we left for his place like he truly was fascinated by what I was doing. So I ended up pulling him into the room and giving him an impromptu coffee lesson.

He did a good job.

He spent half his time kissing the side of my neck while I steamed the milk.

Derek was driving his sister's SUV, and I ended up behind the wheel of his Land Rover. It was a much bigger car than I was used to driving. Yeah, I drove the coffee truck, but not that often anymore because it remained parked at the hospital. My everyday car was a small two-door Honda.

After he'd changed, he handed me the keys and asked me to follow him so he could leave his sister's car at the hospital for when she needed it.

I couldn't say no, so I agreed and drove the thing, nervous I was going to run something over the entire time.

We weaved through the parking lot longer than necessary until he found two spots toward the back, beside each other. Once we were parked, I took a minute to sip at my coffee and fuss with my hair.

Not that it needed it. Since I hadn't blown it dry after our shower and we'd rolled around in bed most of the day, I'd just pulled it up into a high ponytail. I was dressed down in a pair of denim shorts (not the daisy duke kind, thank you very much) and a loose white top made out of some floaty gauze material. Beneath it was a simple white tank, and on my feet were a pair of white flip-flops.

Derek wasn't too happy with my choice of footwear. He thought I should wear something more steady to walk in since I was limping.

I told him too bad and did what I wanted.

I think it amused him.

I hadn't bothered with makeup. Derek had already seen me at my worst. Plus, there was no point in even trying to cover up my bruised face.

I must have procrastinated too long, because there was a light tap on the driver's window. With a sigh, I opened the door. Derek pulled it open all the way and leaned in.

"You don't have to do this," he said knowingly.

"I want to." I lied and got out.

The door shut definitively behind me.

Derek stepped up close. He smelled like a mixture of my soap and his aftershave. You'd think the combination wouldn't be too appealing, but, oh, it was. It was like I still lingered on his skin… and my scent mingled with his.

See? Primal. He made me feel something I could only describe as primal.

The coffee was plucked out of my hand, and I tried to snatch it back. He moved it up and sat it on the roof of his car. Both hands came to rest at my hips. I leaned back against the cool metal and took all the weight off my injured leg.

Carefully, he slid one thigh between mine.

"I don't think I've ever seen you dressed so casually," I said, smoothing my palms across his T-shirt covered chest while I reminded myself to breathe.

When he'd come out of his room in a pair of faded loose jeans and a faded cotton red T-shirt with a large pale star in the center, I'd nearly choked on my spit. He filled out his clothes in all the right places, the worn fabric practically molding to his body.

God, he looked even better in jeans than he did in a suit. I only ever saw him at the hospital in scrubs or some kind of suit with a doctor's coat.

Yeah, he'd been dressed in sweats when we were in the silos, but that didn't count.

I loved his closeness. I loved the way everything about him crowded me, like there were no boundaries between us. I knew in my head it seemed like we were moving so very fast.

But in my heart, and in a sense, we weren't at all.

I'd known Derek for several months.

I saw him on almost a daily basis. Sure, we mostly engaged in light, flirty conversation, but he was no stranger. And after what we'd survived together… it felt like we'd been through more than what some couples experienced in years.

"Get used to it," he told me. "You're going to start seeing me a lot more outside of this place."

"I could get used to that." I stretched up and kissed him quickly.

He smiled against my lips.

"You ready for this?" he asked, glancing up at the huge, imposing hospital.

No. "Yes."

Derek offered me his back, and I laughed. I didn't turn down the ride, though. I hopped on. When I was settled against him, his arms snuggly hooked beneath my knees, he leaned forward so I could grab my drink.

"We need to get you some crutches," he huffed halfway across the lot.

"I like the arrangement we have currently," I said primly.

He laughed.

We got some looks when he strode right through the hospital with me on his back. I told him to put me down, but he ignored me.

Finally, inside the elevator, I was carefully placed on my feet.

"When you want to leave, just say the word," he murmured, taking my hand as the doors slid open.

I nodded. It was suddenly hard to swallow. When we stepped into the hall, my stomach and chest tightened. My palms felt a little clammy, and I felt silly for getting so worked up. But I couldn't help it. I didn't like confrontation.

I supposed some people thrived off this kind of thing, but I wasn't one of those people.

Plus, it was really starting to sink in that I was coming face to face with someone who basically ordered my murder.

It wasn't personal, I told myself. I knew it hadn't been. It'd been about anyone who was a possible match for her son.

Funny thing about kidnapping, though; it felt pretty freaking personal.

When Derek's footsteps slowed near the end of the hall, my heart rate spiked. I swallowed and gripped his hand tight.

The TV was on inside Rocco's room. It sounded like some kind of comedy. I heard a laugh that could only belong to a little boy, and it actually released some of the panic inside me.

He sounded like Derek.

I couldn't help but picture a miniature of the man next to me just beyond the door.

How adorable.

He leaned in and spoke low against my ear. "I'll get Laura."

I held his hand until I couldn't anymore, and our fingers pulled apart out of necessity.

"Uncle Derek!" a voice from inside exclaimed. "I've been waiting for you!"

"Rocco, my man," Derek said. The happiness in his voice made me smile. "Get those cards out, kid. I'm about to whip your ass."

"Derek!" a woman gasped, and I instantly tensed. "Don't teach him to cuss."

She sounded like every other mother I'd ever met. Including my own.

"Aww, Mom, I've heard worse on TV," Rocco quipped.

"Well, if the people on TV jumped off a bridge, would you do it, too?" she asked.

He laughed.

"Hey, uh, someone wants to talk to you out in the hall," Derek said, a serious note creeping into his tone.

I felt the charged silence that bounced between them.

I leaned against the wall outside the door and tried to calm my nerves. This was hard.

"I'll be back in a bit," she said. "Don't beat your uncle too bad. You'll embarrass him."

"Hey!" Derek called like he was offended. "I only lost a couple times."

"Yeah right," Rocco retorted.

Laura chuckled. "No cussing."

"Yes, ma'am," he called.

Seconds later, a thin woman with long, dark hair stepped out into the hall. At first, she didn't see me. She stopped, glanced around, and then spun, presumably to go back into the room.

We locked eyes.

Her face drained of color, and a palm pressed to the center of her stomach like she was suddenly ill.

"Hello, Laura." I spoke softly.

"Rose?" she asked.

I nodded, swallowing thickly. She'd been to my coffee truck before. I recognized her. Of course, I had no idea she was Derek's sister at the time. She'd just been another customer.

Her hair had been haphazardly pulled back that day, too, as if it were an afterthought. I remembered thinking how tired she looked and wondering why she was at the hospital.

Now I knew.

"Are the police with you?" she asked, glancing around with a stricken look on her face.

"No. I came to talk to you," I replied, straightening off the wall.

Derek's dark head appeared out of the room. "Everything okay?"

"I… yes," Laura said.

I glanced at him and nodded.

"I'll just be in here if you need me," he said softly, holding my gaze.

"Thanks."

When he was gone, I turned back to Laura.

"Would you mind if we went a little farther down the hall to talk? I don't want my son to overhear," she requested.

I gestured for her to walk, and I fell into step beside her. At the end of the hall was a large private waiting room. Because it was later in the evening, it was empty. We stepped into the room, and I crossed to a nearby chair against the wall.

Laura chose one opposite me.

"Why haven't you told the police?" she asked, blunt. "Is it because of Derek?"

Her candor was a relief. I didn't want to dance around this. I didn't want to listen to her excuses. I just wanted the truth, and I wanted to look into her eyes.

"It's partly because of Derek," I admitted. "You've put him in a terrible position. You know that, right?"

Her eyes filled with tears, and I resisted the urge to roll my eyes. "Yes, I'm well aware of the damage I've done to my relationship with my brother."

"Even after everything you've done, he still doesn't think you deserve to go to jail." I cocked my head to the side. "Why is that?"

"Because I love my son."

"Loving someone doesn't give you a free pass," I said.

"I know that. I made the only decision I could in an hour of desperation. I had a choice the night I set all this into motion. Kidnap you or continue to watch my son die. I chose the one I could live with."

"You know they planned to kill me, right? Sell off my body parts."

She blanched and wrapped her arms across her middle. "I told them to leave you alive. I told them to take you to a hospital."

"That doesn't make it okay," I said, anger shaking my voice.

"I know that."

"Are you even sorry at all?" I asked, my voice sort of bewildered. She was so matter-of-fact, so willing to just admit it all and make no excuses.

"Of course I am." This time, her voice shook with emotion. "I ruined my relationship with my brother, a man I love and who stepped in to basically help raise my son. I risked his life. I risked your life. I know it was wrong. I knew it was wrong the second I agreed to it. But I did it anyway. I'd do anything for my son."

Her words didn't make me angry. They didn't even make me disgusted. They just made me incredibly sad.

Derek was right. She was just a person who turned desperate, and that desperation pushed her to do things she shouldn't have done.

I really wasn't sure what was left to say. Honestly, I expected more. More arguments, more anger, more need for justice.

Seemed to me she was already in her own personal hell. The only thing worse would be putting her in jail and quite possibly robbing her of the only time she had left with her son.

The meter is running…

How could I take away a child's mother? How could I rob anyone of the precious time that never seemed to be enough.

She tried to take away your time.

But in the end, she didn't.

Maybe I was stupid. Maybe I was in shock. Or maybe I just didn't have the strength it took to punish her.

"I am sorry." She spoke out, interrupting my internal debate. I stared into her eyes. She didn't look away. "You said Derek was only part of the reason you hadn't told. What's the other reason?"

I shrugged. "I guess part of me understands why you did it."

Her eyes filled with tears. "It's so hard to see him this way."

My own tears threatened to emerge. I bolted up from the chair. I refused to cry in front of her. I didn't want to feel sorry for her. I didn't want to feel compassion.

"Derek said he'd introduce me to Rocco," I said, turning away.

"I'll just go get some coffee and maybe get some fresh air. Give you some time."

I wondered about the last time she'd been outside. When she'd left the hospital at all. Did she feel as much a prisoner as I had when I was in that silo? Except her chain wasn't around her wrist, but around her heart.

At the door, she called my name.

I stopped.

"Please don't tell my son."

I walked away without replying.

26

Rose

The sound of laughter washed over me like a ray of sun on a stormy day. The brightness in the sound was so pure it was almost infectious.

Almost.

I knocked on the door as I stepped inside the room. Two dark heads looked up from a pile of cards.

Just like that, I knew exactly how Derek looked as a child. Rocco looked just like him. Except his eyes were blue.

"Hey," Derek said, pushing up from his chair and coming to where I stood. I felt his eyes assess me, his sharp appraisal. "You okay?" he mouthed so Rocco couldn't hear.

"I will be," I said and smiled.

He held out his hand, and I surrendered mine.

"Rocco, this is the coffee fairy I was telling you about," Derek said, pulling me along with him toward the bed.

"Hi!" he said, smiling. He was missing a front tooth. "You make good hot chocolate, too."

I smiled. "That was for you?" I'd forgotten about the day Derek not only grabbed something for him, but an extra as well. At the time, he'd just said it was a treat for a patient.

He nodded. "Uncle Derek never drank coffee until you started making it for him."

I burst out laughing.

"Don't tell her all my secrets, man." Derek hushed him.

Rocco just shrugged like he didn't know it had been a secret.

"So I hear you're good at poker." I moved closer to look down at the cards. "Will you teach me?"

"You don't know how to play?" he asked dubiously.

"I know the basics," I admitted, "but I'm not very good."

After that, I got the kind of card lesson that convinced me the boy was going to be a card shark when he grew up.

If he got the chance. I shoved away the thought violently. I couldn't even comprehend a world in which this boy died because of something like failing kidneys.

How did Derek do this every day? Not just with his nephew, but with patient after patient?

Derek hadn't been exaggerating when he said Rocco was a master at the game. He was funny, too. His personality was bright. Even though he was in the hospital, he still made me laugh.

Just sitting here with him, even though we were laughing and having fun, was so difficult. It was beyond challenging to watch someone be brave, even accepting, in the face of a storm. It was like his condition was all he knew, like he just found the silver lining in his young and limited life.

I'd seen adults with less grace than this boy. I'd heard them at my coffee truck. I'd eavesdropped on the nurses' conversations while they stirred their brew. Most people were bitter, angry, or even resigned.

Rocco's happy personality said a lot about him. It said a lot about the people around him and the love and support he received on a daily basis.

It spoke volumes about his mother, the woman who sat at his side day in and day out.

Every once in a while, I'd glance at Derek, and it was like he knew exactly what I was thinking. He'd only nod imperceptibly and then turn back to the game.

After he'd beaten us both and I was embarrassed, Rocco glanced between Derek and me. "Are you guys dating?"

"Why do you think that?" I asked.

"You're holding hands," he pointed out.

I glanced down, startled. I hadn't even realized. By the look on Derek's face, he hadn't either.

"I asked her out. She said no," Derek told him, making a face like he was sad.

Rocco's eyes bulged. "You must not have done a very good job asking, then."

I laughed.

Derek scowled. "Whose side are you on?"

He shrugged. "Mom says ladies first."

My hand tightened around Derek's. I tried desperately to hide my reaction. It felt like I was being kicked every time more evidence was presented that Laura was just a good mother in a bad situation.

"Your mom's right. Ladies first." Derek relented.

Rocco's eyes wandered to the TV, and I used the moment to compose myself. This room was far too "lived in." Toys and books scattered about, blankets and pillows from home. Rocco wasn't even wearing the horrible hospital gown. Instead, he had on a pair of colorful pajamas and a bright-green robe.

When was the last time this little boy was anywhere but here?

The presence of monitors, tubes, and equipment reminded me he might never go home again.

I cleared my throat and stood the very same moment Laura stepped into the room. The color was back in her cheeks, and there was a Styrofoam cup in her hand.

"I'm thinking someone needs to go to bed," she said, pointedly looking at Rocco.

He rolled his eyes. "Aww, Mom. Can I watch one video first?" he asked, picking up what looked like an iPod.

"Just one," she replied, smiling. The love she felt for her son shone out of her eyes and made her look a little less exhausted.

"We're outta here, Roc," Derek said and stood. "I'll see ya tomorrow." He leaned forward and kissed the boy on his head, ruffling his hair.

Before he could pull back, thin arms wound around his neck and hugged. "Bye, Uncle Derek."

It was hard to breathe in here. I felt hot and a little dizzy. I just wanted to get out. I wanted to go home.

"Bye, Rose," Rocco said after Derek stepped back.

His mother cleared her throat.

"Miss Rose." He corrected.

Laura nodded approvingly.

"Bye, Rocco," I said, pushing out the words. "Thanks for the poker lesson."

"Anytime!"

I rushed out into the hallway and sucked in a deep breath.

Seconds later, Derek appeared, pulling me against his front. My arms wound around his middle, and I clung to him tightly right there in the center of the hall. He wrapped me tight in his arms, and we hugged for a while before he gently nudged me toward the elevators.

Once inside, he said, "How'd it go with Laura?"

"She's just like you said."

He nodded, not looking happy he'd been right.

"He looks just like you," I whispered, my voice like an echo.

"I know," he replied.

Why was life so fragile? Why was love? Why did it seem like such a battle to keep both yet so easy to lose either?

By the time we pulled up to my place, I was so exhausted I could barely keep my eyes open. Derek carried me into the apartment and didn't put me down until we reached my bed. I discarded all my clothes, pulled on a T-shirt, and let down my hair.

After I crawled between the sheets, I glanced up at Derek and lifted the blankets higher, inviting him in.

All his clothes but his boxer briefs hit the floor, and my body fit right alongside his the second he lay down.

Once again, I listened to the rhythm of his heart. I thought about how, when I was kidnapped, I wondered if every heartbeat was a unique sound.

Derek's convinced me it was. I'd certainly never heard a sound so captivating until I'd laid my ear upon his chest. As I listened, I pictured the measure of the heart beat tattoo stretched across his back.

It wasn't exactly as I thought when I first saw it, but more.

It was the measure of Rocco's heartbeat and Derek's resolve to have *faith* it wouldn't cease far too soon.

I don't know how long we lay there, not saying a word, wrapped up in each other's arms. But I knew it had been hours.

"I can't do it," I said finally, knowing he was still awake. "I can't tell the police." Once the words were out, I felt a sense of peace I hadn't realized I was lacking.

It was crazy, some people might not agree, but *it felt right*.

"I know," he murmured, rubbing my back in the most comforting way.

"How did you know?" I questioned. "I only just figured it out."

"I saw it in your eyes when you looked at Rocco." Perhaps he had, because really, it was him that convinced me more than Laura herself that going to police wasn't an answer to what had been done to me. Or to Derek.

It seemed the answer was forgiveness. No, I couldn't lie here and say I forgave Laura, because it was still too raw, still too new. But maybe someday I'd be able to find it within myself to forgive her for what she set into motion.

So many times I'd heard the saying *forgiveness is a choice*. I never understood that until now. I was *choosing* to forgive Laura, even though I wasn't quite there yet, I was working toward it. I was hopeful.

Just like Derek, I had faith.

"Do you think I'm wrong?" I wondered in the dark. Just because I was choosing this didn't mean it was easy. I questioned myself, my decision, but maybe that just meant it was right. The right choice wasn't always easy.

He made a sound, stroking my hip with his palm. "I don't think I'm the right person to ask about that."

"You're glad." It wasn't a surprise. This was his family.

"I want my nephew to have his mother," he stated simply.

So did I.

I also wanted him to have a shot at a normal, full life.

"Derek?" I asked after a while.

"Hmm?"

"Would it be possible to give one of my kidney's to him?"

Under me, his body tensed and went still at the same time. Against my ear, his heart skipped a beat.

"That's a very big decision. One that should take a lot of time and thought." He cautioned me.

"But would it be possible?" I asked.

"There would need to be tests to see." He hedged again, like he couldn't even let himself consider the possibility. He almost didn't dare to hope.

"Derek, is it a possibility?" I cut off the rest of his words, just wanting to know if there were actual proper, legal channels in which I could potentially save Rocco's life without putting mine in danger.

After a long minute, his reply was low and hoarse. "Yes."

I thought a little bit longer. "Could I still have kids if I only had one kidney?"

"Whose kids!" he demanded, forgetting everything else. Against my hip, his hand flexed.

Oh my. He was territorial.

I smiled against his chest. "Yours?"

His hand unclenched, and a sound of satisfaction filled the room. "In that case, yes."

"It's something to think about," I murmured, settling just a little bit closer against him.

Abruptly, he rolled, both his arms tucked around me so I lay in their circle. Through the darkness, I felt his stare, looking up into eyes that hovered so close to mine.

"Giving someone an organ is a big decision. There's risk and pain involved. The recovery is long and hard."

"Good thing I have a really good doctor." I teased.

His teeth flashed in the dark but disappeared almost as quickly. "I'm serious, Rose. Your emotions are running high. You've been through a lot. This isn't a choice to make quickly."

"I know," I whispered and rubbed my palm against his jaw. "I just wanted to know if it was possible."

He kissed me softly. "I would never ask you to do anything like this. Especially for Laura's son."

"I'm not doing it for her. Or even you," I told him honestly. "If I do it, it will be for Rocco. And for me."

"I'm gonna fall hard for you," he vowed. "And I'm never going to let you go."

"Never is a pretty long time," I told him. We were new, too, so new I couldn't even be sure we'd be able to make it work. Or even if after all this dust settled, we'd even like each other.

But *oh* my.

I wanted him. I wanted those words. I wanted to sleep in his arms every night going forward.

"Not long enough." He spoke gruffly and lowered his lips to mine once more.

I smiled as we kissed until my smiles turned to moans and my body succumbed to his. The start to our relationship had been as bumpy as a cab ride in the city… but I had a feeling our destination would only end in wonderful things.

Our meter started now.

EPILOGUE

Derek

Two years later…

Rose saved my nephew's life.

She became a living donor and gave him one of her kidney's.

Even after everything she'd suffered—all of it at the hands of Rocco's mother—she still found the compassion and selflessness to give him what he truly needed.

His body accepted her kidney like it'd been there all along. Even a year after the transplant, his body showed no signs of rejection.

He was healthy and whole again. His cheeks had color; his eyes didn't have bags. He still beat me at poker every Sunday, but it wasn't from a hospital bed, but from the living room while we ate pizza and chips.

It only took me about two weeks to fall in love with Rose. But honestly, it wasn't that far of a fall. I think she claimed a little piece of me the day we met.

We never told anyone about Laura's involvement in our taxi-cab kidnappings. After all this time, I knew we never would.

Laura remained a single mother who devoted all her time and energy to her career and son.

My relationship with her would never be what it was.

Was it the price of Rocco's life or a tragic loss of a bond I thought would always be there?

Both.

We were cordial to each other now. We made an effort for Rocco. Even two years later, Rose never saw Laura except at birthday parties and holidays. They kept a distance from each other even then. My girl would never be friends with my sister, and I would never want her to be.

Rose and Rocco were close, though, so close sometimes it made me jealous. She thought it was cute.

I didn't.

Holy fuck, did I love her.

I loved her more than I ever thought I could love anyone. It was a different kind of love than I felt for Rocco. This was all consuming. It was chest tightening, it was the strongest kind of bond I'd ever known.

I glanced down at the black velvet box resting open in the palm of my hand. A square diamond sparkled up at me, the rays of the sun reflecting its brilliance. The ring was mounted on a thin silver band, the square center stone two carats, and it was outlined in small red rubies.

I had to get the red in there. 'Cause you know, her hair.

And because of the fire she ignited inside me, the heat that always burned between us when we touched. Turns out (frankly, I never doubted it, but I was pretty sure Rose had) the intensity between us wasn't just a product of how we were brought together.

Two years later, she still melted when I stroked her skin, and my dick still throbbed with just a single look or thought.

Beyond the physical, Rose was my best friend.

We were meant to be. Plain and simple. She didn't mind my hours. In fact, she worked just as hard as I did, if not harder. She even learned to live with my snoring, and I still teased her she farted in her sleep.

(She really didn't.)

I was going to marry her. She was going to say yes. I was going to spend the rest of my life loving her and the kids she was going to give me.

FYI, she had no complications living with just one kidney. I'd performed both surgeries myself, and I'd monitored her recovery with such care she told me I was worse than a hovering grandma. Was that supposed to be an insult? I liked grandmas.

After my morning rounds, I left work early. I didn't do it often, but more than I did before Rose. Turns out I wasn't as much of a workaholic when I knew I had someone I truly loved waiting for me at home.

I dressed in a pair of loose jeans and a T-shirt with the green logo for Curbside Coffee on it and headed outside. It was a typical summer day here in North Carolina. Hot and humid with a bright blue sky.

There was a breeze today, something that made the usually stifling heat just a little more bearable. It pulled through my hair as I walked along the sidewalk, peering through the sunglasses wrapped around my eyes, toward the light-green coffee truck parked a short distance away.

There was a line in front of it, and as I moved closer, the breeze carried the sound of her laughter to my ears.

I loved that sound. It was the sound of my entire life.

The minty-green Vanagon was parked where it always was, shiny without a speck of dirt on it. The vehicle had been modified, of course, which made it only more of a reflection of my (hopefully) bride-to-be.

The roof had been extended so it rose higher than the roof above the driver's head. It sort of looked like a little pop-up that always stayed up. The sides of the extension were also painted the minty green, and the new roof was shiny white. It extended out into an awning that stretched over the open bar beneath it.

The entire side of the Vanagon opened to reveal the small café. It was simple, just like Rose, but it was neat and professional, too. The inside was decorated with a richly stained paneling. The back wall was all chalkboard where Rose would write the featured drinks and specials. Above that was the regular menu in bold letters that were easy to read. The back counter stretched the whole length of the interior and held a small sink, espresso machines, and coffee makers all in stainless steel.

White paper cups with Curbside Coffee written on them in a unique font were in dispensers, and rows of flavoring and unique toppings took up the rest of the space. The back end of the vehicle was one large window, but it opened like a door.

Under the awning was the counter where people ordered. It was a plain butcher block with all the usual coffee necessities. Over the heads of the customers were strung-up blubs that lit when the days were cloudy and dim.

Rose was always standing behind the counter in her jeans and Curbside Coffee T-shirts with her hair pulled up off her face.

The fact that she loved this place made me love her more.

I got in line behind the customers. She'd yet to see me because she was so engrossed in what she was doing.

Plus, she had no idea I'd taken a half a day. She had no idea I had a ring in my hand.

We'd taken our time with our relationship (not the sex, though; I wasn't about to keep my hands off her sexy ass). I wanted to make sure it was absolutely right. I wanted there to be no question in my fairy's mind about why we were together.

Two years was long enough. I wanted to see my ring on her finger.

Her back was turned when I stepped up to the counter. "Be right with you!" she chirped, rinsing out something in the sink.

"I'll have my usual," I said.

Her head whipped around; a smile lit up her face.

"Hey, you!" She turned. "What are you doing here?"

"Took the day off. Missed my girl."

She shoved away from the sink and came forward, practically diving across the counter, sliding right up to my face. "Kiss me!" she demanded.

Our lips met and parted, my tongue slipping deep into her mouth and stroking against hers. She smelled and tasted like coffee.

I loved coffee.

When I lifted my head, she smiled. "Still want that coffee?"

"What do you think?" I asked.

"Coming right up!" She leapt and turned around to her supplies.

"So," she called behind her as she moved around. "What do you think? I could close up early. We could go grab some lunch, maybe drive to the beach…"

I set the open velvet box on the counter, facing her.

Her words fell away when she turned.

The green eyes I loved so much rounded and nearly fell out of her head.

Around the coffee she'd just made, her knuckles turned white.

"I was thinking maybe you'd marry me?" I said, my focus fully on her.

"Derek." My name sounded sort of like a prayer when she said it.

"I can't live without you, fairy," I said, pushing the ring across the counter just a little closer to her. "I want the rest of our lives."

"You want to marry me?" she asked like she couldn't quite catch up.

"I've never wanted anything more," I answered.

She stared at the ring, her eyes glittering.

"You gonna put me out of my misery, here?" I asked, nerves coiling in my stomach, I just wanted to hear one word.

That's all I needed, just one three-letter word.

She made a sound and set the coffee behind her. Rushing forward, she climbed over the counter and leapt down into my arms.

Her legs wrapped around my waist, and her fingers delved into the short strands of hair at the back of my neck.

"Yes," she said. "Yes, of course I'll marry you."

People around us clapped and cheered. We'd drawn an audience, but neither of us cared.

I kissed her again. My world never felt more whole.

I pulled back. "Wait a minute."

I set her on her feet and snatched the ring off the counter.

She held out her hand.

I slid the diamond past her knuckle, exactly where it belonged. "I hope you like it," I murmured, lifting her hand to kiss the stone where it now lived.

There. Now I was whole.

"I love it." Her words were watery, just like her eyes. Rose pulled her hand back and looked down, turning her hand this way and that. "It's stunning."

"I just want you to know…" I began. "I'm not waiting two more years to get you down the aisle. This is gonna be a quickie engagement."

She laughed. "Sounds good to me."

"I love you, fairy." I caressed her cheek. "So much."

"I love you, too." She smiled, stepping into my arms.

* * *

We got married two weeks later on the beach.

Rocco was my best man.

Rose not only saved his life, but mine as well.

Being a doctor would never give me a God complex.

But living with an angel might.

Author's Note

It feels entirely weird to be back here at the end of another *Take It Off novel.* It's almost, in a sense, like stepping back in time. I have to admit I struggled a bit when writing this. I kept looking around on every page for Romeo or Trent. Or any of my *#Hashtag* family. I think I suffered from a hangover like you readers sometimes do, except mine was from writing and not reading.

In other words, moving to a book that didn't contain any of the characters I've spent the last year and half with has been very difficult. More so than I thought it would be. In fact, I really wanted to write this book. If you really know me, you know I have an overactive mind (shocker, I know), and I pretty much look at every situation I'm in as a potential kidnapping or hostage situation.

I mean, really, though. I can't be the only person who stares at everyone in a movie theater before the movie starts, trying to decide if they're suspicious and what type of plan I would use if I needed to escape… right?

In the past year and a half, I've traveled to a lot of book signings and events. It's at these events I'm often in need of a cab. You see where this is going, don't you?

Well, it was in the backs of these cabs that I realized just how precarious riding in one is. I could be taken anywhere. The driver is a complete stranger. In fact, I've often said the words while I'm traveling, "If I don't call, my taxi driver kidnapped me."

So basically, this book is born out of my own twisted nightmares (just like *TEXT* was, lol). With some romance sprinkled in, of course. We all love romance.

And hot doctors.

Anyway, so I've been thinking of this book for a long time. It's always been on the backburner. So when I finished up *#Rev* (*GearShark #2*) I decided before moving on to Lorhaven's book, I would write *Taxi*. Over the past year, I've had some requests (even some rather rude demands) for more *Take It Off* books. I know I put a blurb for *Trace* in the back of *Trashy*, so I'm sure many of you saw this book and wondered what the hell I was thinking.

I was thinking I might get kidnapped. By a weirdo in a taxi. Totally legit.

Anyway, this idea was in my head, and I wanted to write it. I hope you guys enjoyed it and it brought you back to the *Take It Off* days. LOL. This book is like a giant #TBT (throwback Thursday)… See… I'm obsessed with hashtags. I can't stop… #itsasickness.

That being said, as much as I wanted to write it, the entire time, I kept thinking people might be disappointed this isn't Lorhaven's book (It's coming. I promise.) or a *Hashtag* book. (I get emails for that daily. *Daily*.)

But I also really wanted to maybe take a brain break, dive into something fun and dare I say "less exhausting."

Turns out that was dumb. Hahahaha.

This book was exhausting to write as well because I kept pining away for my *#Hashtag* boys. (Sickness, I tell you. I may need therapy.)

Also, in 100% honesty, I'm worried this book sucks. I can say it. It's okay. An author is their own worst critic, right?

Well, maybe not. I've read some reviews… *shudders*

Anywho, I know I've written ten of these (this is number eleven!), but that was a long time ago. Eons it feels like. And to be honest, I feel I'm a different writer than I was in a lot of ways. So it was a little difficult to try and keep the tone, etc. similar to the other books in the series.

And please realize this is fiction… even though black market organs are a very real and scary thing. I've Googled. I've seen… *shudders*

I've said to my husband on numerous occasions, "I need to slap a warning label on this book that reads: CAUTION: No Trent and Drew."

All my *GearShark* readers are totally gonna know what I mean.

That being said, I think Rose and Derek are awesome in their own right. This story is intriguing in the sense I think things like this happen more than we realize. Especially in other countries. I think "real" fear is scarier than any kind of made-up fear could ever be. Know what I'm saying?

So I sincerely hope you enjoyed *TAXI*. Next up, I'll be going back to finish the *GearShark* series… and I have another idea on the backburner for something new.

Will I ever write another *Take It Off* novel? I'm not sure. I do have ideas. So we'll see. Maybe let me know what you think!

As always, thank you for reading. Thank you for reviewing. And for more of me (cause you know you just want more, haha), sign up for my newsletter (it's in my bio on the next page or on my website) for book news, giveaways, and more!

See you next book!

xoxo—Cambria

Cambria Hebert is an award winning, bestselling novelist of more than twenty books. She went to college for a bachelor's degree, couldn't pick a major, and ended up with a degree in cosmetology. So rest assured her characters will always have good hair.

Besides writing, Cambria loves a caramel latte, staying up late, sleeping in, and watching movies. She considers math human torture and has an irrational fear of chickens (yes, chickens). You can often find her running on the treadmill (she'd rather be eating a donut), painting her toenails (because she bites her fingernails), or walking her chorkie (the real boss of the house).

Cambria has written within the young adult and new adult genres, penning many paranormal and contemporary titles. Her favorite genre to read and write is romantic suspense. A few of her most recognized titles are: *The Hashtag Series, GearShark Series, Text, Torch,* and *Tattoo.*

Cambria Hebert owns and operates Cambria Hebert Books, LLC.

You can find out more about Cambria and her titles by visiting here:

Website: http://www.cambriahebert.com.
Email: cambriahebert@rocketmail.com
Facebook: http://smarturl.co/CambriaHebertFanpage
Twitter: https://twitter.com/cambriahebert
Pinterest: https://pinterest.com/cambriahebert/pins/
Instagram: @cambriahebert
Sign up for my Newsletter: http://eepurl.com/bUL5_5

Taxi